WEAVER

BOOK TWO OF THE
FOUR HORSEMEN TALES

Kacey Ezell & Mark Wandrey

Seventh Seal Press
Virginia Beach, VA

Chris Kennedy/Seventh Seal Press
2052 Bierce Dr.
Virginia Beach, VA 23454
http://chriskennedypublishing.com/

Publisher's Note: This is a work of fiction. Names, characters, places, and incidents are a product of the author's imagination. Locales and public names are sometimes used for atmospheric purposes. Any resemblance to actual people, living or dead, or to businesses, companies, events, institutions, or locales is completely coincidental.

Ordering Information:
Quantity sales. Special discounts are available on quantity purchases by corporations, associations, and others. For details, contact the "Special Sales Department" at the address above.

Weaver/Kacey Ezell & Mark Wandrey – 1st ed.
ISBN 13: 978-1948485357

Prologue

The dark catacombs went on for kilometers under the surface. Deep, deep, deeper than any light could penetrate. Endless spaces of quiet contemplation and design. Far away from the war that waged among the stars. The Caretakers watched over their world and the mundane things needed to keep it working. Most importantly, they dealt with the Masters.

"I asked to talk to Kut'oja," the visiting Master said, "not to a mere Kehra'aja."

"The Kut'oja is deep in the work and cannot speak." She looked at the Master and bowed slightly. "Not even to you."

"We have tolerated your eccentricities for many years during this cleansing, but we cannot afford this dance of delicacies any longer!" Although they were the same height, the Master was imposing, as Masters always were. The power they wielded was inconceivable.

"I am sorry."

"Sorry?!" the Master raged.

"I will speak to you." The Master turned and looked at the Kehra'aja. Her dark bulk was just at the edge of the light and dark, where they preferred. Ever in darkness.

"I said I don't want to speak to you; I want to speak to the Kut'oja."

"She cannot speak now, and if you were to try, you wouldn't understand what she said."

"You have unleashed this abomination upon us," the Master raged. "We are undone; we are defeated on all fronts!" The Kehra'aja regarded the master without comment. "What have you to say for yourself?"

"The Kut'oja did what you asked of us," the Kehra'aja said, splaying a set of arms wide and affecting a bow.

"And now I am telling you to stop them. This is not what we wanted."

"As the Kut'oja says, consequences often do not match intentions."

"We should destroy you for this!"

"Fate often doesn't match consequences either." The Caretaker looked between the two in growing fear and horror.

* * * * *

Pa
Lea

Chapter One

Teeno examined the data presented on the Tri-V before her. She didn't use her eyes; they no longer functioned. She used a pair of image-scanning goggles, linked directly to her brain via pinplants. As steward of Brood 37F2, she had a massive responsibility. Unfortunately, it was one she hadn't wanted. It would have been better to retire, but there was work to be done.

"Here's the additional data you wanted," an assistant said, handing Teeno a data chip. She grunted her acknowledgement and inserted the chip into the computer. Instantly the Tri-V was updated. She'd been waiting for this, the results of the late addition breeding. She made a face. More than half were small. Unusually small.

"These are yours, are they not?" she asked toward the ceiling. A tiny Tortantula, less than a half meter across, slowly lowered from above on a gossamer strand and looked at the data.

"They are mine, yes," he said.

She looked from him to the data and shook her head. "The males seem fine; more than 90% of them escaped into the male brooding alcoves. But the females," she pointed a clawed digit at the data, "are 5% below mean average, and over a quarter of them are six deviations from the norm."

His six eyes, all situated forward, examined the data. "It is a bit substandard, but male breeding cycles often result in poor female results."

"I should flush all the females," Teeno said. The male didn't react.

It was only thirty or so, she decided; maybe a couple would be worth the effort. She'd let it go and see what happened. The survivors would be moved into a standard training dome. With no further comment, the male climbed back and disappeared.

* * * * *

Chapter Two

I t was warm and squishy. She didn't like it.

"Can't I have a different one?" she whined. Her mother smacked her to the other side of the alcove with an idle flip of her second foreleg. The youngster lay stunned for a moment while her mother left with no further answer. Then the air came back, and she could breathe again, though it hurt.

She untangled her legs and gathered her feet under herself, then stood up as steadily as she could.

It just lay there, watching her.

She'd seen her mother's Flatar, and he didn't look anything like this ugly, hairless thing with enormous eyes. Hranou was sleekly furred and laughed all the time. She liked him more than she liked her mother, truth be told. He was the reason she'd looked forward to this day. Today she was going to meet her infant Flatar.

This, though? This was not what she'd expected.

"Look at you," she said. "Who would want to bond with you? Ugly, weak thing as you are! You can't even move properly. I think Mother made a mistake. I think you're supposed to be food. I think maybe I'll just eat you."

It kept watching her with those huge eyes. Like all Flatar, it only had two, but they dominated the little face. She watched it back and took a step toward it.

It was so small! She wasn't very large herself, having hatched only a few days ago. She'd barely made it out of the nesting carcass alive, too, as she was one of the smaller of her mother's offspring. The big ones always hatched first, and they immediately began consuming the majority of the meat that surrounded the smaller ones as they emerged from their eggs. Then, when the carcass meat got scarce, the larger hatchlings turned to eating their smaller siblings. She hadn't known much at that moment, but she'd known she wasn't ready for her seconds-old life to be over. She fought back, and when that worked, she followed suit and consumed the body of the sister who'd attacked her. A few more of those, and she'd managed to fight her way free of the bloody tangle of egg sac and bone, and she'd run. She'd finally collapsed in this alcove.

When mother showed up, she thought for sure she was dead. Mother was so big, and she was exhausted. And Mother had seemed so displeased to see her.

"Too small," Mother had said. "She should never have survived Hatching."

"But she did," a small, chittery voice had answered. She hadn't dared rise from her defensive crouch, but her left side eyes caught the movement as a furry head poked up beside Mother's. That was the first time she'd met Hranou.

They visited her every day after that, and the experience was always the same. Mother dismissed her as not good enough, while Hranou laughed and told her not to be so blind. He, at least, seemed to think there was something redeeming about her, so when they told her they'd bring her a Flatar pup, she was excited.

But again, this was not what she'd expected.

She rose up over the thing, staring back at its obscenely large eyes. She supposed it did look a little Flatar-ish...and up close, she could see that it did, in fact, have fur. It was just very, very fine and colorless. It was wrapped in some kind of drab cloth, and as she watched, it kicked its back legs free. Then the cold air hit it, and it began to whimper.

Stupid baby. She reached down and pulled the blanket over it again.

It kicked it off again. The cries got louder.

"Stop that," she said. She pulled the blanket over it again, but to no avail. It kicked loose and let out an ear-piercing wail that echoed off the stone walls of the alcove.

"Quit!" she said, keeping her voice a low hiss. "You'll tell my siblings where we are, and if you do, we're both food!"

It just kept crying.

"Stop it right now, or I will sting you," she said. "And then you'll die, and I'll eat you! It's better than being eaten myself!"

More wails.

Something clenched inside her, but she didn't really have much choice. She looked down at that red, wrinkly face all screwed up in a cry and gave it a good jolt with her stinger.

The cries stopped. The tear-filled eyes opened wide, and the little mouth parted with an "O," revealing the little Flatar's milk teeth. Then it did the strangest thing.

It glared at her.

Or rather, he glared at her. Since the stupid baby insisted on lying uncovered on the ground, it was obvious he had male sex organs. She didn't know how she knew what they were, she just knew.

Kinda like she knew how to fight, she guessed. Small she might be, but she was clearly not stupid.

Unlike the baby, who seemed not to know he'd been stung. He glared at her, then reached up and rubbed the sting site.

"Why did you do that?" he asked in a piping voice.

Now it was her turn to stare.

"You can talk?"

"Of course I can talk. All I've heard since I was born was your ranting and raving."

"You were just born?"

"Why else would I be so small? Are you going to eat me now? Because I'm not afraid to fight you."

She laughed, her mandibles clicking together.

"I'm twenty times your size! You're just a baby!"

"So are you! Why else would you have stingers and be afraid your siblings would find you?"

"I don't...why are you still alive? That sting should have killed you."

"Maybe I'm stronger than you...what are you?"

"Me? I'm a Tortantula."

"That's your name?"

"No, that's what I *am*. I'm a Tortantula, and you're a Flatar. And don't ask me how I know; I just know," she said. Then she paused. "...I don't have a name."

"Why not?"

She shrugged, her foremost legs lifting and dropping.

"My mother doesn't like me. She said I was too small and should have died in Hatching. Maybe that's why she didn't give me a name."

"That's stupid. You look plenty big to me. I think your mother's an idiot."

That surprised her so much she laughed again.

"What's your name, then?" she asked him. She was beginning to revise her initial impression. He was still small and gross looking, but this little Flatar pup had guts.

"Sadek," he said. "At least, that's what my father said when I opened my eyes earlier."

"Sadek—"

She never got to finish what she was saying. A whisper of sound warned her, and she barely had time to collapse her body over Sadek and roll to the side before her attacking sibling could strike them with the full force of her charge.

She wrapped Sadek's tiny body up in her center limbs and came up on her feet, stingers ready. Her sibling lunged, forelimb slashing out toward her eyes. She ducked and skittered forward, holding Sadek close to her abdomen. She came up under her sibling and jabbed with her two front stingers, right at the wasp waist. The small one heard her sibling gasp, but she was already down and rolling again. She took out her sibling's left-side legs and managed to get in a bite on the rearmost ankle. The sibling went down with a scream.

"Get up on me!" the small one shouted to Sadek and gave him a boost in that direction. She could feel his tiny, clawed hands and feet scrabbling to find a seam in her exoskeleton to hold onto. She didn't have much time to worry about him, though, because her sibling was rolling over, and if the small one was going to survive, she had to beat her sibling *now*.

The small one leapt, causing Sadek to let out a "meep!" of fear and dig his claws into the seam he'd found. It hurt, but she ignored it. Instead, she focused on coming down hard on her sibling's head with her back four feet. The sibling was rising, but her front legs toppled back down under the small one's sudden weight, and she managed to scrape her back right stinger across the sibling's eye ring.

The sibling let out another scream as several of her eyes on the right side burst. Her back legs buckled, and she fell to her abdomen on the stone floor. The small one scrambled backward, getting the bulk of her body positioned over her sibling as she started to thrash and try to rise again.

"Stay down," the small one growled, and bit her sibling's head off.

Well, not all of it. The small one was smaller than her sibling, after all. But she did take a big chunk out of the side where the pierced eyes leaked black ichor. The taste of her blood filled the small one's mouth as her sibling screamed again. She tasted delicious, like metal and strength.

The small one ate until her sibling stopped screaming, then she ate until there was nothing left of her but a few fragments of exoskeleton and her stingers. Only then did she slow down and let out a large burp.

"Wow," Sadek said. His little voice echoed softly off the walls of the alcove, emphasizing the silence. If there had been other siblings lying in wait, they'd decided to go elsewhere.

"Are you all right?" the small one asked. She hadn't realized she cared, but suddenly, she did.

"I am," he said. "You're...really good."

"How do you know?" she asked. "You're just a baby."

"So are you," he said, "and look what you did! She was half again your size, and you took her right out! And saved me at the same time! I wish you liked me."

"Why?"

"So I could be your partner! We would be unstoppable! Plus, if you keep eating everyone that attacks you, you're going to be plenty big soon enough."

"I do like you," she said. Again, she didn't realize it was true until she spoke, but there it was. She liked Sadek. He was important.

So be it.

"You do?" he asked. "Why?"

"Because..." she thought about it. Why *did* she like him? He was small and ugly. But he was also smart and tough. He hadn't even flinched when she'd stung him, and...

And he liked her. He was the first being who did. That was something.

"I like you because you like me. So give me a name, and let's be partners," she said.

"Yeah? All right!" he said. "I will name you...Azah."

* * * * *

Chapter Three

There was no more food. Time had passed without much meaning. When it was dark, they hunted for food. When it was light, they were hunted as food. Sadek and Azah learned each other's strengths and weaknesses without conscious effort. The pairing that began with surviving that first attack grew with every passing lightless period.

"Is this the world?" Azah asked one dark time as they huddled in a place out of view of the other, much larger, Tortantulas.

"I don't think so," Sadek said.

"Why?"

"Because my food is coming from somewhere." Every few dark times, they'd find batches of berries and tasty shoots, all wound together with succulent greens. Little bunches in odd places, and never the same place twice. Sadek loved them, while Azah did not. The big predator could barely stand the taste of them when she used a leg to hoist them before racing back to concealment. "There isn't enough room for these creatures you eat, either."

Azah's prey were usually smaller four-legged animals, which usually showed up around the same time as the plant bundles. They seemed lost or confused and were easy prey when she got to them soon enough. The trouble was, the other Tortantulas were usually there first. She had, more often than not, been forced to settle on sucking the remnants of juices from one already preyed upon. A few times, she'd gotten remnants of her own kind who'd lost a squabble over the prey.

The cannibalism bothered him at first. The idea of eating his own kind, or Azah's, made his stomach roil in protest, but watching her suffer when there was nothing else to eat was worse. And she moved instinctively, not like she enjoyed it. Maybe...maybe it was just the Tortantula way.

Once they'd found the remnants of a Tortantula and a Flatar, both consumed. That had been harder to see, and it confirmed there were other pairs there, as well. He'd known there must be; he still remembered being in the comfort of his mother's litter chamber. That warm place, surrounded by his brothers and sisters, possessed a dreamlike quality about it, like the taste of his mother's rich, warm milk.

Life had a sharp, bitter edge to it now. They hung on to the edge of survival, and he never knew if they were going to make it. Regardless, he had no intention of giving up. Azah depended on him.

Eventually, the food all but disappeared. It had been several dark times since they'd last found the plant bundles, and no animals were about. They only found the remains of dead Tortantulas, with all the edible parts consumed. Further proof the food was gone. The next time the light came on, Sadek made an announcement.

"We need to get out of here," he said.

"Out to where?" Azah asked, the eyes around her head looking every which way. Pillars rose from the ground in various places, some climbing toward the top. Elsewhere there were shapes that could move; boxes, Sadek called them. He'd tried to learn their placements but insisted they weren't always in the same place. The walls went around their place, and held various hiding spots such as the one they were currently in. The near distance held the curve of white bones, remnants of the brooding carcass Azah had been hatched into. They'd visited it a few times lately, in hopes of finding some bits of food remaining. They'd only found her biggest sisters using the carcass as a sort of home.

"How about up there?" Sadek asked and pointed a short arm up. High up the walls toward the top were more holes, hundreds of them. Around the holes were wispy places. If he squinted, he thought he could see movement up there.

"I can't climb the wall," she admitted. "Maybe right after I was born, but I doubt it now." Sadek examined the heights and wondered what was up there moving around. As they waited for night, the pair watched more than once as their much larger kin raced past, sometimes chasing each other, sometimes for unknown reasons. It was clear to both that all were starving and desperation was setting in.

Sadek thought again of his litter chamber. Of the comfort, safety, and love he'd felt. It was a little of what he felt from Azah, yet different. What he shared with Azah was trust, as well. She was so big, so powerful. A Tortantula was all raw emotion, strength, violence, and determination. He was inventive, intuitive, and curious. *It's up to me to get us out of here,* he thought. *This isn't about strength.* They hadn't seen another Flatar recently, and that supported his idea.

"Stay here," he told her, and he began to crawl out of their hiding place.

"Where are you going?" she asked, concern in her voice. He didn't think she was capable of fear.

"To get us out of here."

"I should come too."

"This requires stealth," he said. "Trust me?"

"Yes," she said without hesitation.

"Then wait, I'll be back." She waved her pedipalps up and down in a nod, and Sadek was off.

Maneuvering around in the daylight wasn't easy, especially with an unknown number of famished Tortantulas running everywhere looking for food. As a tiny bipedal mammal, he was definitely in that category. He had to race up and over one of the columns more than once in the first few minutes. It was then he realized he could leap from one to the other and stay off the ground entirely.

One particularly persistent Tortantula followed his progress for a time. He ran along, hoping his high road didn't vanish before she did. He negotiated one particular curving section as she gained on him. His heart raced, and it was all he could do not to think of Azah with despair.

Without warning, another, larger Tortantula crashed through the passageway, barreling into Sadek's pursuer. He couldn't suppress a scream, but he kept moving, leaving the sounds of a titanic, savage battle behind.

It turned out being on the column had more than the benefit of putting him out of the reach of hungry Tortantulas; it also gave him a new perspective on their world. Not all the columns were in the open; some were near the walls, as well. He angled back toward the wall and came to one only a short distance from the wall. He waited for a moment on that one as a huge Tortantula raced by in the direction of the fight Sadek had inadvertently started. Once the coast was clear, he went to the edge and peered at the wall.

* * *

Azah watched the entrance to their hiding place, never using less than two eyes, and usually more. The pair often slept during the day, alternating watch lest they be discovered and caught unaware. She kept her fangs ready and stayed wide awake, just in case. For some reason the time after Sadek left felt like it stretched on and on. After a while, she was convinced her partner was gone, devoured by her sisters.

The sound of two of her sisters locked in battle echoed across the world. She moved forward slightly and let her topmost pair of eyes look out. The light slowly dimmed, but there was no sign of the battling Tortantulas. In a moment, one of her sisters appeared. Azah lowered herself a little more so her eyes barely poked out. The other slowed as it passed the cave, her feet probably tasting either Azah or Sadek. There was another clash of battle, and she was off in that direction. She dearly hoped it wasn't her only friend.

Quite a bit of time passed. The light continued to dim. The sounds of battle didn't decrease; instead, they seemed to intensify. Azah began to wonder what was happening, enough to get curious. Her empty digestive tract wasn't helping. Even if she was too small to fight, she could possibly pick off a wounded straggler. As big as the others were, it would be enough food for days.

"Don't even think about it," Sadek said, making Azah jump in surprise. She looked around; she was quite a way out of the cave and heading toward the noise. She hadn't realized what she was doing.

"I just…" Azah started to say.

"I know, I'm hungry, too. But I have a solution." He explained what he'd found. It was a cave entrance at a slightly lower level than the last column he'd scouted. "I felt wind coming out of it, and smelled plants. There's food in there."

"What good will plants do me?"

"If there are plants, there are animals who eat them." Azah bobbed her cephalothorax slightly, considering. "You'll have to jump," he explained and marked a spot on the ground, then walked to another spot, "this far." Azah examined the distance. He could almost see her mind working.

"How far do I have to run before I jump?" she asked.

"Less than the distance I just showed you." Her fangs scraped against each other.

"Maybe," she said. "I'd do better if I had some food." She pointed with a pedipalp toward the sounds of fighting.

"You don't want any of that."

"How do you know?"

"I might have started it." All her eyes fixed on him, and he looked away.

"What did you do?" Sadek reluctantly told her. "You're lucky none of them came up after you."

"They can't," he said, whiskers twitching in amusement. "They're too fat! Now you? I bet you can. After I found that tunnel, I went looking around. That's what took me so long to get back. I found—" A hiss of triumph cut him off as a massive Tortantula with a rider flew around a column at high speed, right toward Sadek. They were far too close. He knew he was dead. He prepared to die.

A pair of legs snatched him roughly and jerked. Fangs snapped mere inches from Sadek's feet, clawed feet reaching as well. Everything missed, and the Tortantula roared by, legs working maddeningly to stop her headlong charge now that she'd missed her mark.

"You missed!" her Flatar screamed as he slapped the Tortantula on the upper thorax. "Turn around, stupid. Hurry!"

Sadek felt himself thrown more than handed up onto Azah's back. Her partner was already accelerating. His smaller size gave her a huge advantage over their attacker. She raced around the nearest column in a zigzag pattern, going faster than he'd ever seen her go.

"That way," he said and pulled the hairs behind her head. He hadn't failed to notice how the other Flatar treated his ride, like she was stupid. Maybe she was.

"Why?" Azah yelled back.

"No time, hurry." Trusting her friend and partner, she altered course.

The other Tortantula lacked her acceleration, but easily matched her top speed. The two huge spiders raced through the towering columns, one hot on the tail of the other. Every so often, Sadek would pull the hairs on her left or right thorax, and Azah would deftly maneuver around a column. Sometimes their pursuer would lose ground; more often, she'd gain. With the advantage of wide-spread eyes, Azah could see they were going to be caught.

"I hope you have something real soon," she said; he could feel her lungs working, her entire thorax throbbing as she struggled to feed her straining muscles, "we don't have any time left."

On her back, Sadek had been noting landmarks. A column with a slight tilt. Another with a chunk missing out of it. A big pile of chewed Tortantula exoskeleton. There it was, he realized. He tapped the back of her head and pointed.

"That one!" he crowed. "Jump for the top."

"I'm not sure I can make that," she huffed.

"You have to," he said. Sadek looked behind, and the other Tortantula was close. Damned close. "Jump!" he urged.

Azah dug deep and put on a burst of speed, vaulting her huge body into the air. She didn't make the top, so much as crash into the side most of the way up. Sadek yipped in fear as her 10 legs scrambled for purchase. They slid back for a terrifying second, then Azah found a hold and pulled herself up. The other Tortantula slammed into the column with enough force that it rocked, threatening to go over with them on top.

Azah accelerated across the top and leaped to the next closest one. Sadek had been too shaken up to give her directions, so he looked around frantically to get his bearings. She sped across the next column and leaped again before he pinpointed their location; right on target. He guessed that only made sense, as she couldn't jump much farther than he could. Especially with the narrow column tops, which happened to be flat.

This is all on purpose, some voice whispered in the back of his mind. "To the left," he yelled and pulled those hairs as she landed. Azah angled and jumped. While they were in the air, Sadek looked over the side, between her splayed legs. He gasped; there were five or six Tortantulas following their path below. *Oh, what have I done?* he wondered. *Have I killed us both?*

Sadek looked ahead. Three more jumps before they reached the last one. At the next landing, Azah stumbled with two legs missing their purchase. For a terrible second, Sadek thought they were going to plunge over the side and be instantly set upon by the crowd chasing them. It was all he could do to press his body against her thorax and hang on, both hands and feet grasping tufts of the thick, bristly Tortantula hair.

"Is...that...it?" Azah asked, gasping between breaths and pointing with a pedipalp as she made the second to last jump.

"Yes!" he said. "You can do it, we're almost home free." She made the last jump as Sadek saw Tortantula legs appear over the edge of the column they were about to land on. One had gotten far enough ahead and climbed up to get them.

Azah let out a surprised yell as she landed, and with more power than Sadek thought she had, almost instantly rebounded ahead like a bouncing ball. He saw the other Tortantula clearly. She was well within grasping distance, and there was a rider on her back. He was sure it wasn't the one they'd eluded earlier. This one was smaller, though not as small as Azah. It didn't try to grab them; instead, it watched where they were going.

Azah's powerful legs vaulted them so far that, for a second, he was afraid they were going to smash face-first into the wall above the tunnel entrance. He cried out and flattened himself even more against her thorax, and the rough-hewn tunnel roof passed over him only a hair's breadth away. Azah hit the ground, her legs not quite managing a proper landing. It turned into more of a pancake landing. They spun down the sloped tunnel, bouncing and bumping over the rough floor. Sadek was wondering if she'd knocked herself out when he heard her speak.

"Oh, great." He turned to look in their direction of slide as they flew out over open space and began to fall.

"Eeeeeeahhh!" he screamed in a most undignified voice. A second later, they cannonballed into water with a thunderous *Booom!*

Sadek was lucky she hadn't rolled over during the fall; instead, they hit armored belly first. Azah was stunned, but apparently Tortantulas were buoyant; they bobbed to the surface in only a second and both spluttered water from their lungs.

"That was kind of fun," she said, making a strange sound. *Was that a laugh?* he wondered.

"Dung if it was!" Sadek cursed. He'd never been more terrified in his short life. Descended from an arboreal race, he didn't like falling. "Can you get us to the shore?" He looked and realized what he was seeing. Pointy things were coming out of the floor. *Trees,* he thought. The floor was at all kinds of weird angles. *Ground,* his mind again corrected. The trees continued out of sight. In the distance, he could see a…*hill.* It was a whole new world!

"Sure," she said, and her legs started churning with a rhythmic motion. In no time, they were moving along at a pretty good clip. Sadek reached over and cupped the water, putting some to his mouth. It was clean and pure, different than it had been in their old world. He looked up, high above, and saw the roof arching far, far over their heads. This place was *huge.*

As soon as they made it to shore, Azah climbed out of the water and all but collapsed. She was completely exhausted. Sadek wandered around a bit, looking at all the vegetation growing. He tasted a few things and found several items he liked. The world was edible! But what about Azah?

He turned back when a four-legged animal about twice his size came out from around a tree. It was munching some of the plants on the ground, and when it saw him, it looked up curiously. Sadek froze, but it simply chewed and looked at him, so he stooped, picked up a rock, walked over to it, and crushed its skull. It let out a squeak as he bashed in its brains. Dead, he dragged it back to the beach where his partner lay asleep.

"Azah, wake up?"

"I'm too tired," she said without opening her eyes. "Just let me sleep."

"You might sleep better with a snack." He dropped the dead animal in front on her. She opened a pair of eyes and looked. Instantly all her eyes opened and focused on the animal. One of her pedipalps reached out and touched it, tasting the creature's skin, hair, and the blood. Suddenly she rose up, moved forward, and impaled it with her razor-sharp fangs with an audible *Crunch* of breaking bones. Sadek smiled. "You eat; I'm going to go find some more for me."

"I like this new world," she said. He patted her closest leg.

"So do I."

* * * * *

Chapter Four

"**S**omeone's coming."

Azah looked up sharply at Sadek's words. He stood still, his small feet in the shallow stream, tail quivering as his big ears twitched in the wind. Azah pushed herself up higher on her legs and lifted her front two legs to the breeze so she could taste the air. Sure enough, the taste receptors on her feet picked up the coppery tang that signified another Tortantula…or possibly two, given the way the taste thread seemed to be coming from different directions.

"Hide?" she asked, looking around. They'd come to this stream bed to gather up the green shoots of water plants Sadek liked to eat. It wasn't the best terrain for stealth, but it wasn't hopeless, either. Large boulders and rock shards lay tumbled about—remnants of some old landslide down the hill that rose to her left.

"Yeah," Sadek replied, leaping free of the stream and grabbing onto her exoskeleton with the ease of some practice. She didn't know how long it had been since they'd left the warren of caves where she'd hatched, but it had been long enough that Sadek had become quite good at pulling himself atop her pedicel waist. She felt his tail curl back along the topside of her abdomen and launched herself up the hill, looking for a defensible place to crouch and watch the streambed below.

Azah found it. A pair of boulders had rolled to a stop together during that ancient landslide. Over the years, sticks, old tree limbs, and debris had piled up against this barrier to create a natural deadfall with a small gap on the downhill slide. Azah had to do a little digging, but she was able to get herself and Sadek concealed in the shadowy space between the boulders under the deadfall, moments before the first Tortantula came tearing up the stream at a breakneck pace.

"She's hurt," Sadek whispered. He'd wormed his way forward and now lay on his belly, directly beneath Azah's thorax. He peered out from between her pedipalps at the scene below. "See how she's limping on her right front foreleg?"

"Mmhm," Azah replied. "And there's the one who hurt her."

A second Tortantula, this one much larger than the first, exploded onto the scene with a stellar leap. She landed atop the smaller, wounded Tort, and struck for the other's eyes with her fangs. The wounded one screamed and tucked her own legs into a roll, sacrificing her balance in an attempt to knock her attacker off. It wasn't a terrible gamble, Azah figured, especially since she landed on her back in the flowing water, blinding her opponent.

"Are these your sisters?" Sadek asked.

"I don't know," Azah said. "Maybe, but they're both so much bigger than me."

"Well, you did say you were small."

"Yes. But I don't think these are my sisters," she said. "They look bigger than all the ones we fought in the caverns. There must be other Tortantulas. They can't *all* be my sisters."

"How do you know?" he asked.

"I don't know how I know, I just know," Azah said, and it was true. For no reason she could name, she knew on an instinctive level that the two Tortantulas were not from her brood. She watched as the smaller one managed to flip herself over atop the larger attacker. She struck down hard once, twice with her fangs, opening large, weeping gashes in the bottom of her prey's thorax. The larger Tortantula's legs spasmed, and she fought to claw the other off of her, but it was no use. She was hampered by the rush of water in her eyes and mouth, and her movements became first frantic, then weak and ineffective as she drowned, pinned by the weight of her "victim."

"Whoa," Azah said softly. "That was impressive."

"Yeah," Sadek said. "I thought she was dead when the other one attacked."

They'd seen a few such scenes since emerging from the hatching caves. Most of the time, the bigger, stronger Tortantula emerged the victor. They'd managed to survive by being clever and doing the unexpected, like the wounded Tortantula in the stream, currently preparing to consume her prey.

"I wonder if she's like us," Azah said. Excitement at the idea rippled through her. "Maybe she could join us, and we could help each other."

"I don't think—" Sadek started to say, but he cut himself off as Azah bolted from their concealment out into the open.

"Are you wounded?" she called down the slope to the other Tortantula. "My partner can help! He has clever digits on his front legs—"

She never got to finish, because the wounded Tort let out a snarl and launched itself at her. Azah was not expecting the attack, since she'd taken pains to be friendly and not approach the other's kill, so she stumbled in surprise. The loose gravel under her feet slid, turning her stumble into a full-fledged fall, and she landed badly, out of position to defend herself.

The wounded Tort continued to charge up the hill, her fangs raised and ready to come slashing down into Azah's unprotected eyes, when she stopped short and let out a scream that was half-surprise, half pain.

Sadek, who had scampered up to the top of the boulders, let fly with another deadly-accurate stone and hit her squarely in the eye cluster. One of her eyes burst, and she stumbled and slid backward down the hill. It wasn't a life-ending injury, but it was enough to make her pause, and let Azah get her feet back under herself.

"I only wanted to help you," Azah screamed in fury. She whipped out her foreleg and swept the other Tortantula's wounded side. The wounded one crumpled to the ground, slashing out ineffectively. Azah neatly sidestepped her and stepped down on her thorax with a sickening crunch. "I don't know why you had to attack me!"

The wounded Tort let out a horrible, high-pitched keening kind of scream as Azah stomped her again and again. Her thorax continued to crumple, her abdomen spasmed uncontrollably, and the coppery tang of her blood filled the air.

"I only wanted to be friends!" Azah cried out, her anguish-fueled fury causing her voice to break on the last word. She reared up and drove her fangs deep into the other's eye cluster for the last time. The other Tortantula heaved, then went still. For a moment, everything but the water in the little stream was still.

"Azah?" Sadek asked, his words gentle.

"I only wanted to be friends," Azah said again, this time without the fury.

"I know," Sadek said. "But she was a savage one. She didn't know anything but fighting and dying."

"I know," Azah said sadly. "I hoped, when I saw how clever she was…"

"I know," Sadek said again. "I did, too, but savages can be clever and cunning, too. We should remember that."

"We will," Azah said, and for the first time in the encounter, she looked up at the little Flatar who had, for once, saved her. "You're my friend."

"Always," he said. "Together until the end."

"Zha Oort," she said. Azah didn't know where the words originated, but she knew their meaning like she knew her own breath. She reached out a foreleg to him. He took the invitation and leapt from the rock to her, then scampered into place on her pedicel. "Yes. Zha Oort. Until the Ending."

* * * * *

Chapter Five

Azah grew rapidly. As Sadek had predicted, it didn't hurt that she continued to eat her vanquished opponents, whether they were Tortantulas or animals she and Sadek hunted. She never grew larger than the other Torts they saw, but her thorax and abdomen filled out, her legs lengthened and grew strong, and her fangs became sleek and wickedly sharp.

Her body changed in other ways, too. It took her a while to notice, but her stinger became less and less effective. She could still produce venom from her fangs, and it seemed to do the job on her prey as effectively as ever…she just had to deliver it via a bite, instead of having the option of the stinger. Luckily, her pedipalps had grown along with the rest of her, and her reach with her fangs was much greater than it had ever been before.

Then one day, the stinger just…fell off.

Well, it didn't just fall off, exactly. It sort of came off by accident.

They'd gone to a forested area, where thick-trunked trees stretched high above even Azah's head and spread wide limbs adorned with deep green and red leaves. The red-leaved trees made an acorn that Sadek particularly liked. He'd climbed up the trunk of one of them, and was leaping from limb to limb, knocking the nuts down to the ground. Azah would then kick them into a pile, which he'd gather up in a mat he'd made by weaving river grasses together, and they'd take them back to their sleeping place. It was a rather clever little arrangement, and Azah admired her partner's ingenuity for thinking it up.

"Ugh," Sadek called down to her at one point, "these acorns here are stunted and puny. I think we need to go further up away from the river, where the trees are thicker."

"Come down, then, and we'll go," Azah said, rearing back and leaning on two of the tree trunks to look up at him. The bark of the tree tasted strange under her feet. Spicy and warm...not bad, but not good, either.

"Take too long," Sadek said. "I'll just go through the trees. Follow along on the ground."

"I won't fit."

"Yes, you will. Don't be a baby. You'll be fine. Keep up!" Sadek's voice carried a current of chittering laughter that made Azah grind her fangs together in frustration, but she pushed forward after him anyway. Where he led, she followed. That was how it was.

The trees crowded in almost immediately. She felt their rough bark scraping along her exoskeleton as she wove between the trunks, trying to find a way through to remain under Sadek's maddening laughter. She could always move fast, that wasn't the problem. The problem was trying to find a path between the increasingly small gaps on the forest floor.

"You're falling behind!" Sadek called back to her in a sing-song tease as she tried to push through a section that had looked wider than it apparently was. A low-lying branch scraped against the underside of her thorax and snapped painfully up into her pedicel. She lifted one of her mid-legs and stomped on it. The branch cracked and bent, but didn't entirely break. The wood inside was green and tasted sweet and green like sticky plant sap. It was revolting, and only amped up her growing anger.

"I'm stuck!" she called back. "This is why I didn't want to come in here!"

"You're not!" Sadek called.

"I am!" she bellowed and shifted her weight from side to side, trying to back out from between the trees that held her abdomen like a vise. Slowly, millimeter by millimeter, she began to move. Though she could feel the gouges on her exoskeleton, and more of the green, springy branches began to scrape against her.

"You are?" Sadek said, and this time his voice carried worry instead of laughter.

"I just said so, didn't I?" she snarled, and then returned her attention to getting free. She found that, if she wiggled from side to side and sort of pushed backward, she could manage to work her way back out of the trap into which she'd blundered. It was hard work, though, and she soon found herself gasping and holding her breath as she pushed.

Suddenly, she felt something low in her abdomen pop and release, and the dried-up husk of her stinger shot off the bottom of her body.

"Whoa! What was that?" Sadek asked, above her. He'd come back through the upper branches to see if he could help. Azah wondered if he felt guilty for getting her into this mess.

"What? I think I lost my stinger. That happens when we grow up."

"No, the white stuff you shot out. It's like...string? A fiber of some kind?"

Azah wanted nothing more than to turn around and look to see what under the bleeding sun Sadek was babbling about, but she was still stuck. Her anger ratcheted up another notch, and she let out a scream as she shoved herself backward. She felt more of that strange pressure release from the back of her body, and suddenly she was free, slamming back out of the grasping, tight trees, fighting to keep her balance on the sticky-sweet detritus of the forest floor.

Strands of something began to float down around her, drifting in the still air. Like Sadek said, it was some kind of stringy fiber, but it was like nothing Azah had ever seen before. The light through the red and green leaves caught at the slowly drifting strands, lighting them up in an iridescence that drew Azah in. Somewhere in her mind, she felt a door starting to open as she watched that strand of silk float down through the dappled light, winking at her with all the secrets of the universe inside...

"Azah! Azah!" Sadek's voice, edged with panic, broke through her mesmerized reverie.

"What?" she asked, trying to focus her eyes on his little face. "What's wrong?"

"You...where'd you go? You just sat there for so long, watching that stuff—"

"Silk."

"What?"

"It's called silk. Don't ask me how I know, I just know. It's...special."

"How, special?"

"I don't know," she said, frustration rising as the door in her mind slammed shut, and the drifting fiber of silk touched the forest floor. "It just is."

"Okay," the Flatar said slowly. "Are you okay? I'm sorry I didn't listen to you."

"It's all right," Azah said. "You will next time."

"I will," he confirmed. "Always."

"Did you get your nuts?"

"Some. Enough. Let's go home," he said, pulling himself up into place on her pedicel. Azah took one last look at the mysterious silk lying on the ground then turned and headed back the way they'd come.

* * * * *

Part II

Teamwork

Chapter One

The year had passed so quickly, he'd had to be told it was a year, and then she'd needed to explain what a year was. Azah and Sadek had grown into a team. When they'd first met, he'd needed her completely in order to survive. Now he was able to fend for himself, mostly through stealth and subterfuge. Those two things came naturally to him. They didn't to Azah.

Together they had grown stronger and more able to fend for themselves. Their world was a dome that took a good part of two light cycles to move across, full of hills, valleys, trees, and water. Prey could be found to feed them both. Azah ate most of what they caught, giving tender pieces of flesh to Sadek to complement the various edible plants he'd discovered. A routine was established, and they flourished.

The world wasn't without challenges, though. Other pairs roamed the dome, and hundreds of solo Tortantulas. Most of the solos were no worry; they didn't plan ambushes or work in pairs. They hunted each other as often as they did the prey animals. It was the teams who were the real threat. At first, they'd avoided them, only glimpsing them at a distance, but eventually the other teams figured Sadek and Azah were targets because she was smaller than all the other Tortantulas. What they hadn't counted on was how devious Sadek was becoming.

Time and time again, they evaded ambushes with ease. None got close enough to even put a claw on the pair. All the while, Sadek kept coming up with new ideas. He'd recognized the benefits of being able to strike from a distance. Some of the prey animals were small, not much bigger than he was. He'd always found plenty of plants to eat, but Azah couldn't consume them. Only animals kept her healthy, so he'd crafted several spears. He used flaky rock to make razor-sharp points, which Azah helped attach to the branches.

"How did you know how to make those?" Azah asked.

"I just did," he said. Deciding he needed a way to carry them, he used some more branches and vines to craft a place to sit on her back that held four of the spears. With the—it was called a harness, he realized—in place, he was able to do more without having to hang on. He hooked his legs through the straps, and off they went. The whole process left Azah amazed, and Sadek a little confused. How did he know such things?

Finally, one day a pair of Tortantulas and their riders ambushed Azah and Sadek. One came at them from a hidden spot along a game trail. Sadek had recognized the ambush spot and, using foot signals, redirected his partner away. Then a huge Tortantula, bigger than any they'd ever seen, leaped out of a tree and pinned Azah against its trunk. The monster clicked its fangs together in delight as the Flatar yelled, "Kill the runt, I'll get the rider!" and threw a good-sized rock at Sadek. He ducked under the whizzing bullet, snapped up one of the spears, and stabbed.

Not all the game were herbivores. A few were cats twice Sadek's size. They liked to run and leap at him, thinking he was an easy target. Azah was fast, but not always fast enough, so Sadek had gotten good with the spears. His thrust was true, and the razor-sharp tip of the spear punched through the center left eye of the attacking Tortantula. Blinded by pain, she tried to back away, and Azah used all her strength to flip her over. In a flash, she'd sunk her fangs into the other's sternum. Venom shot straight into her circulatory system. They were resistant to their own venom, but not immune to such a direct injection. In seconds, her heart stopped.

The Flatar rider crawled out from under the dead Tortantula, a look of horror on his face. He looked up as Sadek screamed and flew at him, another spear held in both hands. With a sickening crunch, Sadek impaled the other Flatar through the chest, his weight and momentum slamming the enemy back and pinning him to the ground.

The second Tortantula came around a bend in the forest to see its much bigger partner upside down, Azah on top of it, her fangs glistening with blood. With Sadek dismounted as he was, if they'd attacked, the pair could well have been split up and taken out.

"Run!" the other Flatar screamed, high and shrill. The Tortantula spun and raced into the underbrush. Azah gorged herself. Sadek tried not to wonder if the pinned and dead Flatar was one of his siblings. It didn't matter; he was alive, and the other wasn't. He slept well that night.

The next day, he woke up, and Azah was gone. He was in a room, not the world of before. Its floor was covered in grass, and the walls looked like the woods, but they weren't. It was fake. At first, he panicked, running around, feeling all the walls for an exit.

"Azah!" he called repeatedly. "Please, help me!"

"Azah is not here," a voice said. Sadek spun, searching for a weapon, and found another of his kind. Bigger, older, with fur flecked with grey in places. "I am Teacher Pidek."

"Why did you take me from Azah?" Sadek asked.

"You will call me Teacher Pidek," he said with a stern voice.

"Where is Azah?" With a blinding fast move, Pidek shot across the space and kicked Sadek, hard. He went flying into the wall and slid to the floor, stunned.

"You will learn humility, or you will be fed to the brood mothers." Sadek sat up, putting a hand to his face. It came away wet with blood.

"I want Azah," he said, but not loudly. He raised a hand. "Teacher Pidek, I want Azah, please." The hand lowered.

"You will see her at the end of the lessons."

"What lessons? We don't need lessons; we're doing fine," he said, then added a hasty, "Teacher Pidek."

"Running around the brooder dome killing each other has winnowed out the worthless of your brood. The Stewards have deemed you worthy of being educated with the other teams and bade me to make it so." Sadek didn't understand all of what was said but remained silent. He didn't want to get hit like that again, and he also wanted to know if part of the education would be to learn to do that himself. "Are you ready to follow me, youngling?"

"Yes, Teacher Pidek." The older Flatar nodded and gave a little smile.

"Good. I see the Steward was again wise in her choice. This way," he said and walked back to the exit.

The teacher led him down a series of corridors, all painted in comforting woodland views, until they reached a big round room, higher on one end and sloping down to the other. The higher end was full of what looked like stumps covered with moss, but they were all the same height. On most, a young Flatar like himself sat patiently waiting. Sadek noted that more than a few were bloody as well, though a few were not.

"Sit there," Pidek said and pointed to an empty stump. Sadek did as he was ordered. After a while, more older Flatar arrived with other younglings, as they called the students. Again, some were bloodied, and others weren't. Two teachers entered alone, and Sadek wondered about that, too. Finally, no more younglings arrived, and the speakers all gathered at the lower end of the room.

"This is the first-year classroom," one of the teachers explained. "Having lived through the first year, you will all now begin basic education. Your Tortantulas are being instructed as well, though not in the same manner. You are free to discuss this with your Tortantula if you wish. There are new rules." Another teacher stepped forward. Sadek was sure it was Pidek because he looked right at him.

"You are now forbidden to prey on other teams such as yourself. Any caught doing so will be fed to the brood mothers. You may defend yourselves, and this rule does not extend to those without riders. They can attack you, and you may attack them. Do you all understand? The proper answers are 'Yes, Teacher,' or 'No, Teacher.'"

"Yes, Teacher," the room chorused. The ones who were injured were the fastest to answer.

"Very good. Reach down to the stump you are sitting on. You will see there is a recess, a hole in it, and inside is what we call a slate. Take it out and touch the light. You must keep this slate and not lose it. There is a belt inside to hold it, as well." Their education began.

* * * * *

Chapter Two

Azah woke, disoriented. Her pedipalps and feet throbbed with a sickly-sweet taste that seemed to cling to her. She badly wanted water to drink and something rich and meaty to eat, but that wasn't the concern that rose to the top of her sluggish thoughts. Something was wrong. Where was Sadek?

Her eyes flashed open, and the light outside stabbed into her brain from all directions. She pulled her legs under her and tried to stand, though her body felt loose and limp, slow to obey her commands. His warm furriness was nowhere to be found, and panic knifed through the thick fog that wrapped her mind—

"Sadek is safe."

The voice was dry and cold, and vaguely familiar. Familiar enough that Azah paused in her panic and let the words register. Safe? How could he be safe without her?

"Stupid child," the voice said. "You've earned the right to live, thus far. Don't make us regret that choice. Your Flatar runt is safe with his own kind right now, as are you. You survived a year in the brooder dome together, so you get to progress to the next phase in your education. I admit, I didn't expect to see you live to exit the caverns, let alone get this far. You were so small. You're still rather runty."

Memory rocketed through Azah. That was her mother's voice. She blinked and slowly forced her misbehaving eyes to focus on the hulking figure crouched before her. Sure enough, the features were the same as that misty memory from the day she'd first met Sadek.

"Mother?"

Mother struck out with her foreleg, sending Azah spinning thorax over abdomen to land in a crumpled heap against a white, featureless wall.

"Address me as Zorm, or Teacher. I won't acknowledge birthing such a puny thing as you outside these walls. Do well in school, and you may sometime call me 'mother'…perhaps."

Azah picked herself up on heavy limbs and crouched submissively. Zorm went on.

"As I said, your Flatar is safe. He is with his own kind, getting his own instructions. From now on, the two of you will be separated a few times a week for lessons. If you learn well, you will progress. If not, you will die. But for now, there are a few rules you must understand. You are no longer on your own, living a lawless life. You may not attack another team consisting of a Flatar and a Tortantula. Unpartnered Tortantulas are fair game. You may always defend yourselves. You may ask questions when you do not understand something. You must complete all tasks assigned to you. Do you understand these rules, Azah?"

"Yes, Zorm," Azah said.

"Do you have questions now?"

"Why do I feel so strange?"

"We drugged you. Sometimes, in the past, Tortantulas have reacted badly to being separated from their partners. We slowed down your reactions to give your brain time to hear me before you got yourself killed out of panic."

"When will I see Sadek again?"

"When you complete your lesson."

"What is the lesson?"

"That is for you to figure out," Zorm said, and Azah imagined she could see the malice dripping from her mother's words. She blinked again, trying to keep her eyes focused as Zorm turned and disappeared through a door that slid open, then closed with a sickening finality.

Azah took a deep breath and blinked all her eyes once again. She wished the fog wreathing the edges of her brain would dissipate. Zorm had said she must figure out the lesson, then complete it, in order to see Sadek again. All right, so there must be something in the room then, right?

She rose up and looked around. The room was largely featureless, with curving white walls and a light that came from somewhere in the ceiling. Azah couldn't even see a seam where her mother's door had been...so maybe there were other doors? Was that the lesson? She had to escape this strange, blank room?

Azah walked toward where the door had been, focusing her eyes there. Sure enough, there was no seam whatsoever, but when she reached out and touched the wall, she caught a trace of something...meat, perhaps, tinged with malicious curiosity? It certainly seemed like her Mother's traces. Were there more?

She shuffled around the room, sweeping her foreleg across the surface of the wall as she walked. The wall itself tasted strange, like rock, but different. Less...natural. She didn't know how to describe it, except that it left an unpleasant not-quite-metallic taste on her receptors.

Wait...yes! There, that was something different. She'd made it about a quarter of the way around the room before she tasted another faint trace. This was different: furry and soft. Like Sadek, yet with a sharper tang. An older Flatar, perhaps? She focused on the portion of the wall with the trace, but still no seam betrayed itself. She swept her foreleg over the wall again and found the trace one more time. It seemed to concentrate down lower…

She crouched and prodded at the wall where the trace tasted strongest. Sure enough, the omnipresent light flickered, and a small section of the wall slid noiselessly out. It was a shallow tray, and it held a small object, about as wide as two of her feet side by side. She reached into the drawer to lift the object out, and it came to life.

"Well done, Azah," the screen said. She pulled it closer and focused her eyes on the Flatar face it showed. The voice tickled at her memory, but she couldn't have said why. "You have passed the first test. This is a slate, and it will be one of your most useful tools for learning. Right now, we're going to work on language. I will show you a picture of a sound, then the sound itself. You must learn to automatically associate the sounds with the pictures. This is called an alphabet, and it is the basis for written language. It is imperative that you learn to read and write with facility. You will begin now."

"When can I see Sadek?" Azah asked. The Flatar on the screen ignored her and disappeared from view. An unfamiliar arrangement of lines replaced his face, and his voice uttered the sound that began her name.

"Repeat it," the Flatar said.

"When can I see Sadek?"

The slate delivered a shock so suddenly Azah almost dropped it. It wasn't damaging, but it had surprised her, and it stung.

"Repeat the sound."

"Aaa," she said obediently.

"Good. You may see Sadek when your lesson is complete. Now, this is the next sound…"

They worked for a long time. At least it felt like a long time to Azah. Long enough her stomach began to rumble with hunger, and her patience to fray thin. Still, she fought to master the symbols and sounds they represented, because it seemed that was the only way to be reunited with Sadek. But as the time dragged, the symbols and sounds began to swirl together in her head, and she grew more and more tired until her legs drooped, and she rested her abdomen on the floor.

"Recite it for me from the beginning," the Flatar said. Azah glared at the little screen but complied. To her surprise, she got all the way through without him interrupting her with a correction.

"Excellent. The lesson is finished. Exit through the door and follow the path to your new sleeping quarters. Sadek will meet you there."

Joy surged through her, stiffening her legs and giving her new strength. Sure enough, a seam appeared in the far wall and a door slid noiselessly open. Azah barreled through without another thought and followed the short corridor beyond until she burst into a room. It was about four times the width of her body across. The floor was covered in grass that tasted…unnatural. The walls sloped up to a small, circular roof that glowed softly.

But Sadek stood there, looking up at her with relief. She surged toward him, reaching out a foreleg to assist him up into place without even thinking about it. Once his warm furriness was safe upon her pedicel, she felt the horrible tightness of lingering fear start to ease.

"I thought they'd taken you from me," she whispered.

"Me too," he said.

"Are you all right?"

"I'm fine. They put us in a classroom and started to teach us. You too?" he asked, and Azah belatedly realized she was still holding the slate. How she'd managed that headlong charge into the room without cracking it was anyone's guess, but it was intact. She laid it carefully down. Something told her if she broke it, she wouldn't like the consequences.

"Yes. Although there was no us. I was alone."

"Did they hurt you?"

"No. At least, not as long as I did what they said."

"Same. So, I guess, for now, we do what they say," Sadek said. It was almost a question, though they both knew the answer.

"I guess so. I'm so glad to see you," Azah said.

"Me too. Are you hungry?" Sadek asked, as her stomach began to rumble again. He could probably feel the vibrations through her exoskeleton.

"Yes."

"There's food. They showed us earlier. Let's go eat, then I'll show you our new sleeping place. Believe it or not, I think we're actually kind of safe here."

Azah clicked her fangs to indicate she wasn't sure. Sadek laughed and tapped on the top of her thorax.

"Fair enough. But there's food. Let's go find it. I missed you."

"And I, you."

"But we're together now," he reminded her. "We'll survive this, too. As long as we're together."

* * * * *

Chapter Three

One of the first things Sadek learned was how to read and write. It was surprisingly easy. At the same time, he learned they were both, Azah and he, one year old when their education started. He began to understand the passage of time in units. That was, surprisingly, harder than language. With that new knowledge, he understood they were in class one day in every three. They would be summoned by flashing lights to an exit that led to their sleeping chamber. They'd rest there, then go to their separate learning. Afterward, they'd sleep in the room again, and then leave in the morning. The rest of the time, he spent with Azah, and that was wonderful.

Like him, Azah went off to her own class while they were in the rooms. She didn't talk about what went on in her class, so he decided not to share, either. At least for a time. Every two classes were called a week, every four weeks was called a month, and every 10 months was a year. They were expected to learn and keep track.

The classes were meant to only be places of learning. The lessons became progressively more difficult once language was learned. At the end of the first month, he finally found out how he'd known some things before learning them. "Certain elements of knowledge were imparted to your brains as infants," the teacher explained; "this was done via implants into your brain while you slept. That knowledge is passive, and only used if you have the wherewithal to access it." All the young Flatar were looking with mixtures of confusion, surprise and, as with Sadek, revelation. He knew by that expression which had experienced the moments of knowledge.

Even though education was fun—and he was enjoying it, most-ly—the time with Azah was more enjoyable. Every day their effectiveness as a team became more pronounced. However, the prey became harder to find. At first, it was only a few days between making kills. Then a week. Then two weeks. Azah became increasingly moody and unhappy. Finally, when Sadek barely missed a small animal with a thrown spear, she lost her temper with him.

"You missed!" she yelled and shook so strongly, Sadek almost flew out of the saddle.

"I'm sorry!" he yelled and hung on.

"I'm just so hungry," she said. "I could barely finish the lesson in school last time."

"Lesson," Sadek said as he swung down to the ground and retrieved the spear. As he jumped back on her thorax, he snapped his fingers. "Lesson!"

"What are you going on about," Azah asked and moved up off the path where they'd been tracking the animal.

"This is just another lesson," Sadek explained, "a lesson of life and death."

"Aren't they all?" Azah mumbled.

"What did you say?"

"Nothing," she said, kicking over a rock as she passed.

Sadek grunted and thought. They used to provide food to them in the classrooms, back at the beginning. That had stopped a few weeks ago, at the same time prey began getting scarce. That prey must come from somewhere.

"Azah, head for the school dome."

"Why?" she asked. "School isn't for another day."

"You need to trust me," he said, "I have an idea."

Whether out of faith or from being too tired to argue, Azah turned in the correct direction. The school dome was in the center of their home dome, about a half-day's steady pace for Azah. By the time they arrived, the light was going, and night was coming on. They no longer feared other teams like theirs, but wandering solos were always a threat. For whatever reason, they were always the largest of Azah's kind.

"Okay, we're here," she said as they reached the edge of the school. As Sadek expected, the doorway the students entered through was invisible, though they knew from the lay of the land where it was. The grass was heavily trampled, as well. He swung down and walked along the wall. Azah followed, her eyes scanning in all directions. Some sort of machines kept the solos away when school was called. No such defenses protected them now. "What are you looking for?" she asked him.

"Shhh," Sadek said. He was on all fours, moving with his face next to the ground, searching for something, anything. There must be some sign. He moved halfway around the dome before he found it. A pattern pressed into the ground. Like a footprint that never stopped, going on and on. There was another one a short distance away. They both ran parallel to each other and looked to be at least a week old. Something had been moving here, before the food became scarce, and the tracks went right up to the dome.

"Look at this," he said to Azah, who came over and examined the marking.

"I've never seen any animal make these sorts of tracks," she said.

"Nor I." Sadek looked in the direction they went. After a short way, they moved into some trees. "I think we should follow them."

"It's an unknown," she said. "It could be dangerous. I'm not as strong or as fast as I was even a few days ago."

"It could be food," Sadek said. "We haven't heard any sounds of hunting in days. I don't think there's any prey left here at all." He indicated the strange tracks. "I think these are the marks left by the teachers bringing food to the school, before they stopped." Azah considered, her eyes looking in all directions, pedipalps rubbing together in a sign of confusion.

"Okay," she said at last, "let's see where it goes."

The tracks were easy to follow at first, but eventually became more subdued as they passed through a rocky area. Sadek struggled to follow them.

"Let me," Azah said, "I've been tasting the tracks, and I think you're right. It reminds me of the inside of the school." Sadek slung under her thorax for a time as Azah picked her way along the rocks where no evidence of the strange tracks remained. Then, there was soft ground again, and Sadek could see where the thing had gone through.

"Well done," he said, patting a fang. Azah clicked in satisfaction. Sadek again raced along the ground, his little legs moving him quick enough that Azah had to hurry to keep up. The tracks then led directly to a huge rock and ran into the side, not unlike they had at the school dome.

"Dead end," Azah said dejectedly.

"Not necessarily," Sadek said as he examined the rock. Unlike the school, there was evidence of a door, and several holes in the rock. Sadek reached into each one and felt the inside. They were all what they appeared, except one. Inside that one, he felt metal. "Ah," he said and examined it with his fingers. "If feels like a lever…"

"Pull it," Azah encouraged, all sense of caution gone at the discovery. Sadek gave a shrug, wrapped his hand around the lever, and pulled. Nothing happened, so he pushed. There was an audible *Click* and the door moved inward an inch. "Yes!" Azah said.

Sadek gently pushed the rock door inward until it stopped, revealing a metallic door behind it. There were no handles, but a small square hole. He leaned closer and saw a glowing keypad inside. By leaning in and stretching, he could touch the controls. Sadek took his slate computer from the pouch around his waist and looked at it. By bringing it alive, he was able to take a picture of the keypad and examine it closely.

"It is a locked door?" Azah asked.

"Yes," he said and held up the screen for one of her eyes to see. The picture was the display showing a series of words:

"Heaviest—Terbium, Ytterbium, Dysprosium."

"What does that mean?" Azah asked.

"Atomic weights," he said, "we just learned about that." Azah remained silent as Sadek thought hard. His little face scrunched up and he tried to remember the lesson. Those were all rare elements and were very valuable. They hadn't explained why, only that they were sought after. He didn't remember the precise number but thought Ytterbium was the highest. He reached in and touched the word. There was a beep. He looked, and the display had changed, so he took another picture.

"More puzzles?" she asked.

"Yes," he grumbled and examined the words.

"Water, Rock, Air." *What in entropy does that mean?* he wondered. Did it want to know which was heavier? What was useable? Or...was it flow? That was the only thing that could make sense. He stuck his hand in again and tapped air, rock, and water last. Another click, and another screen.

"How many?" Azah asked.

"I don't know," he said and took yet another picture. This was only two things—a Flatar and a Tortantula. He blinked for a second and reached in to touch a picture. There was another click, and the door swung inward.

"You did it!" Azah cried.

"I did," he agreed. The entrance was too small for Azah, so he activated the slate's little light and went inside.

"Wait," Azah called and he looked back. She was holding out one of his spears. "Just in case?"

"Good idea," he said and patted her furry leg. "I'll be fine."

"Please come back?"

"I will."

He moved into the dark space, which was a sort of tunnel. It was smooth, like the walls in the school, and cooler than the air outside. Before long, he came to a larger room. To one side was a machine he'd never seen. It had strange circular devices on the side. *Tracks* he heard in his mind, more of the information he'd been given at birth. He realized that was how it moved and left those marks in the ground. The rear of the machine was a box big enough for a dozen Flatar to ride. Then he saw there was a line of them.

He scanned the room as far as his light would allow him. It smelled mechanical, not of animals, and he was worried they'd come all this way for nothing. Then he saw a big stack of boxes to one side. He'd seen boxes like this when he'd been given water in funny little containers. He skittered over and examined them.

"Standard Tortantula Field Ration" one of the boxes said. He knew the first three words, but not the last. What was a ration? He took down a box and tore the paper top open. Sure enough, it was the funny little containers. Like a ball of water contained by a clear material. Only, these weren't pure water inside. It was black and seemed to have stuff moving inside. He sniffed one, and it only smelled of the container.

It said Tortantula, so it was meant for Azah. He put it back in the box, and after a last look around, took the box and quickly moved back up the corridor. There was little light left outside, but Azah could see him coming by the light from his slate.

"Is that you, Sadek?" she asked.

"Yes," he said, and in a moment, he was back outside in the fresh nature-smelling air. For some reason, he felt more relieved.

"What do you have there?"

"It says they're Tortantula rations."

"What's a ration?"

"I don't know," he said and took out one of the funny containers. He decided it reminded him of a flower bulb, so that's what he called it. "It had a couple dozen of these."

"Is that a liquid?" she asked him.

"Yes," he said, and showed her how it squished in his hand. As he was squeezing it, one of his finger claws pierced the side. The dark liquid spurted out onto his hands. It was putrid smelling. "Ugh, what is that—"

"Incredible smell?" she finished for him.

"It's the black stuff," he said.

Azah reached a foot out and touched the wetness on his hand. Instantly all her eyes flashed with excitement. "Put it on the ground," she said, "quickly!"

"Okay," he said, and did as she'd asked. Immediately, she leaned forward and punctured it with a fang. In less than a second, she'd sucked it dry, and the empty shell of the container fell from her fang.

"Ahhhhh!" she said in a contented sign.

"Was that…good?" he asked, more than a little revolted. He'd watched her eat the dead of his own kind and only shrugged (mostly), but *that* stuff was absolutely disgusting.

"Yes," she said, "give me another?"

"Sure," he said and set a second one out for her. Again she pierced it and sucked it dry. Her thorax quivered with delight.

"Another?" he asked when the empty fell away.

"No," she said and let out a little burp, "that's enough. Wow, they're filling!"

"That wasn't very much," he observed, "not compared to what I've seen you eat from an animal."

"I know, but those are different somehow."

"I guess ration means food," he said. She lowered herself to the grass and made contented sounds as he counted the containers. There were twenty more in the box. He closed it as best he could and was about to jump up in the saddle, then went back to the door. He was surprised to see it was already closed. The rock covering was, as well. "Huh," he said and picked up the shriveled empty ration bulbs. "No reason to help anyone else," he said, then managed to get on her back while holding onto the box. "Let's get out of here before anyone else comes looking," he said.

"Thanks," Azah said, "I mean, really."

"We're partners," he reminded her and patted the fur behind her head, "it's what we do." The two moved off into the night.

* * * * *

Chapter Four

They continued to raid the school for food at night. Sadek said that someone was replenishing the supplies, which probably meant they were doing what they were supposed to do, so that was good. Azah felt the strength returning to her body, and she thought she might be growing a little. Still, though, something was off.

She continued to complete her lessons, both with Sadek and away from him. They rarely had trouble with the solo roaming Tortantulas any longer, and the other teams kept their distance in deference to the school rules. None of them seemed interested in working together. Which was fine with Azah. Sadek was all she needed. But still, she felt out of sorts.

"Azah," her partner called one afternoon. "Azah! Pay attention, Azah, we need to move to the other side of the hill. I swear, you're so spacey lately—"

"Maybe you should just go and leave me then," Azah growled back. "If I'm so much of a burden! It's not like you need me to gather up these nasty berry things you like to eat."

Sadek stopped what he was doing and turned to stare at her.

"What's wrong with you?" he asked, his tone hurt. "You've been snappish all damn day...for several days now. Why would you say something like that?"

"Nothing. I'm bored. Let's go find a solo to kill."

"What? Azah, what would that do? It's not part of our lessons—"

"Oh, rend our lessons! I'm so sick of hearing about our stupid lessons! Maybe I want to do something useful, did you ever think of that?"

"You don't think the lessons are useful?" Sadek tilted his head to the side, his big eyes blinking in confusion.

"I don't think *I'm* useful! You're the one who figures everything out! And with your spears, you don't even need me to protect you anymore. You're smart and deadly and all of the teachers like you, and I'm puny, worthless me…" she trailed off, and let her body droop down to the ground.

"Azah," Sadek said softly. He walked toward her, until he could rest his furry face against her cephalothorax, above her eye ring. "You're not worthless. Not to me. We're a team. I can't do any of this without you."

"Yes, you can," she said. Her pedipalps twitched in misery. "You figured out how to get us food."

"We did that," Sadek said. "I couldn't have found the cache if you hadn't been able to follow the taste trail."

"You would have found it eventually. You're smart."

"So are you!"

"No, I'm not, I'm—"

"Shut up, Azah. Just stop it. I hate it when you do this."

"What –?"

"You get so down on yourself! I wouldn't even be alive if not for you! Just because I'm getting good at things, that doesn't mean that you can't also be good at stuff!"

"That's not what I mean—"

"Then what do you mean? Because it seems like you get angry every time I do something for us. It's not all about you rescuing me, you know. We're a partnership, right?"

Azah opened her mouth, but no words came out. She felt completely blank, blindsided by the perspective she hadn't considered.

"Right?" Sadek insisted, rearing back and staring into her eyes.

"Right," she whispered.

"Right. You're not my mother, I'm not your father...we're partners, and that means your strengths compliment my strengths. Sometimes we'll need what you can do, and sometimes we'll need what I can do." Sadek stomped his foot on the soft dirt as he spoke, making Azah blink at his vehemence.

"I just..."

"What?"

"I just don't want you to leave me," she said softly. "I know I'm small, and you could partner with anyone, because you're so smart."

Sadek pressed his fuzzy lips together and shook his head. Then he leaned back and smacked Azah hard on the side of her cephalothorax.

"What—? What was that for?"

"For being mean. Never, ever suggest I find another partner," Sadek said, his voice low and throbbing with anger. "I am yours. I don't even want to think about bonding with someone else. We are *together*, Azah. You and me against the entire bleeding world! And whatever's beyond these domes, too. So don't you ever say something like that again, all right?"

"All right," Azah whispered.

"All right?" Sadek said again, louder.

"All right!" Azah snapped.

"And I don't care what size you are. You're big enough, fast enough, and deadly enough for me, all right? None of the rest of them matter. Just you and me. We must survive our training, and we can't do that if we're not in harmony. Which means you handle the stuff you're good at, and I'll handle the stuff I'm good at...and we never mention working without one another again. Got it?"

Azah couldn't speak. Emotion wrapped so tightly around her lung she couldn't make the sounds come out, even though she moved her pedipalps. From the first moment of her life, all she'd known was she was too small, too weak, too worthless to do anything right. Only Sadek had ever seen anything else in her. She'd protected him, and he'd wanted to be partners...only it wasn't just that, she realized.

The thought opened in her brain like a door to another side of the world. It wasn't that she protected Sadek...it was that Sadek protected her as well! He wanted to be her partner, not because she was tough or fast or terrifying...but because she was Azah. She didn't want to be his partner because he was quick and clever, but because he was Sadek. He was the only one who had ever liked her, ever wanted to know her, and ever cherished her.

"I'm sorry," she said finally. "You're right. We're partners, we do things together."

"Until?" he asked, stroking the curve of her cephalothorax.

"Until the ending," she said, clicking her fangs on the final syllable. "Zha Oort."

"Zha Oort."

* * * * *

Chapter Five

"The Trefalon 62 flier is one of the most common we use in operations. They are affordable and useful." Sadek made a note in his slate, glancing around the room at the other Flatar. School was a time he used to study the required material presented by the teachers and to study the others of his kind. The interest in lessons varied from indifference (lessons like this one on fliers and remote operations), to extreme interest (Tortantula biology and psychology).

"Moving on to another topic," Pidek said and touched a control. The flier being displayed on the classroom's Tri-V became a weapon. They'd been educated on many different weapons, though only to teach familiarity. None of them was made for use by either the Tortantula or Flatar. Sadek wondered if they were afraid to teach the students about weapons at this point. Only, the weapon now displayed was obviously meant for them. Sadek knew, because it was the weapon he'd seen his mother wearing.

"This is the XT-12 magnetic accelerator pistol," Pidek explained. The image of the gun became a cutaway and transitioned to a graphic of an exploded view. Individual components were listed. "The standard sidearm of riders. Designed by Jeha engineers, who pushed the absolute limits of accelerator technology." He pointed to the drawing. "The capacitors which power the weapon are housed in the magazine. Due to the power restraints, it only holds 10 rounds."

The display changed to a Flatar on a firing range, several targets a dozen or so meters away. "The weapon is far too powerful for a being our size to handle its recoil, so the engineers built in an ingenious recoil cancellation system, taking advantage of both blowback and gyroscopic compensation."

Sadek examined the internals, now off to the side of the display, as the Flatar fired the weapon. A tongue of flame a half-meter long blew from the barrel. Four muzzle brakes redirected the blast, further reducing the recoil. The shooter switched to a single hand, holding the weapon at arm's length with ease, despite it being a quarter his size. It fired again, and this time the wielder used his arm to take up some of the hit.

"The XT-12 can be fired with great ease and at point-blank range. Barrels must be changed every 20 rounds, two magazines. It's a fast swap." The image showed how quickly the barrel slid out and was replaced. "Your standard Tortantula's assault saddle holds five replacement barrels, and nine extra magazines."

"Why only nine?" one of the others asked before Sadek had the opportunity.

"Because after 10 magazines are expended, the magnetic buffers have degraded and must be replaced." Anticipating the question, another Flatar was shown breaking down the weapon. "This isn't a complicated operation either, but it is not field expedient. However, the functional use of the weapon doesn't often exceed a team's deployment time."

Sadek considered the meaning of that statement. Did it mean that he wouldn't need to fire more than 100 shots? Or did it mean they wouldn't live long enough to need to use the gun more than 100 times? Or was it both? He wasn't sure if he liked that idea much. "Not replacing the barrel can cause a critical failure, compromising the massive power loads in the magnets. That constitutes a catastrophic event."

They spent another hour of study on the XT-12, then Pidek went through several other arms individually, though in much less detail.

Some were designed to be mounted on the Tortantula-standard saddle, others used by hand. There was a small semi-automatic ballistic weapon meant for a sidearm, as the XT-12 was simply too bulky to carry around. Then a somewhat underpowered laser carbine, the first energy weapon the class was introduced to. He finished with a bolt-actuated ballistic rifle, magazine fed, with optical sights. It seemed to be of limited utility, and Sadek wondered why they even bothered with such a simple weapon.

"Now," Pidek said after they finished the rifle, "we go to the range."

The class was as excited as Sadek had ever seen them. He himself was almost giddy. Were they about to be introduced to the legendary XT-12, at long last? If so, that meant their training was almost done. They hadn't known the school contained a firing range. It was located through a door, which had never opened for them before, and down stairs into the ground underneath. There they found a large firing range with a dozen lanes and Tri-V targets.

Once they were assembled, Pidek was joined by a squad of other teachers. There was one for each of them. This was a day of firsts, it seemed. The first time they learned about guns, the first time they'd get to fire them, and the first time they would receive individual instruction.

The instructor who paired with Sadek was one he'd never seen before. After just a few minutes of talking with him, he realized it wasn't a teacher exactly, but a Flatar soldier brought in for the introduction. That was a first as well. They didn't treat the young Flatar with the dismissive, almost resentful scorn most of the teachers reserved for the students. The soldiers were patient and didn't mind questions.

Sadek's instructor produced an XT-12 mockup and gave it to his student. "This is not a functioning weapon, but the feel, finish, controls, and even weight are identical." When he handed it to Sadek, he almost dropped it. The thing was *heavy*! The instructor chuckled, but not in a scornful manner. They'd just shared an experience the rider had himself gone through in the past. "Yes, they are heavy, but you'll get used to it."

Behind each range lane was a Tortantula standard saddle mounted on a hump in the floor. One at a time, they sat on the saddles and were given the mockup XT-12s to practice with. They learned how best to maneuver the ungainly weapons to get it around the saddle's front protrusion (called a horn), and how they could move their entire body to bring the weapon to bear in all directions.

Finally, Pidek spoke up. "Live fire, who's first?"

"Me!" Sadek said instantly. As it turned out, he was a half a second faster than any of the others.

"Come up here," Pidek said. "Sadek, isn't it?"

"Yes, Teacher Pidek." The teacher nodded and gestured to the saddle closest to him. Sadek walked over and mounted.

"Have you listened to your instructor?" He nodded. "Very well." Pidek went a short distance to a locker and swung it open. Inside was row after row of XT-12s. Sadek knew these wouldn't be mockups. Pidek took one out and walked back to Sadek. "This is a live weapon," he said and held out the gun.

Sadek took the weapon and following his instructions, instantly aimed it at the ground and checked its condition. The electrically-actuated bolt was closed, the safety was off, and there was a magazine in the grip. With sure movements, he clicked the safety on, removed the magazine, and manually drew back the bolt. The controls were designed for his short, dexterous fingers and pointy claws. Sitting the magazine on the saddle horn, he looked to the teacher, who had watched his every move. After a second, Pidek nodded in approval.

"Satisfactorily done," he said and turned to the others. As he lectured about the moves used to make sure the weapon was safe, Sadek looked down at the magazine charge display. It was empty. He wasn't surprised. Had Pidek actually given him a loaded weapon? That would have been a surprise.

"Now, Sadek," Pidek said, and the saddle began moving forward to the lock at the entrance to the range lane. The teacher held out a magazine. Sadek could immediately see the glowing charge indicator. This one wasn't empty. He accepted it and, still keeping the gun pointed at the floor, slid the magazine into the XT-12's handle. It locked into place with an audible click. Immediately the weapon came alive in his hand. It seemed to hum for a second, and then stopped. "The gun is primed," Pidek explained. "It draws power from the pack for all its functions. Point it down the range and load it."

Sadek did as he was told, keenly aware that everyone was watching only him. The charge control was under his right thumb. He pressed it hard, as he'd been instructed; the gun gave a 'click-*whirr*,' then was silent. "It's loaded," Pidek said. The teacher took a slate and tapped on it. Down the lane, a simple multi-ring target appeared. "Take a proper grip, aim, release the safety, and fire a round."

Sadek raised the gun, letting his small hand settle tightly into the grip designed and molded for his people. As it settled in place, he heard a beep, and felt the gun come truly alive. It almost seemed to resist his aiming.

"What you feel are the gyros," Pidek said, "they are essential for us to be able to wield such a weapon, but they are a double-edged sword. It also means you need to take care how you move, aim, and control the weapon. Riders who weren't completely cognizant of that fact have had the gun pull itself right out of their hands when their Tortantula made a sudden turn or jump."

Sadek spent a moment moving the gun, changing the aim, and feeling how much force and control it took to make it do his bidding. "Fire when ready," Pidek said. Sadek settled the glowing site on the target and squeezed the trigger. *Crrack!* The gun bucked in his hands. The sound was deafening, and the flame bright enough to blind him. The target was flashing to indicate Sadek's round had passed through the inner ring. A perfect shot.

Pidek nodded. "What do you think?"

"I like it," Sadek said with a grin, imagining what he and Azah could do if he had an XT-12.

"Very good. Continue until the magazine is expended, and then we will retire to practice breaking down and stripping the weapon for service." All around them, other Flatar were mounting the saddles and being given weapons. In moments, thunderous cracks reverberated through the range. Sadek raised his weapon and fired again, scoring another direct hit. He was really going to like this part of his life.

* * * * *

Chapter Six

They'd been doing lessons for almost another year when everything changed again.

Azah had managed to embrace the idea of teamwork with Sadek as his capabilities grew. No longer was she the protector and he the protected. Rather, they learned to work as a team to continue procuring food for them both, learning their lessons, and generally keeping away from the other Tortantula teams. The other teams were forbidden to attack, it was true, but that didn't mean they had to be nice to one another. Azah never forgot the lesson of the wounded feral who'd attacked rather than accepting Azah's friendship, so she preferred to avoid others altogether.

Besides, Sadek's company was all she needed, and he seemed to feel the same. After a year, they'd gotten pretty good at avoiding the others as they went about their lives, solving the problems that presented themselves. Sometimes those problems were obviously lessons, sometimes Azah wasn't so sure.

Not that it really mattered. She learned anyway.

She continued to grow, though she was still smaller than any of the other Tortantulas that had a Flatar partner. It seemed to her that the other teams avoided her and Sadek because of this. She didn't care so much for herself, but it grieved her that Sadek should suffer isolation. The other Flatar seemed to relish interacting with one another. Sadek simply spent all his time and energy with her.

"I don't like them," he said one day, when she asked him about it. They'd reported for lessons separately as usual that day but had then been reunited in a larger room. Azah had been so happy to unexpectedly see Sadek, she'd almost missed the way he led them away from everyone else. Almost, but not quite. "They're mean, they say mean things, and they're stupid. I'd rather just hang out with you."

"What do you mean they're stupid?" Azah pressed.

"They can't look beyond the obvious," Sadek said, shaking his little head in disgust as he pulled himself up into his seat on her pedicel. "Not like you. All they want to talk about is who's biggest, who has the most feral kills. Do you know, some of them go hunting for ferals after lessons? They actively try to track them and eat them. That's how they've been living since the food situation changed."

"Well," Azah said, wondering at the disgust in his tone. "I mean...they have to eat. If they weren't smart like you, maybe they couldn't figure out how to raid the store room."

"Oh, it took them awhile, but they figured it out. I told them, even. There's plenty of food in there. We're supposed to eat it, and they always put more back. But they keep hunting ferals, because they like it. They don't eat them anymore."

"Oh," Azah said, turning that thought over in her mind. Killing others to eat and live was one thing, but killing only to kill? When there was no mission or objective to meet? Was that what she was supposed to be doing? It didn't sound either fun or right to her. Especially not when their raided rations gave them everything they needed.

"Come on," Sadek said, patting the top of her cephalothorax. "Don't worry about them. Look there on the dais, a teacher is about to speak."

"Today you will try something new," the Flatar teacher said as Azah turned to focus her eyes on him. "In the center of your feeding grounds is a small hill, upon which we've constructed a basic stockade. Today, you will take that stockade, using all means at your disposal, including the feral Tortantulas that inhabit your feeding grounds. This is a lesson in leadership, and your performance today will have a direct bearing on your assignments once you leave the training environment. No questions will be allowed at this time. Figure it out. You have until nightfall to complete your objective."

While Azah was still wrapping her mind around that extraordinarily short brief, the teacher pair left, and a large door opened in the otherwise featureless room. The cool morning outside beckoned, and Azah found herself swept up in the tide of the other teams as they flooded outside.

"This is about leadership," a Flatar named Hyree said. He sat proudly atop the pedicel of the largest Tort, who stalked ahead with deadly, liquid grace in each of her ten limbs. "That means we have to get the ferals to attack the stockade for us."

"We'll herd them," his partner Nura said, her voice low and deadly. "If we can get them to jump off a cliff all in a mass, we can get them to attack a stockade."

"You get them to jump off a cliff?" Azah asked before she could help herself.

"Of course," Nura said, turning to focus her near-side eye on Azah. "It's a basic hunting technique. They'll run from us, so we coordinate to push them together in a group, then we run toward the cliff. It's funny to watch them fall, and sometimes, they're broken but alive at the bottom. They let out the most piteous cries."

Azah's feet faltered, and she nearly stumbled under the wave of teams following closely behind.

"Azah?" Sadek asked quietly, leaning down so only she could hear his words as she fought to keep her feet. She sucked dust-laden air into her lung and tried to flow to the side of the group, away from the center clustered around Nura and the other large frontrunners of the class.

"I'm okay," she replied as she pushed through to the edge and took in a lungful of clearer air. "I just...I wasn't prepared for her..."

"I tried to tell you," he said, his tone grim.

"She enjoyed their cries..."

"I know," Sadek said, patting the top of Azah's thorax again.

The group of them continued to surge forward down the length of the largest valley. At a short, low-voiced command from Nura, the group spread out like a net, ready to capture any hapless ferals hiding within the trees and creeks of the feeding grounds.

As soon as they reached one of the more thickly wooded areas, Azah broke off from the main group and headed away from the main student body toward the center of the feeding grounds. She stopped beneath a large, heavy-barked tree and crouched. Without a word between them, Sadek leapt up from her body and scampered into the tree's branches overhead. Azah kept herself perfectly still and listened to the faint rustle as he climbed to the top of the tree and looked out.

Not more than thirty heartbeats later, Sadek flipped down from the tree and landed atop her abdomen. He slid into place and leaned forward to speak softly for her ear slits alone.

"The stockade is up ahead, in the direction we thought, another two klicks or so. It sits on a hill at the bottom of a box canyon, with a stream running to it," he said.

"Oh! I know that place," Azah said. "The canyon cliffs are good for hiding, with lots of creases and holes in the rock."

"That's what I thought," Sadek said. "What do you say we head over there and take a look down at the stockade from the top of the cliffs? Maybe we can figure out how to take the stockade by ourselves! Wouldn't that be awesome?"

"Yeah, except Teacher said this was a lesson in leadership."

"Well, we'll lead by example!" Sadek said, sounding happier and happier as he spoke. "We'll take a look, come up with a plan, then lead the others through it."

"What if they don't listen to me?" Azah asked.

"They will. When they see how incredibly smart our plan is, they'll listen. You watch. This is going to be fun!"

Despite her misgivings, Azah found Sadek's enthusiasm infectious, so she followed his navigation with a lighter, easier disposition. The conversation with Nura still bothered her when she thought about it, so she simply *refused* to think about it and pushed forward to their goal. They moved at a quick pace, though Azah took care to place her steps carefully and listened hard for the sound of anyone following them.

"I'm taking us a bit out of the way," Sadek informed her, after the second time he scampered up a tree to check their position. "But it's going to keep us within the forest until we're well clear of the opening to the box canyon."

"I don't want to be late," Azah said. "It would be bad if we got there and all the others had taken the stockade already."

"Not going to be a problem," Sadek said, his tone confident, "they're stopping to herd the ferals, remember? They'll have to go slow and deviate the other way down the main valley to gather up as many as they can from the riverbank before pushing them back up and into the box canyon."

"That's true," Azah said. "Ferals do like to hang out near the river."

"That's probably because it's easier to get water there."

"You think?"

Sadek huffed out a soft puff of laughter, but let her sarcasm go. Azah felt a wave of good feeling pass over her. It was a beautiful day. The ground tasted fresh and alive beneath her feet. She was out on a mission with her partner...Life was good, at least for the moment.

They kept moving on, through the depths of the woods, to where the sunlight dappled the ground, and the trees thinned, then disappeared altogether. Azah crouched low in the tall grass that covered the slope and crept up to the cliff's edge overlooking the box canyon and the stockade below.

"Careful," Sadek said, leaning low over her thorax, "it would suck to fall down there. It's got to be a hundred meters or more."

"I will—" Azah said, then cut herself off as she caught sight of movement down below. Something was happening.

As the pair of them watched, a formation of fliers lifted off a launch pad deep within the confines of the stockade itself. There had to be at least ten of them, and they moved in perfect concert with one another to fly an orbit of the wooden walls.

"I wonder what kind of fliers those are," Azah said.

"Trefalon 62 Bravos, I think," Sadek said. "Maybe Charlies, but those would be expensive to use for a training exercise."

"How do you know that?"

"I'm guessing, based on their lifting fans. We had a class in flier recognition recently."

"What did you learn about these?"

"They're armed reconnaissance and scouting fliers," the Flatar said. "They've got an auto-targeting MAC, as well as active laser-ablative shielding on the body. Their one big limiting factor is they're vulnerable from above."

"Above, you say?" Azah said, tasting the words and finding them sweet. "Isn't that interesting?"

"What are you thinking?"

"Well...we have this whole lovely, crumbling cliff here. If I climbed down on it, with you strapped in, do you think you could make a shot at one of those fliers?"

"You'd have to get down maybe fifty meters...but yeah. Of course, we'd have to be quick, because we'd be super vulnerable hanging on the side of the cliff like that."

"Yes, but what if we weren't alone?"

Azah felt Sadek go still beside her.

"What do you mean?" he asked.

"What if we found some of the other pairs, maybe some ferals, too? We can lead a group up and back around this way, then down the cliffs toward the stockade. Meanwhile, Nura and the others can drive the rest of the ferals up through the canyon as they'd planned. They'll still have casualties, but not nearly so many if we're taking the fliers out and keeping them busy looking for us."

"That's...a really good idea, Azah," Sadek said, his voice shading more and more enthusiastic with every word. "That's a fantastic idea, and it shows off our leadership abilities, too! You're a genius!"

Azah let out a low chuckle.

"I don't know about that," she said, "but I've got you, and you're a genius, so I guess that's close enough."

* * * * *

Chapter Seven

It didn't take them long to find the others.

Sadek had been correct; the mass of feral Tortantulas being herded by Nura and the others moved slowly, pushed along by cruelty and fear. In the time it had taken Azah and Sadek to circle around the back of the canyon's cliffs, scout the stockade from above, come up with a plan, and backtrack to the central valley with the river, Nura and the others had covered about half the distance from their starting point to the entrance of the box canyon.

Azah heard them before she saw them. The ground rumbled with the force of their passage, and the cries and growls of the massed ferals combined to create a dull roar that blanketed the valley in noise. It made it hard to focus.

"Come on," Sadek said. "Nura's there, in the rear. Let's go talk to her first."

"Right," Azah said, angling that way. Nura was, naturally, still in charge of the gaggle. It made sense to present their plan to her. She'd be the one to order some of the other pairs and ferals to follow Azah and Sadek up around the back of the canyon. Azah poured on the speed and ran down into the valley toward the larger Tort.

"Nura, Hyree," Sadek called as they got close. "We have a plan for you."

"Hello, little ones," Nura's partner called out. "I'd wondered where you'd gone. Look, Nura. The babies are back."

"We're the same age," Sadek snapped. "But that doesn't matter right now. We've got information you need to make this work."

"Oh?" Hyree asked, his cheeks stretching in a condescending grin. He shifted his training rifle from one small shoulder to the other. "And what might that be?"

"There's a way around the box canyon where the stockade sits," Azah said, her tone flat and carefully emotionless. "Up over those hills, through the woods. We got all the way to the top of the cliffs and looked down into the enclosure."

"Can't herd this many ferals through the woods, stupid," Nura said, "They'll get lost, and we'll have to round them all up again. Are you trying to make me fail this exercise?"

"No!" Sadek said, raising his free hand in placation. "Not at all. We're trying to help you win! See, Azah has a plan—"

"Oh, I bet she does," Nura said.

"No, it's a good one! See, we thought you could order some of the pairs and a few of the ferals to follow us back around the cliffs—"

"Why? So you can take away from the numbers I'm leading? I don't think so," Nura said. On her pedicel, Hyree chuckled. "This is a leadership challenge, that's what Teacher said. I'm leading hundreds of ferals and all the teams. So if you want to meet the objective of taking the stockade, get in line and help push the ferals forward."

"They have armed fliers," Azah said. "Your ferals will be obliterated in minutes if you don't do something about them. Our plan will take care of them for you."

"Not my problem," Nura said. "They're only ferals."

At that moment, one of the cries from the mass of charging feral Tortantulas drifted back to them, and Azah slowed her running gait. Nura and the others started to pull away.

"See you later, little ones!" Hyree called out, laughing and waving with the hand that wasn't holding his rifle on his shoulder. Azah skidded to a stop.

"I hate them," she said in a low growl that started deep in her abdomen and worked outward.

"Me too," Sadek said. "You're not stupid. They are. They're going to get so many of their ferals killed…and for what?"

"For fun," Azah said. "I'd like to see the ferals turn on them and eat Nura's eyes out of her head."

"Me too," Sadek said, "but that's unlikely to happen. You said it yourself; the ferals are going to get destroyed by those fliers."

"What if we go alone?"

"What?"

"What if we go alone and take out some of the fliers? There are hiding places in those cliffs. We won't be able to take out as many as we could otherwise, not without covering fire, but if we pick a careful spot, and time it right, we might be able to help at least a little bit. I don't want to fail this exercise, but I'm not participating in that," Azah spat as she spoke and shuffled her feet in the torn-up dust left in the ferals' wake. It tasted like their cries had sounded: hopeless and enraged.

Sadek was silent for a long moment.

"You'll be careful?" he asked.

"Of course I will," Azah said. "I'm not letting you get hurt."

"It's not me I'm worried about," he said.

"I know," she replied.

Sadek took a deep breath and hefted his training rifle.

"All right. But you promise you won't take crazy risks."

"I promise."

"Then let's do it."

Azah didn't need any more than that. She turned on her back legs and attacked the hill down which they'd come, heading back up the slope toward the path that would take them to the cliffs above the stockade.

By the time they arrived, the sun had passed its zenith and was beginning to slide toward the western horizon. Azah and Sadek picked their way along the edge of the cliff to a spot where a steep rock fall had happened sometime in antiquity. The rock fall had left behind a sharp vertical crease in the rim of the cliff.

"How about here?" Azah asked Sadek. "This cut in the rock is big enough to hide me from the stockade, see how it's angled into this curve in the rim?"

"Yes, but Azah, it's straight up and down! And look how smooth the sides are! How do you plan to climb down it?"

"Well, I was thinking about that," she said. "You know how strong my silk is? How we can't break it, we have to cut it?"

"Ye-es," Sadek said, tilting his head warily.

"I think it's strong enough to hold us, and if you look closely, the sides aren't that smooth. There are footholds and stuff. The silk would really just be a backup."

"A backup? What would you anchor it to?"

"I don't know. I figured you could find a rock or something to tie it around."

Sadek slid out of his saddle and crouched at the top of the crease, looking closely at the surface of the stone and the area around it.

"How much silk can you make?" he asked.

"I don't know," Azah said. "A lot, I think."

"Enough to tie to that shrub right there and make it down the cliff?" Sadek asked. "See how the roots tangle together? I think we could loop around that root right there and it should anchor us. Those shrubs have deep roots. I know, because I tried to dig for them once, and they just kept going down. I still don't know if they taste good or not…"

"That should work," Azah said. Sadek blinked, shook his head as if refocusing his thoughts, and looked back at her with a nod.

"All right," he said. "If we're going to do this, let's do it."

It worked pretty well, actually. It took a few misses before Azah could coordinate herself well enough to provide a stable firing platform for Sadek, but she managed. It was disconcerting, though, as she walked headfirst down the vertical face of the cliff. She tasted the coppery-iron tang of the rocks with every step and crouched to ensure she and her partner stayed hidden inside the crease.

"Keep your straps cinched tight," she warned Sadek as the silk continued to play out behind her. "If we need to retreat, I'll swing my body up and around and climb back up the silk cable. That'll put you hanging head down, though, so make sure the straps aren't going to slip and let you fall."

"Got it," Sadek said. "And worst case, I'll drop the rifle and hang on to the straps meant to hold it on the side of your thorax. I really don't want to drop the rifle, though," he said, finishing up with a note of awe and longing in his tone.

"You like it, huh?" Azah asked.

"Hmmm? Oh, the rifle? Yeah. I mean, it's just a crappy training model—bolt action, single shot—but ever since they let us try these out at the range the other day, I've wanted to try them out for longer. Shooting is fun. You should give it a try...if you could figure out how to pull the trigger, that is."

"I think I'm good with my fangs," Azah said, laughter in her tone. "There's a small ledge up here. I think it's a good place to stop and see what we can see."

"Okay," Sadek said as her front legs touched down on the floor of a ledge just big enough to hold them both. She let enough slack play out that she could stand comfortably, then let the rest of her legs touch down in the fine, powdery rock dust that covered the solid surface. Sadek let out a deep breath and released the catch on his harness straps, then slid to the ground beside her with a thump.

Distant cries started to drift up to them, echoing off the stone walls of the canyon. Azah focused all her eyes on the canyon's entrance and saw the darkness of the massed army of ferals start to spill in through the gap.

"Here they come," she said.

Sadek grunted in response underneath her. He'd climbed down on his belly, lying flat below her chin, his head and the barrel of his rifle sticking out from between her pedipalps. She crouched lower over him, using her body as a shield against whatever would come.

Down below, a high-pitched whine echoed up to them, heralding the launch of the combat fliers.

As they'd both predicted, it was a slaughter.

The fliers launched together in a unified formation before splitting off into elements of three. These trios then accelerated to meet the mass of charging ferals blotting out the ground of the canyon floor and raising such a dust cloud Azah could no longer see the entrance to the canyon. The whole place thundered with the sound of their running feet. Dust from the cliff above trickled down on her and spilled into the seams in her exoskeleton. It itched, and her already angry mood got worse.

An explosion blossomed on the right flank of the charging ferals, throwing body parts in all directions. The trio of fliers overhead followed the rocket strike up with what seemed like three lines of energy fire…though from the sound of it, Azah realized it was only tracers fired at an incredible rate. She'd seen Tri-V vids of tracer fire in training, and the knowledge that most combat loads carried one tracer round for every four ball rounds surfaced in her mind.

"Wow," she said, impressed at how dispassionate she managed to sound. "They're really chewing them up down there on the right."

"Yeah," Sadek said slowly, drawing the word out as he shifted underneath her. "I think I can…"

Crack!

It wasn't as loud as the explosion had been, but the sound of Sadek's rifle shot echoed off the canyon's walls in such a way that Azah was sure every attacking flier would turn and fly straight toward them. They didn't, however. Apparently, the noise of the battle was enough to muffle a single gunshot. One of the fliers harrying the right flank faltered, then flipped over and fell out of the sky, smoke trailing from its inverted body.

"Nice shot," Azah said. "Right in the stabilizer!"

"Thanks," Sadek said absently. Then he worked the bolt, loaded another round, and stroked the trigger again. Another cracking gunshot rang out. Another of the fliers on the right flank fell. She felt rather than heard him working the bolt action before he shot the third one as well. Then he rolled toward the cliff wall and wormed his way out from under her.

"Let's go," he said. "I don't want to take too many shots from here. Let's go further down, where there's that scrub on the lower ledge. Think you can get there?"

"You know I can," Azah replied, feeling her angry mood pass. Yes, it was horrible that the ferals were dying out there. Their throaty screams battered at her ear slits, but she couldn't do much about that right now. Nothing other than what she was doing—which was working with Sadek, and therefore her favorite thing in the world to do.

Four more times they took out a trio of fliers, moving after each trio crashed and died. None of the fliers turned to come find them, which was a comfort. By the time they downed their last trio, the army of ferals still standing had swarmed over the walls of the stockade and were busy murdering every robotic construct and caged animal that had been left inside.

Azah thought for a long moment about just continuing her descent to the bottom, but that would leave the army of ravening ferals between them and Nura and the other pairs. Retreating and going around the long way seemed much the better option.

"Do you think we helped?" she asked Sadek as they scaled the topmost portion of the cliffs and climbed back up onto the shrub-dotted slope above. The setting sun had ignited the sky, and the canyon below sat in gloom.

"Sure we did," he said. "At least a little bit. Nura and the others might not have noticed, but I guarantee someone did. You watch, Azah. Our actions today are going to have a big influence on our graduation placement; I'll bet anything you like."

"I hope you're right," she said. "I hope we helped, at least a little."

* * * * *

Chapter Eight

"Pathetic, absolutely pathetic." Teeno tossed the slate aside and turned to look at Esrin, who bowed his head. "How can you bring these sorts of results to me?" The goggles she used to see unnerved most of the Flatar trainers, and she liked it that way.

"Brood 37F2 was a male birthing," Esrin offered without looking up.

"You don't think I know that?" she snarled and pointed at the slate. "The failure rate is unacceptable in any birthing. We should have just flushed the females and been done with it, instead of wasting two years."

"Do we get rid of them now?" one of the other trainers asked.

"No, you fool," Teeno said, "and compound the waste?" She picked up the slate and looked at the figures again. A shocking number of solos survived. So few teams, and of the few who had completed to reach this point, many were loners or schemers. The loners would go to special operations, the schemers into regimental combat teams. There were only a few driven types to send to command. One of the driven was an outlier.

"Have the solos corralled and moved to assault compounds to start the controlling process." The trainers all bowed in understanding. She ticked off decisions next to each of the surviving teams. The trainers responsible for them received notification of their outcomes in real time. Finally, there were only three teams left. She scratched her head where the vision goggles rested as she considered. Despite her outward reaction, she hated wasting talent that might have a use. Any use at all. She was under considerable pressure to deliver teams, but they needed to be useful teams.

One at a time, Teeno assigned the last. One went to special operations, another to command, then she paused on the last. The data was conflicting. "I think we'll send them to command," she said aloud.

"A risk." She glanced up at the long-legged figure dangling from a strand a few meters above her.

"Risk? That team? They have instincts."

"Yet they acted poorly in their final test." Teeno glanced again at the results, though she'd memorized them hours ago.

"That one, this Azah, is yours, is she not, Loof?"

"She is," he said. Teeno used the slate to pull up data on the male Tortantula. A long, illustrious, and amazing career. He'd earned the position he had now.

"What would you have me do with her?" The male made his suggestion. Teeno considered for a second, then made the entry in her slate for the resolution of the last team in Brood 37F2.

* * * * *

Part III
Combat

Chapter One

The day after the stockade exercise, the student teams had the day to themselves. Azah and Sadek set out first thing, hiking back into the hinterlands at the edge of their world. The terrain grew rough and rocky, and the trees became short, stubby scrub the higher they climbed. Azah felt her lung expanding more and more with every breath, until it felt as if she were stretching herself to her fullest capacity simply to breathe.

"I like it up here," she said, coming to a stop at the crest of one of the taller hills. The majority of their world, their training space, stretched before them. She could see the river winding through the central valley, glinting in the morning sunlight as it filtered through the massive dome stretched above them. A breeze swept by, tickling the receptor hairs on her body and tasting of cold dryness.

"Me too," Sadek said. "It's quiet, and we don't have to be around the others."

"Are you still bothered by yesterday's exercise?"

"A little," Sadek said. "Mostly because they were so mean to you. You had a good idea, and they wouldn't even listen."

"I knew they wouldn't," Azah said. "I'm too little."

"But—" Sadek started to protest, squirming in his seat atop Azah's pedicel.

"No, listen. I know I have good ideas, and you know I have good ideas, but this isn't the first time things like that have happened. My kind don't like smallness, Sadek. It indicates weakness, unworthiness. Maybe it's not right, but that's the way things are."

"Entropy," Sadek said, spitting the curse word into the wind. "Pure entropy. Maybe that's the way things are, Azah, but it's not the way things should be. We'll show them, you and me! We'll defeat every obstacle they put in our path."

"Considering the other option is to lay down and die, I agree with you," Azah said, dry humor leaking into her tone. "Because I certainly intend to survive."

"That's right," Sadek said. "That's exactly right."

Azah turned and looked at the low set of school buildings on the far edge of the central valley.

"I wonder what will happen tomorrow," she said. "Before the exercise, the Teacher mentioned something about leaving the training environment. I wonder what that meant."

"It's been a year since we started school. Maybe we're getting ready to move on to something else."

"Yes," Azah said, "but what?"

The breeze and the vista held no answers for them. They spent most of the morning up there anyway, just spending time together. Azah found herself thinking hard about each moment, trying to implant it in her memory. She might not know exactly what was happening, but she couldn't shake the feeling that something was about to change, and she didn't think their lives would ever be the same.

The next day, she found out she'd been right.

"Student pairs will gather in the large classroom immediately."

The voice came from everywhere and nowhere, and it startled Azah before she realized she recognized it. It carried an electronic edge due to its amplification, but it was undeniably Teacher Pidek.

She raised herself up from her sleeping nest and waited while Sadek boosted himself up into place on her pedicel.

"Here we go," Azah murmured as soon as she felt him strapped in. She stepped forward into the flow of other pairs, who looked just as sleepy, curious, and nervous as she felt.

"Together," Sadek reminded her. "Here we go *together*."

"Right."

They filed in alongside the others and entered the large, mostly featureless classroom where they'd been briefed on the box canyon mission. As before, their teacher stood alone on the dais. A hush filled the room, despite their numbers.

"Congratulations on a successful mission," Teacher Pidek said. The gathered Tortantulas and Flatar began to stomp and yip in thunderous applause, but Pidek held up his hands, indicating he wasn't done. The roar quieted quickly. Azah figured it was because the other pairs had learned, as she and Sadek had, that the Teachers weren't long on patience.

"Some of you did very well in the leadership portion of the exercise," Teacher Pidek went on. "Some of you less so, but all of you standing here participated in the assault and survived to see the accomplishment of your objective, so all of you have passed. You have now completed the primary portion of your training, and you're ready to move on to more specialized skill sets. Over the last year, you've been graded on your problem-solving skills and styles, your aggressiveness and teamwork, and your leadership and ability to follow. Those grades have been tabulated, and you have been sorted into groups based upon your demonstrated aptitudes. Your assignments will be displayed on your slates...now."

Azah fumbled to pull her slate from its pouch on the underside of her abdomen harness.

"Uh, Azah," Sadek said, his voice tentative as she caught the slate and stabbed at the screen to get it to light up.

"What?" she asked, just as her slate lit up. Letters scrolled across the screen, bright white against black, filling the slate.

Azah and Sadek. Assault Company Bravo. Shock Troops. Command Track.

"Shock troops?" she whispered.

"Yeah," Sadek said. "Um...maybe we should go somewhere?"

Azah looked around the room. Chaos filled the space as pairs moved around in celebration and excitement. Teacher Pidek stood on the dais, his hands folded across his furry belly, watching over them all with an indulgent smile. He caught sight of Azah looking, and his smile faded as his gaze zeroed in on her.

"Yes," she said softly, so only Sadek would hear. "I think we should...if we can."

"Pretend to be happy," Sadek said. "Teacher's still watching. Let's move back toward the back of the room, maybe?"

"Right," Azah said. Truth be told, she had no idea how to "pretend to be happy," so she let Sadek handle it. As they moved through the crowd toward the back, she could hear him calling out cheerful congratulations. Once, he reached out to slap his hand against another Flatar's outstretched digits. Azah snorted a soft laugh but kept moving until they were at least out of Teacher's direct eyeline.

"Shock troops."

The word fell like stones from Azah's mouth.

"Azah..."

"They think we're no better than ferals, Sadek," she said. "They want to use us in a swarm like we saw at the canyon."

"Azah, we won't let them. We're smart, remember? We can handle this, as long as we're together. I don't think they want us to be in the swarm, more like we'll be pushing it, like Nura did."

Revulsion rose up inside Azah and threatened to spill out of her mouth, taking her last meal with it.

"I won't be like Nura," she hissed. "I won't."

"No," Sadek agreed. "You're smarter than she is. You won't get your troops killed for no reason. You'll listen to others. You'll survive, Azah. We both will."

"Right. Together. Zha Oort," she said.

"Zha Oort—Entropy!" Sadek cursed, and Azah felt a thunk and a clatter as her partner dropped his slate. Less than a breath later, her own slate shocked her as well, and it, too, fell to the floor. She glanced around with several of her eyes and reached out to pick it up. It didn't look like anyone had seen anything, so she focused through her detail eyes on the screen itself. Had they noticed she wasn't happy about her assignment?

More letters scrolled into place, then stopped, flashing.

I don't know how you learned the forbidden language, but you must never say those words out loud again. For your own safety.

—A Friend.

* * * * *

Chapter Two

Graduation day, it seemed, was also moving day. Immediately after being given their assignment (and a nasty shock from their anonymous "friend" over their choice of language), Azah and Sadek were told by their slates to gather their belongings from their sleeping quarters and report to one of the large meadows just outside the school. They didn't have much to take, really. Just their slates, Sadek's harness, and his weapons...most of which they were already carrying.

So Azah followed the hallway out to the meadow and found several her classmates already waiting there.

"Oh no," she said softly as she stepped onto the grass. She bent her knees deeply and tried to slink around the edges of the group, so as not to be noticed. "Nura's in this group. She got selected for command, too."

"Of course she did," Sadek said. "I'm sure it's what she wanted. Let's just try to stay away from her. Maybe we won't have to talk to her at all."

As it turned out, they didn't. Before long, a tiny black slit appeared in the sky above. It widened, becoming a black square no bigger than the size of Sadek's smallest claw before closing again behind something that had entered the world.

It looked like one of the fliers they'd seen at the stockade. Only bigger, Azah realized. Much bigger, with a wide central body as big as the wing of the school building behind them. It came closer and closer until the wind from its rotors blasted through the meadow, and Azah had to fight to stay on her feet. The roar from the four engines reverberated through her body like a physical force and left her feeling shaken and nervous.

Once the huge flier touched down on the grass of the meadow, the massive engines cut off, and the rotors slowed. The noise level dropped sharply, leaving Azah feeling bruised in its wake. One side of the central body dropped down from the top, forming a ramp that led up and into the flyer.

"Command track!" an unfamiliar, squeaky voice echoed through the meadow. It carried a tinny edge that told Azah it was being electronically amplified and came from the opening on the ship. The rumbling undercurrent of conversation ceased, and a figure stepped into view at the top of the ramp.

It didn't look like any being Azah had ever seen before. In shape, it was roughly like a Flatar, but about three times as tall. It didn't have the large, fluffy tail at all. Rather, it had some kind of hairless, whipcord type appendage instead. Its face was small, with a pointed nose, and it wore tinted goggles over its eyes. Except for the tail, and the round ears atop its head, it was covered all over in cream-colored fur.

"What is that?" Sadek whispered.

"I don't know," Azah replied. She would have said more, but the strange creature with the amplified voice spoke again.

"My name is Shuroo," it said. "I am the commander of Assault Company 889. That means I am your commander. Follow my orders, and we'll get along fine. Fail me, and that failure will likely be your last. Any questions? No. Excellent. Board the ship. No fighting. Fighting amongst yourselves constitutes failure."

Shuroo turned and disappeared back into the belly of the ship. Azah hesitated for a second, unsure what to do.

"Should we go?" Sadek asked.

"I think so," Azah said and stepped forward. The metal of the ramp tasted like ordinary metal when she stepped on it, though it carried hints of strange chemicals she'd not yet encountered. She walked up the ramp and, soon enough, the other pairs in the command track followed. Even Nura.

"What are you doing here, little ones?" Hyree sneered in his fake-friendly way as Nura pushed past Azah to be first on the ship. "This is the command track. Are you sure you're in the right place?"

"Our slates said so," Sadek responded. Azah could feel his body trembling with anger, but her partner did a fantastic job of keeping his voice neutral.

"Huh. Musta been a mistake. Don't worry, though. It looks like things will sort themselves out soon enough." The Flatar gave them a nasty smile and then laughed.

Azah stayed very still, letting the rest of the pairs flow into the ship around her.

"Don't get in my way again," Nura said, her voice a low growl.

Azah said nothing.

"It's been great to see you both," Sadek said. "I'm sure we'll have a chance to catch up later."

Hyree let out another evil laugh, and the larger pair turned and began pushing their way through the crowd toward the front of the vessel. Sadek let out a long breath.

"I hate her," Azah said.

"I know. We're okay though, for now. Let's just see what happens next."

Once all the pairs had loaded onto the transport, the ramp lifted and resealed the compartment. For a moment, they were plunged into impenetrable darkness. Then several round openings about the size of a Flatar opened in a row along the walls, and daylight streamed in once more.

The noise of the rotors got louder again, and with no more warning than that, the ship lurched slightly and lifted into the air. Something moved unpleasantly in Azah's stomach as she watched the ground recede through one of the windows. It got even worse when the ship tilted to the left and sent some of the other Torts sliding across the floor into her.

All across the floor of the ship, recessed rings had been set. Azah crouched low and used two of her legs to hang on to these rings. They, too, tasted of unfamiliar chemicals, but Azah was glad she had them when the ship tilted back the other way, and she wasn't one of the ones sliding and scrabbling for purchase.

"You're so smart," Sadek said, stroking the sensory fur on top of her cephalothorax. "I'm so glad you're my partner."

"Me too," Azah said. "Z—until the end."

"Right. Until the end."

The ship climbed higher and higher, until they got close to the structure Azah had always known as "the sky." As before, a black line appeared and widened to make a roughly square-shaped hole. Only it wasn't tiny, as she'd thought before. It was huge. Bigger than the school building. Big enough to send ten of these ships through and still have room on all sides. The engines gave a whining sound, then a different, deafening roar shuddered through the frame of the ship and they jolted forward through the hole, out into the blackness beyond.

"Azah!" Sadek squeaked, excited. "Look! We're outside the world!"

Azah blinked and focused her detail eyes on the vista outside their window. Sure enough, as they continued to climb, she could see the wide, pale curve of a dome. It was massive, but it was, in fact, finite. Which made sense, when she remembered the way she and Sadek had explored to the limits of their world, where the curving "sky" came down and melded with the ground.

"So not sky, then," she murmured. "A dome. Not the whole world at all."

"Yeah," Sadek said, awe in his voice. "Not even close. And look! There are more of them!"

There were many more of them. Separated by narrow lanes of blasted, lifeless rock, more huge domes lay scattered in all directions. Most were even bigger than the one from which they'd come.

"I wonder what's in all of them," Azah said.

"I don't know," Sadek replied, "but I'm starting to wonder if there's any part of the world that isn't covered by domes. Except for the bits in between. But those just look like rock…no plants or water or anything."

"Maybe plants and water and everything can't exist outside the domes," Azah said. "Maybe this world isn't really made to support life."

"Then why were we born here?"

"Your guess is as good as mine."

They lapsed into silence then, and Azah continued to feel a growing sense of her own insignificance as row after row of gargantuan domes passed under them to reveal the true size of the world. As the ship maneuvered, she could occasionally see the inky blackness studded with bright points of light that stretched above them and seemed to wrap all the way around the curve of the world. Was that just another dome? Or was it something different?

Eventually, the pitch of the ship's engines changed again, and Azah felt a pressure pushing her forward. She gripped the floor rings once again and realized they were slowing relative to the surface of the world. Another huge dome came into view, and it rapidly became clear that this was their destination.

"We're going into another dome," Azah said. "Another world. I wonder what this one will hold."

* * * * *

Chapter Three

The huge dome Azah and Sadek had left was a flurry of activity as its interior was processed. Hundreds of robots moved through it, clearing out debris, tending to damaged foliage, and disposing of the odd rogue the harvesting teams had been unable to bring in. There were always a few; too smart to be solos, too savage to be in a team.

Eventually the robot work was done, and the drones moved in. Hundreds of stunted females lacking the mental capacity of their higher born sisters and brothers. They did work either too complicated for the robots, or that required discretion above what a robot could manage. Their main job was to disarm booby traps left by the various teams during their time. It had been determined over the years that those traps could be quite inventive, and often lethal enough to be hard on robots. Drones were easy to replace; robots cost credits.

Loof lowered himself from the male brooding alcoves. They were many times easier to process than the lower floors of the domes. The males tended to form groups based on their interests. Because of their nature, when disputes arose, they weren't often as explosively lethal as it was with the females. There had been exceptions, of course. Loof was one of those exceptions. Unlike the females, when males did exceptional things, they were usually rewarded for it.

He could see a few other males moving through the dome, inspecting what the robots and the drones had accomplished. A group was supervising a robot team removing the corpse of a monstrous rogue solo. The big ones were often the least controllable.

Eventually he reached the far side of the dome. It was a less favorable living area, often home to the smaller teams that were creative enough to avoid having to work with others. He'd been sure that arriving here would seem to be a matter of fate, not on purpose.

At the base of a small hill with a tiny artificial stream running down between the rocks, he found a pair of drones piling items found in a little cave. The spot was a favorite of teams, it seemed at least one found it every brood. Sometimes there was even fighting over it, if the brood was extensive. This time it hadn't been.

He moved over to examine the items the drones had piled up. A fair-sized stash of carefully preserved fruits and nuts, preferred food for the Flatar. There were several cases of the liquid Tortantula ration packets as well. This team had been well prepared, but it wasn't the food that interested him. He went over to a container designed to be moved by robots, a disposal unit. The drones looked at him then fell back, their bodies low to the ground.

Loof rummaged through the various detritus until he found what he wanted; one of Sadek's spears. He lifted it close to his mouth parts, tasting it with his feet and gently tearing at it with his fangs. Sure of what he'd found, he tossed it back into the metallic container and removed a device from a utility clip on his thorax. Clicking the control, he tossed the device into the bin with the spear and turned to go.

Behind him, there was a popping sound, and in seconds, the bin was burning brightly. The thermite charge consumed everything in the bin in seconds. The circle of drones watched the fire silently until it had burned down to ashes. The bin was untouched, made of an alloy too tough for the thermite to damage. A short time after the fire was extinguished and the metal cooled sufficiently, they resumed their duties.

* * * * *

Chapter Four

The ship landed in a place unlike anything Azah had ever seen. Instead of a wide-open meadow covered in lush grass with trees around, the ship descended into a monochrome landscape of rigidly squared-off corners and blocky, stacked towers. The landing area was the same size as the ship, and Azah wondered at the skill required to pilot the thing into such a tight space.

The ship settled to the ground with a light *thump*, and the lights in the cabin area brightened.

"Exit down the ramp and enter the building immediately in front of you," Shuroo's voice echoed through the space. "Form up once inside."

The side of the ship to Azah's right let out a hissing sound and began to fold down to create another ramp like the one they'd used to board the ship. It hit the bottom with a *thunk*, and the Torts around her began to jostle and push in their eagerness to comply with the commander's orders.

Conscious of Sadek's soft vulnerability on her back, Azah let herself be carried with the crowd down the ramp and into the dark entrance of the grey, hulking building beyond. Once they stepped over the threshold of the open door, bright lights came on, harshly illuminating the cavernous room beyond. It was an open space with a dais at one end, and interesting pictures covering the walls.

"Maps," Azah said as she glanced around using her peripheral eyes. "They're different kinds of maps. I recognize them from school."

"Yeah," Sadek said. "Me too, but I don't recognize what they're maps of."

Once they had room to do so, Azah pulled herself from the mass of the crowd and took up a position at the back of the emerging formation. She ended up on the far-right end in the last row. It wasn't ideal, since she was still on the end and thus vulnerable to being noticed, but at least it was far away from Nura and the dais at the front.

The lights dimmed slightly, and Shuroo walked in. Immediately, the excited undercurrent of conversation ceased as the commander took the dais. Azah thought that must have pleased her, to see how well disciplined her new recruits were, but the commander didn't remark on it, and Azah couldn't read her strange body enough to guess.

"Because of your demonstrated performance while in training, you have been selected to command the ranks of assault troopers that make up my company," Shuroo said, forgoing any kind of preamble. "The assault troopers are made up of the feral Tortantulas you have seen before. They are not intelligent. They are barely even sentient. They are ruled entirely by fear and rage. This is desirable, for that allows us to put them to productive use. You will learn how to manipulate that fear and rage in order to lead them into battle. When you have learned enough, I will accept a mercenary contract. You will then utilize what you have learned and direct the shock troopers to achieve our objective and earn our commission. Adequate performance ensures your needs will be met by my company.

Unsatisfactory performance constitutes failure, and your life is forfeit. Are there any questions?"

Shuroo looked around the room through her tinted goggles. No one moved.

"Very well. This building is assigned to your group. You have the run of the entire building, but you may not leave it without orders. The next hour is yours to find and establish a den spot. No fighting amongst yourselves. Fighting constitutes failure. Are there any questions?"

Again, none.

"Very well," she said again in her inflectionless tone. Either that was just the way beings like her spoke, or Shuroo felt absolutely nothing about what was going on. Either way, it was an interesting bit of data for Azah to file away. "Return in an hour. Do not be late. Dismissed."

A general hubbub ensued as the pairs immediately began talking and plotting. Nura announced she would den close to the map room, and she sauntered out the door that slid open as she approached.

"Let's go up," Sadek said. "I saw when we came in; this is one of the tall buildings. If we climb, I bet we can get away from most of them."

"As long as we can get back to the map room quickly," Azah said. "I don't want to be always running in late. I'm guessing that would constitute failure."

"Right," Sadek agreed. "Good point. I'll set my slate to alarm at half an hour and three quarters, just so we can make sure we're back on time."

"Good idea."

As it happened, they found a terrific compromise. The building itself had little internal consistency—with one exception. It was designed to direct traffic up. However, the methods of getting "up" were astonishingly varied. Everything from ramps to stairs to sheer walls with cutouts for climbing...it was interesting, and Azah couldn't help but think learning to move up and down in these ways was part of their training. The other pairs quickly staked out alcoves and rooms accessible by the ramps and stairs, leaving Azah and a few of the other, less desirable candidates with little option but the climbing walls and ladders.

"I can get up them fast enough," Azah said, looking up at one of the climbing walls, "but I don't know if I can get down quickly enough without falling. I'd probably be all right, but that might kill you."

"You could rappel," Sadek said. "But I still don't think it's a good idea to reveal that you have silk. None of the others do, and nothing I can read about Tortantulas anywhere on the GalNet mentions it."

"Yeah..." Azah said slowly. Her eyes tracked across the climbing wall to the corner, where an unmistakable hatch sat high in the wall. A warning sign was painted across the hatch. "What is that?"

"Incinerator chute access," Sadek said. "I already checked it out while you were climbing the wall. It's for garbage and stuff. No good, it gets flame-blasted three times a day."

"What times?" Azah asked.

"What?"

"What times does the incinerator ignite? Are they the same times every day?"

"Um...maybe. Let me see. I just found the tech data on this building on my slate..." he trailed off as his fingernails clicked across the screen. A moment later, he gave a chittering laugh of glee. "Oh, this is perfect! It goes like clockwork every day at an hour after sunrise, an hour after sunset, and at the middle night hour. The blast lasts for fifteen minutes and reaches a temperature of 1,000 Kelvin."

"That ought to be hot enough to melt silk, wouldn't you think?" she asked. "That hatch looks big enough for me if I squish. Nura wouldn't make it, though."

"I think you're right. You're a genius, Azah."

"We just have to make sure we time our movements properly so we don't get incinerated…but my silk does. I'll climb up to the top, and we'll find a spot just above that hatch, all right?"

"Sounds perfect. I'll program in alarms on my slate and yours for the incinerator schedule so we don't forget. This is going to be awesome."

Sure enough, they found a nice little alcove with quick access to the incinerator chute. Azah was right; she could just squeeze in through the hatch. Once inside, she made another discovery: the hatch was narrow enough she could climb up inside it, too.

"So as long as we stay clear of the blast times, it's like we have our own passageway!" Sadek said, enthusiasm making his ears quiver. "Maybe we can avoid the others entirely!" With their route between the map room and their den spot unimpeded, Sadek and Azah made a habit of arriving early, before the others, in order to study the maps and puzzle over what, exactly, they depicted.

"These ones on this wall are all cities," Sadek announced one day. "Houston, Paris, Beijing, London…they're all labeled 'urban,' and the scale on them is much smaller. Meters per square instead of kilometers."

"Yeah, but where are the cities?" Azah asked. "And why do they have such weird names? And why do we have city maps over here and topographical terrain maps over there?" Part of their lessons every day included how to maneuver and direct a force of assault Torts in different environments. The maps played a large role in their discussions. Azah could understand the theory well enough; it was the practice that frustrated her to no end.

Their job was to intimidate the assault troopers and direct them toward the slaughter. Once the fighting began, some primeval part of the feral Torts' brains seemed to take over and they simply reveled in the carnage. Azah found it strange and slightly frightening. She would kill as readily as anyone, but she just couldn't wrap her mind around the pure joy the troopers exhibited. It was like some strange, transcendent experience she was forced to watch from the outside, looking in.

As usual.

It probably didn't help matters that she continued to be smaller and less imposing than all the other paired Torts, or "junior officers," as Shuroo now called them. Despite this lofty title, they acted like little more than thugs, using their size, savagery, and Flatar weaponry to force the troopers to follow their orders and move in the right direction. Azah was smaller, and she truly hated having to operate in that way. She couldn't bring herself to be effortlessly cruel like Nura and the others. Consequently, she lagged behind, rarely being able to "push" more than a dozen troopers at a time.

According to Shuroo, this was passable, but barely.

"I expect you will be one of the first to die, but your performance meets the minimum standard," the commander said, during one of their one-on-one feedback sessions. These sessions happened every ten days and consisted of Shuroo speaking to each pair indi-vidually. Azah wouldn't have minded so much if they'd been con-ducted in private, or if she or Sadek were allowed to ask questions. Instead, Shuroo simply walked down each rank of the officers' for-mation and spoke to each pair in front of all the others. Nura almost always received great praise for her unquestioning obedience and inherent savagery. Azah was usually called "a disappointment."

"Many of you will die," Shuroo went on, turning away from the formation and heading back up to the dais. "But your time in train-ing is now done. Tomorrow we will depart on our first mercenary contract. You will prove your worth in battle, and if you survive, you will have the type of great slaughter your kind is always after. Re-member to follow my orders and push your troopers toward the fight. Be ready to go in this room at first light. Dismissed."

The commander, who Azah now knew was called a Veetanho, turned and left without a backward glance, the way she always did.

"We're not going to die," Sadek whispered, a low growl under his words.

"No," Azah said, her tone matter of fact. "No, we're not."

* * * * *

Chapter Five

Sadek had experienced more than a few unique situations in his short life. Traveling into space was by far the strangest. Azah took to it like nothing he'd ever seen. With her ten legs and natural three-dimensional sense, it took almost no adjustment for her.

"*Caverns in the deep*," Azah whispered the first night in space, while they were waiting for their dropship to mate with a transport.

"What was that?" Sadek asked her. They shared a padded space that would be tight for the other pairs but was roomy thanks to Azah's smaller size. For once, it seemed her stature was an advantage. The other teams complained constantly.

"What was what?" she asked, her eyes focusing on Sadek. He'd just returned from the disposal room where they all voided. Unlike the Tortantulas' internal systems, Flatar didn't take to space as naturally. Sadek kept getting dizzy and vomiting.

"You just said something about caverns."

"I did?"

"Yes, and you sounded funny when you said it."

Azah clicked her mandibles in confusion. "I…don't remember saying anything."

"You're acting really weird," he told her and dug out his slate. They'd spent so much time cramming information on alien races' combat tactics in the last few weeks that Sadek thought his brain would melt. Now she was acting strange. As if space wasn't strange enough. He pulled up the view of their *planet* from the dropship's external camera. A few months ago, the brooding dome where Azah and he had spent the first two years of their lives was the entire world. Then they'd flown to assault training, and the world had expanded many times as both realized their dome was but one of hundreds on the planet Hok.

Now they orbited a planet that held…what, millions? It was a dark, monotone of a planet. Large greyish seas were scattered around the world, and on land, geometric patterns of domes were everywhere. Some training, some brooding, others just agricultural. A factory, he thought. A factory to make us. *Is that all we are, a product?* Azah floated in the center of their space, all but a pair of her sensory eyes closed in half slumber. He didn't want to share that thought with her. She thought too much as it was sometimes, and they were going into battle in just a week.

Sadek went on to study the configuration of saddle he'd be allowed to use, and the heavy weapons Azah would carry. They'd trained on the weapons systems without ever being allowed to fire them. He thought it was a crazy plan, not letting them do live-fire exercises. He'd been allowed to fire the XT-12 plenty of times. Why wasn't Azah permitted to practice with the heavy MACs—the magnetic accelerator cannons—and missile systems? Of course, he'd never dare say anything to Shuroo. You didn't question a Veetanho leader. Ever.

There was an echoing boom and a sense of motion that pushed Azah over to one side of their space. Sadek moved clear to avoid being pinned as naturally as he brushed his tail out of the way when sitting. "We're docked," he said to his partner. She made a noncommittal humming sound. Sadek cast her a sidelong glare as they were pushed into one wall of their space with a fraction of what they were used to as regular gravity. According to the short briefing before being blasted into space, and this horrid zero-gravity, they were now headed for the stargate.

"Are they going to feed us?" Azah asked suddenly. Sadek lurched in surprise, dropping his slate and looking up to see a group of his partner's eyes examining him.

"Back finally, are you?"

"Back?" she asked, confusion obvious on her expression. "I never left."

"Part of you did," he complained, "you've been zoned out, half asleep or something."

"Oh, well, I was enjoying the feeling of space."

"Glad one of us likes it," he muttered.

"What?"

"Nothing. In answer to your question, not until we're in hyperspace. They have to corral all the feral Torts in the assault deck, or they can go nuts." He realized what he'd said and looked at her. Space did something to the Tortantulas. It did something to the Flatar as well. He'd seen at least two other riders puking their nuts up.

"Space is cool; I wonder what hyperspace is like?"

"I have no idea," Sadek admitted. He'd looked up some of it on the GalNet, and it was mostly just numbers and stuff. There was something about it feeling like you were 'uncreated,' whatever in entropy *that* meant.

"Prepare for transition," a computer voice said over the intercom, and thrust cut off, letting them float again.

"How do you prepare for something when you don't—"

He was unable to finish the sentence because he was screaming as he was torn apart. Then, just as quickly, he was whole again. Gasping, the Tortantula and the Flatar stared at each other. Azah snagged Sadek and pulled him close. He grabbed onto her cephalothorax and held her close.

"That was horrible," she chittered.

"It was," he agreed, "but I'm here with you."

"And I'm here, too." Somewhere in the huge dropship, they heard the sound made by hundreds of feral Torts roaring in confusion and fear. Sadek bet it was quite a job for the handlers to get them under control. At least now, he understood why they hadn't bothered telling them much about hyperspace. How could you prepare someone for that? He called up the outside camera again and saw only the endless white expanse of nothing he'd read about. He showed it to Azah.

"It's like the reverse of space," she said. "I wonder what's beyond this?"

"I hope I never find out," he said.

"All command teams report for meal time," the PA said, "then briefing in one hour."

"Back to work," she said. Sadek slid into his familiar place on her back, and she easily headed into the hallway with her natural zero gravity ability. Sadek felt a little better now and hoped he could keep some food down. It didn't sound like the time in hyperspace would go to waste.

* * * * *

Chapter Six

"Your target," Shuroo said, her voice tinny through the speakers as the dropship's engines whined in the background, "is an outpost of Besquith mercenaries guarding the main approach to a very lucrative mining concern. They know we're coming, so the only hope we have is to hit them hard with overwhelming force. They're armed with magnetic accelerator cannons, as well as projectile and plasma rifles, but there are only about a platoon of them. We need to make this outpost fall so we can open up the approach for our client. If you do this right, this will be what your kind calls "a great slaughter." If you don't do it right, you will likely die. So, push your troopers hard and use their rage to your advantage."

She fell silent without asking for questions, and the click through the speakers indicated she'd turned her mic off and finished her transmission. Azah looked over at the commander, who rode in their ship. She looked the same as always, no visible emotion, and no indication of anything at all.

"Don't screw this up, little ones," Hyree said in his snide way. Nura and Hyree had been chosen to fly in the lead dropship along with the commander, as had Azah and Sadek. For Nura, it was an honor, a testament to her ability to control huge numbers of the ravening troopers who currently rode beneath their feet, caged in the cargo hold below. For Azah, it was less of one, since Shuroo had told her that she was putting her with Nura to balance out Azah's shortcomings.

"Maybe they should screw it up," Nura said softly so Azah and Sadek could hear but the commander could not. "Then they'll die, and we won't have to see their worthless smallness anymore."

Azah felt Sadek rumble a low growl, but she said nothing. Instead, she went perfectly still and didn't move a muscle. She simply stared at Hyree and Nura unblinkingly. She knew very well how small and useless she was, but that didn't matter. Because she knew something else, as well.

She knew, no matter what, she and Sadek would survive the day. No matter what.

The pitch of the dropship engines' whine dropped, and Azah swayed as the ship accelerated on their approach.

"Here we go," Nura said, a deep, sensual satisfaction in her voice. "Let's make the slaughter great, Hyree."

"As always," her partner said. The two of them turned back to ignore Azah and Sadek, and they focused on the door that would open and signify the beginning of the assault.

The ship bumped around quite a bit more, then settled to the ground with a *thump*. The door in front of Nura dropped open, and she stepped out and leapt to the ground. A flood of feral troopers began to pour out of the hold in response to Nura's bellowed orders. Shuroo turned and looked pointedly at Azah.

"Go," Sadek whispered, and Azah leapt after Nura, down into the roiling mass of troopers.

She hit the ground and immediately lashed out at one of the troopers who turned to attack.

"Not me!" she yelled, though she knew their language skills were, at best, limited. "That way!"

It didn't look like much, just a cylindrical building patched together out of scrap metal and half-covered in the planet's oddly green dust. The top edge of the outpost glinted in the orange light from the planet's primary, and the heat seemed to reach out and wrap around them all like a punishing blanket. They'd landed on a berm that overlooked a road, which was cut between two hills and led to the outpost. The whole place tasted like metallic blood.

Sharp whizz-cracks started to ring out all around. Some of them resulted in a little puff of green dust as a projectile hit the dirt next to where they massed. Behind them, Shuroo exited the ship and it lifted off, only to be replaced by another holding the rest of their company.

"Don't let the fire scare you," Shuroo called out. "We're well outside the range for their MAC and plasma, and their puny projectile weapons shouldn't be able to do much dam—" She stopped suddenly as a red-rimmed hole appeared in her forehead. She stumbled, then crumpled to the ground with the back half of her head missing.

"Sniper!" Azah screamed. "Get down! Onto the road!" For once, the massed troopers seemed inclined to obey her. Maybe it was the intensity of her scream.

"No!" Nura bellowed, causing the troopers to stop and mill about in fear. "We don't have any orders! The commander didn't tell us to move!"

"The commander is dead!" Azah yelled back as more *whizz-cracks* echoed around them. "And we will be too if we don't move!"

"Then we die," Nura replied. "We will die looking for the great slaughter!"

"We have a mission to accomplish," Sadek snapped and pointed toward their objective. "We can't complete our objective if we're *dead!*"

"You stupid coward," Hyree shrieked. "More worried about your own life!"

"Shut up!" Sadek said and fired his rifle into the other Flatar's face. The rider's head exploded in a fountain of gore. Then he turned and fired a burst into Nura's head and eye cluster, causing her to slump to the ground before she could recover from the surprise of his attack.

"Right," Azah said. "I guess that's a solution."

"The idiots would have had us sit here and be slaughtered," Sadek said. Pushing her own surprise away, Azah leaped forward to the marginal cover provided by the road. "Now into the road! Let's go kill these fuckers!"

Whether they understood her words or just her tone, the savage troopers followed her en masse, as did the ones pouring off the additional transport that managed to land before a shot from the outpost's MAC turned the cockpit into a smoking ruin. Left with no other option, the remaining officer pairs followed suit.

"Hell of a range they've got on that MAC," Sadek said, his voice calm and dry. The air above them went *Craack!* as another MAC round thundered over. "They musta upgraded it beyond published specs."

"So what does that mean?" Azah asked.

"Means we're dead meat if we get out in the open, just like Shuroo. I think our only option is to attack from the road."

"Right to their front door?"

"Yep, and they're going to have plenty of crossing fields of fire trained right on that spot, but we'll never make it against that MAC. And with the commander dead, I think our only way out of here—"

"Is through them," Azah finished for him. She looked around at the other officers who joined her, their eyes wide. "All right, here's what we're going to do. We will lead the majority of the company straight up the road and kill anything in sight. I don't know if they're expecting that we can climb, so push your troopers up and over the walls as you get close. In the meantime, we need a distraction. I need two officers to do a flanking maneuver starting up there at that cut in the hill, see it?"

"Yes," one of the officers said. Azah had never learned her name. She'd always followed Nura's lead and Azah had worked to stay out of their way.

"Good, you and another pair take that cut and attack the south wall. Get their attention. Kill as many as you can, as messily as you can. You probably won't make it back, so if you're looking for the great slaughter, this is your chance."

"The great slaughter is the highest goal," the officer said, her tone reverent. "It is the ultimate state of being. Yes. We will do this."

"Fine," Azah said, refusing to think about how fatalistic that sounded. Whatever got them listening to her was good; it meant a better chance for the survival of most of their forces. Still infinitesimal, but better.

"We have to hit the front gate and the south wall at the same time," Azah said, "so you've got about a thirty count. Don't die needlessly on the way, because the great slaughter will be inside. Did you all hear that?" she asked, pitching her voice to carry over the mass of troopers that surrounded them. "The great slaughter is INSIDE!"

With that, the troopers let out a deafening roar, and began to surge up the road. Azah nodded to the officers in charge of the flanking attack, and they nodded back before taking a portion of the largest, fiercest troopers off to follow the cut in the hills as Azah had directed.

About thirty seconds later, the mass of her troopers crashed against the metal gate of the outpost and chaos rose all around. Rage-filled screams and the hissing crack of plasma weapons filled the air. The blood-metal tang of the dust deepened with every step.

Wave after wave of roiling black fury hit the outpost as the howling creatures within desperately fought back.

"UP!" Azah screamed. "Climb up the walls!"

Somehow, despite the roll and thunder of combat, they must have heard her. Either that or the battle lust simply drove them on, because the next wave of troopers answered. They used the bodies of their fallen sisters to charge up and over the metal wall. Azah and her officers followed, while their Flatar partners did their best to remove the Besquith sharpshooters from play.

"Mumpee's down!" Sadek shouted into one of her ear slots. "Sniper got his partner. I need his weapon! Mine's too hot!"

"Got it," Azah said and angled through the madness toward the fallen officer pair. In this situation, it seemed, her smaller size was an advantage as she was able to crouch low enough to keep Sadek shielded by the exoskeletons of the dead. Sadek leaned out, grabbed the dead Flatar's weapon, and made a crowing kind of sound as he checked the charge.

"Good to go!" he said. "Now let's see what those fuzzballs can d—"

Something hammered into him, flinging him back over her right side. She felt her harness pop with enough force to make her jump. A snarling figure of fangs and fur rolled around Sadek, teeth snapping in the Flatar's face. Azah heard a wild screaming and later realized it came from her.

She didn't remember moving. All she knew was she landed atop the murderous Besquith. She struck hard and fast, her fangs driving deeply into the base of its skull. She threw herself to the left, rolling and using all her legs to pin the creature's struggling body to herself. He tasted like rage and fear.

Well, fine. She'd been studying rage and fear since graduation. They were old friends by now.

She ripped her fangs free. Red spray fountained up out of the Besquith, blinding her main eyes. Not that it mattered. She didn't need to see for this. She struck again, even as the creature's puny claws scraped great furrows down the side of her cephalothorax. It wanted her eyes.

It couldn't have them. She struck again, and this time, she felt the pop as she severed the main spinal cord. The creature went limp, and she flung it away.

"Sadek?" she called, panic in her tone. "Sadek?"

"Azah! I'm here! I'm okay! It's okay; it's me! Here, let me wipe the blood out of your eyes!"

She blinked as something swiped across her eye ring, and then she could see again. All around them, battle still raged, but he was alive and okay. That was all that mattered.

"Get back into place," she said, half an order, half a plea. "I can't think if you're not safe."

"The harness is broken," he said. "Let me just...there. I re-rigged it. It should hold until we can get a proper repair. Are you okay?"

"Yes. Fine. Get back up. Please!"

"Okay," he said. "It's okay, Azah. I'm fine. Look, I'm back in place, and now I have two weapons! Let's get the rest of these furballs, okay?"

And that was what they did. The rest of the day passed in a smear of blood and a blur of overwhelming noise. One by one, the other officers fell, most of them victims of the Besquith snipers. However, even they were no match for the irresistible tide of a berserk Tortantula swarm. By the time the orange sun sank, and the planet's two moons rode high in the sky, the outpost echoed with the wet sounds of the victorious troopers feasting on the dead of both sides.

"Now what?" Azah asked Sadek.

"Gotta be a comm station somewhere," he said. "Put out a call?"

"To whom?"

Azah didn't have an answer, but as it happened, she didn't need one. As soon as they located the comm suite, the Tri-V screen flickered, and an unfamiliar Veetanho face appeared.

"Objective achieved," she said. "Congratulations to your commander."

"Commander Shuroo is dead," Azah said. "All the officers but me are dead."

"All but you?"

"The Besquith had long-range sniper weapons and MAC fire. We lost one of our ships. I don't know where the other one is. But we took the outpost, and the client can use the road now."

"Who led the attack, if Shuroo is dead?"

"We did."

"Identify yourselves."

"Azah and Sadek of the 889th Assault Company. We're the only ones left."

"So you said," the Veetanho replied, with a bit of heat in her voice. "Very well. This is unusual. Remain where you are for now. We will send ships to retrieve you. Are you still in control of your troopers?"

"I guess so."

"But not certain. Pathetic. Very well. We will be prepared to eliminate uncontrolled troopers. Expect us in an hour," the Veetanho said, then abruptly disappeared.

Azah stared at the blank screen for a long, silent moment, but the face did not return.

"Let's go," Sadek said, sounding as tired as she felt. "Worry about it later."

Azah walked out of the small room inside the outpost that held the comm suite and barely avoided running right into one of the largest troopers still alive. Azah stopped dead in her tracks and felt Sadek raise his weapon as the Tortantula looked up at them.

"Azah," the trooper said, her voice rough and uncertain. Then she did the most extraordinary thing. She stepped back off the Besquith corpse she'd been devouring and moved to the side where she crouched. It was as if she were moving out of Azah's way, or possibly offering her the kill?

"Do you have a name?" Azah asked.

"No," the trooper said. "Good slaughter, Azah."

"Yes, I suppose so," Azah said. "You can keep eating."

"Azah," the trooper said again, and pounced back onto the mangled corpse. Azah squeezed past her and stepped out into the courtyard beyond. Once outside, the troopers there all stopped dead and looked at her.

"Azah," they said. Some, like the one inside, pronounced the word as if they could speak well. Some made a sound that was mostly a grunt...but the meaning was clear enough. They were saying her name.

"They're honoring you," Sadek said. "Because you led them. Because you brought them to this great slaughter. I bet they'd follow you anywhere, now."

"You think so?"

"Ask them."

"Is that true?" she asked, unable to keep a tiny tremble out of her voice. She didn't want to think about why it was there. "Do you follow me?"

"AZAH!" they bellowed back. "AZAH!"

* * * * *

Chapter Seven

The facility was all blood and death. Sadek had thought he'd be used to death by now; he was wrong. Azah was out with the troopers, helping keep them under control. They were used to having more officers to control them, using a combination of intimidation and force. Azah had them in awe, thanks to the slaughter they'd participated in. For most of the troopers, it was their first battle. Sadek kept thinking they should be in as much shock as he was, but the Tortantula seemed unaffected. Besides their near adoration of his partner, of course.

He'd slipped away under the pretense of inspecting the station to be sure there were no more Besquith hiding about. What he really needed was just a minute or two to think, to assess, and to calm down. *I killed another officer,* he thought. *How am I any better than them?* "You're better because Hyree would've had us wait there, and we'd have all been mowed down," he said aloud, answering his own question. Still, his heart was racing and his breathing rapid. Would the Veetanho leaders figure it out? If they did, what would happen to him and Azah?

The Great Slaughter. It's all the other Tortantula and Flatar cared about. It was all they were told to care about. But not Azah and him. Why was that? Azah could kill with just as much brutal efficiency as any other Tortantula. So could he, for that matter. Only they didn't do it for the reasons the others seemed to. For the briefest of moments, Sadek considered running. Just disappearing into this alien world, away from all the death and killing. *And what would happen to Azah without me?* He knew the answer, which was why he could never leave her. Besides, she was a part of him as much as he was a part of her.

Sadek reached the top story of the building he'd entered to "search." It was an administrative facility of some kind, which the Besquith had been using as a defensive point. It was ill suited for the purpose they'd pressed it into, which was why it had fallen. The top story was just computers and communications gear. He looked around for a time, finally feeling his breathing coming under control to the point he'd be able to go back down at last. A sound in the corner made him jump and snatch the holdout laser pistol from his harness.

Sadek squatted even closer to the ground than he was normally as he spun, hoping to gain half a second on whoever had surprised him. His sights fell on a pair of reptilian aliens standing in a recess at the rear of the floor. They're elSha, he realized, remembering them from his classes. They weren't a mercenary race.

The pair put their hands in the air, digits flung wide and eyes bulging in fear. Both were shaking uncontrollably. Sadek's finger was on the trigger. A tiny bit more force, and the weapon would fire.

"Please," one of the two said, "we're just technicians."

Their orders said nothing about surrender or captives. In fact, they'd had little training in what to do with anyone should they surrender. He knew what most of the others would do in this situation, and without hesitation. *It is weakness to not strike when an adversary is helpless,* was part of their training. These were not his adversaries. They didn't deserve to die. Slowly he lowered his gun. The two elSha watched him with unblinking eyes.

"Do not come out here until we've left," he said. "If you do, you will be killed and *eaten*. Do I make myself perfectly clear?" They both nodded. Sadek holstered his weapon and moved back down the stairs.

"Where have you been?" Azah asked. The troopers had all organized the area, moved or eaten most of the Besquith, and piled up the dead Tortantula. "Did you find anything up there?"

"No," he said, and was immediately embarrassed.

"Good," she said. "The commanders will be here soon."

* * * * *

Chapter Eight

Teeno adjusted her goggles. The vision device which fed through her pinplants never sat perfectly. It usually pinched, because it pulled on the longer fur around her eyes. She'd been reviewing the force demands for most of the day, and the numbers weren't getting any better.

"Field report," an assistant said and brought her a slate. She took it and accessed the data. Most combat results were sent in hard copy so they couldn't be compromised en route. The mission on Jacoo had been successful. That was good news. The 889th Assault Company was one of those low expectation units. She'd overseen Brood 37F2, which composed a good percentage of the company. A substantial number of the females in that brood were a waste of food. Then she saw the commander, Shuroo, had been killed by a sniper.

"I knew her," Teeno said to the empty planning center. "A distant cousin." The leadership council had been grooming her for overall command. She'd met Peepo once, and the retired general had liked her. "Fate," she said. Then she considered, *how did the company survive without Shuroo?* The report didn't have a lot of detail.

She accessed the unit roster reports. Most of the command staff had been killed as well, with only four team survivors. She scanned down the names and stopped. "I need the full AAR," she ordered.

"After action report," an assistant said later, handing Teeno yet another slate. She read with increasing annoyance. "Send me Loof," she said after she finished.

The male Tortantula moved into the room; the only sound he made was the tiny clicking of his 10 legs as they moved him along. "You summoned me?"

"Have you heard about what happened to the 889th Assault?"

"No," he said. "What about it?" She regarded the Tortantula. The males were the polar opposites of the females. A necessary risk, as the council called them. Also, they were often valuable assets.

"Their commander was killed," she explained, "and most of the team leaders as well."

"Shuroo commanded that company," Loof said.

"I thought you said you didn't know about it?"

"I said I hadn't heard what happened, not that I didn't know about the unit."

"Azah and Sadek survived. In fact, the report says they took over command and led the company to victory with above optimal losses."

"That's extraordinary."

"It is," she agreed. "The relief company cleaned up the losses. When they did, they found one Tortantula/Flatar team that appeared to have been shot by a Flatar weapon."

"Which ones?" Loof asked.

"Hyree and Nura." Loof didn't respond; he just waited. "Nura was one of yours?"

"Yes," he admitted, "as were most of the team's Tortantulas in the 889th." Teeno looked at the male standing there waiting. He was a tiny fraction of the size of even a small female of his race, yet still several times the size of a Flatar, and about half her size. They weren't fearless, like the females. They thought things through. They could be dangerous, in their own way.

"You suggested placing Azah in that unit."

"It seemed a good idea at the time."

She snorted and looked at her slate. It displayed Azah and Sadek's file, their successes and failures. For such a disappointment, it was a large file.

"What am I supposed to do with them now?" she asked. "Their actions are extremely unconventional for loners. Those types usually don't take command in situations where command is disrupted."

"May I suggest?" Loof asked.

"I wouldn't have called you here if I didn't want your opinion."

"Covert ops."

"Really?" Loof nodded. "I was under the impression you liked that one; now I must change my opinion. The survival rate for covert ops teams is even lower than assault."

"It makes no difference to me," he said.

"Very well," Teeno said, "covert ops next." Dismissed, Loof left without another word.

* * * * *

Part IV

Covert Ops

Chapter One

Sadek was still trying to wrap his mind around the fact that there was more than one world, and now they were heading for their third.

"I don't even know what 'covert ops' is," Azah said, reading from a slate. When they'd arrived back in Hok, the system they'd been born and raised in, a new assignment was waiting. "We only had one fight." Sadek agreed with her; it was confusing. Nobody on the ship would talk about covert ops, and his slate didn't have any details on those units. "Do you think it's punishment?"

"No," he said immediately. The word 'Covert' meant hidden, and the 'Op' had to represent operations. If it was hidden, it only made sense nobody knew what it was. "It's just a new job," he said. *It's not assault*, he thought. *Maybe that means it's less senseless killing.*

"What would hidden operations do?" Azah asked.

"Sneak attacks?" Sadek guessed. Azah opened her mandibles, then closed them.

"That could be possible," she admitted.

"You are to report to the Covert Ops facility on Kutu by most expedient means," Sadek read from her slate. Just like the assault mission, there were no details on the planet to speak of. Sadek was beginning to understand just how restricted their GalNet access was. But why?

"The universe is big," Azah noted. "Do you think all those stars are worlds?" She was floating with her slate displaying a Tri-V of the space outside their ship. Another vessel was slowly floating closer. They would be transferred to that craft for their trip to Kutu. At least he'd become acclimated to zero gravity, though he still doubted he'd ever be as at home in it as she was.

"Probably," he agreed.

"How many?"

"There must be hundreds." She seemed to get this way in space, but not hyperspace. Like she was slightly drugged, or just waking up from a dream. "No," she said suddenly, "hundreds of millions. Billions of planets."

"That's not possible," he said, laughing a little. Then he looked at her. "How would you know?"

"Like some of the other things," she said, "I just know."

"Azah and Sadek, report to Transfer Airlock Two." The PA cut off any more questions Sadek might have had for his partner, and the two quickly gathered their meager belongings and moved through the cavernous transport. A short time later, they moved into the much smaller ship, a Veetanho courier. The ship's crew regarded the pair as extra cargo that just happened to need food, water, and air. They were assigned quarters slightly larger than what they'd enjoyed on the last ship and were largely left alone.

By the time Sadek thought to push Azah for more information about the stars, the vessel transitioned into hyperspace. The moment of destruction and recreation saw her, again, return to normal.

They passed the 170 hours to Kutu looking over training information, which had become available on their slates as soon as the ship left their home system. It was a daunting amount of information. Weapons manuals. Ship's schematics. Details, science, and technology. Details on many alien races. So many races that Sadek began to think Azah had been right about how many worlds there must be. Thousands of races must mean thousands of worlds, even if many shared them, like his people and hers.

They were the most fascinated by a fact they hadn't been told before. The Tortantula, Flatar, and Veetanho were mercenary races. In the seeming thousands of races, only 37 were like them—willing to fight. The newest were called Humans, and they were proving to be a serious problem.

"Look at these things," Sadek said and showed her a Tri-V. "How can this be a problem?" The creature was shorter than Azah, light brown in color, with just four limbs. It had some hair on the top of the mostly-round head that held two eyes and an opening he presumed was for eating.

"They look a little like the Lumar," Azah said and showed him a representation.

"Yes," he agreed, "somewhat, although these Humans look smaller and weaker. Look at that skin; they have to be helpless." The Human wore no clothing and stood with its head down. It had a bloody bandage on its torso, red the same color as Sadek's blood. "It looks…helpless."

"So did you when I first saw you. That proved to be an incorrect assessment." He glanced at her and, after a moment, nodded.

"You're right. There's a lot of data on them. Oh, look, they use combat armor. Well, with that thin skin of theirs, it's no surprise. Entropy, even *my* little claws could rend that flesh!"

"There is a general note of warning," Azah said, apparently having turned to look at them on her own slate. "It says: do not underestimate the race." The two exchanged looks. Sadek wondered if they would ever meet a Human in person.

A few days later, they arrived in the Kutu system.

* * * * *

Chapter Two

"We thought this was a school," Sadek said to the much-older Flatar who greeted the shuttle. Kutu was a nice planet, with slightly lower gravity and mild seasons, but it rained almost all the time. When they'd landed, a pair of elSha techs escorted them off the shuttle and told them to wait. Eventually the Flatar showed up and told them to follow her.

"School?" she asked, looking back at them. Sadek had flipped up onto Azah, and they were following closely behind. The female was fast for being on the ground. Of course, Flatar learned to move quickly when Tortantula were around, or they risked being trampled. "No, there's no school here, just the garrison."

"But our orders were to report for covert ops training," Azah said.

"Training, yes, but we have no school. You'll be learning along with a functioning covert ops team."

"Who runs the team?" Sadek asked.

"I'm second in command," the Flatar replied. "I am Shypik." They followed her down a path from the shuttle landing field, through a vehicle park, and into a nondescript building. Inside, a Tortantula smaller than Azah was waiting. Shypik flipped up onto her back. "This is Ezek. Our commander is named Yeef. Follow us, and you can report."

"She's small, like me," Azah said in wonder. Sadek hugged her cephalothorax from above, glad she was happy. He'd known that other, smaller Tortantula survived early training but, like her, had no idea where they would end up. For a time, he thought they'd ended up dead. That wasn't an encouraging thought.

Inside the structure, Shypik took them to a room on the 1st floor. Ezek waited as she jumped off and went to the door and tapped. It was wide enough for a Tortantula, and a label simply said "Commander."

"Enter," a voice said in the Tortantula's clicking language. A pair of Azah's eyes looked back at Sadek with the same surprised expression he had on his face. Shypik slid the door open and went inside. Her Tort waited outside as Azah scuttled in.

"The new pair," Shypik said.

The office was the strangest place Sadek had ever seen in his life. There was no desk or place to sit; instead it was just like a small cave, with several dark alcoves above them. Out of one of those alcoves, something moved, and for the first time, Sadek felt fear. The worst part was he didn't know why. A ten-legged creature that could only be a Tortantula moved gracefully down the wall until it was just above them. While it was a fraction of Azah's size, its legs were longer. It also lacked the narrowed abdomen she possessed. Other details were more similar.

"I am Yeef," the new arrival said.

"You are a male," Azah said in surprise.

"That is correct, Azah," he said. "Your instincts are as developed as your file says. Sadek, your file also speaks of how accomplished a team you two have become."

"Thank you," Sadek said, all the while trying to get past the idea that he hadn't known there were male Tortantulas. Then he mentally chided himself for thinking like that. *Of course there are males, since there are females!*

"They said they were expecting a school," Shypik said, then laughed. Sadek ground his teeth together.

"Okay, Shypik, you are dismissed," Ezek said. The Flatar bowed and left. "You will please forgive her; she has a great deal of natural competitiveness. She wouldn't be as flippant if she knew how young you two were!"

"What do we call you?" Sadek asked.

"'Commander' is sufficient."

"Can I ask a question?" Azah said.

"Yes, of course. This isn't the brooding group; you are here to become part of my team, not meat for the grinder." Azah seemed to stumble for a second, then recovered.

"Are we here as punishment?"

"You could think of it that way," he said. "The truth is in two parts. One, you are here because the Veetanho couldn't figure you out."

"And the second part?" Azah asked.

"Because someone wanted you here."

"Who?" Sadek asked.

"That, I'm afraid, I can't tell you." He held up a pedipalp. "That is enough questions for now. You are here to be integrated into my covert ops team. For the first time, you are not under direct Veetanho supervision. We are still under their command, of course. The covert ops team director is a Veetanho, and she lives on another part of the planet. We almost never see her, so you can stop worrying about what they think. As long as we produce, they don't care what we do. This isn't a school; you are full-fledged members of my team already, and we'll begin integrating you.

"That means a combination of learning your strengths and weaknesses, and how to leverage the former while mitigating, or even avoiding, the latter. You're assigned to Shypik and Ezek; they'll show you the ropes and start teaching you the few things you have to know, and I'll begin evaluating your abilities. Is that understood?" They both said it was. "Excellent, then; dismissed."

A little bit dizzy from so much so fast, Azah bumped into the wall as she turned and left. Shypik was waiting for them. "He's incredible, isn't he?" the Flatar asked.

"Amazing," Azah agreed.

"So small," Sadek said, shaking his head.

"You are one to talk," Ezek said with a grumble. "You will learn that, in the universe, physical size has nothing to do with power." With that, the other two led Azah and Sadek to their new home.

* * * * *

Chapter Three

While they really weren't in a training facility anymore, as Yeef had insisted, that didn't mean they weren't training. Unlike before, though, they weren't subjected to all varieties of situational exercises; instead, they were submerged in technical data and more advanced instruction on how other races conducted operations. Now they spent most of their time learning about non-merc races, which left them both mystified.

"I don't see what you're complaining about," Azah said in their new quarters. They had freedom and space they'd never enjoyed before. She gestured with the slate she'd been reading from. "We're out of assault and away from the damned teachers."

"All this studying about non-merc races doesn't make any sense," Sadek said. "We don't fight non-merc races."

"They get slaughtered if they get in the way," Azah agreed.

"But they hire us, and those credits pays for our races' needs." Sadek pointed out. "Why are we studying them like they're enemies?" Azah focused a pair of eyes on her partner. He knew she was thinking, because she just sat there. She was always quiet when she was thinking.

"I think you have a point," she said finally, "but what does it mean?"

"I don't know," Sadek admitted.

The base wasn't very large. It was just a tiny piece of a much larger world. Unfortunately, they weren't allowed to explore. The covert ops teams were sequestered in the installation day and night. The best they could manage was to go together on the roof of the main building. There was a wide-open area there, the largest they had access too. It was intended for exercise and close-combat training. The pair used it most often to look at the lights in the near distance.

"It's a city," Sadek told Azah the first night they'd seen the lights. "An elSha technician I met yesterday lives there."

"They can leave?" Azah asked.

"Yes, they can. They're not part of the team. He said he was a civilian."

"What's that?" Azah asked.

"I had to look it up. Nearest I could understand, it means they're not mercs and not part of the team."

"They can just leave…" Azah repeated. "I wonder what that's like."

"I don't know," Sadek said. Their life was all they knew. They served their superiors. They carried out orders. What else was there to do? Sadek looked at the distant sea of lights and wondered. *What do all those beings do there? Whom do they serve, or do they serve anyone?* He struggled for a minute with a word at the edge of his mind. *Freedom,* he finally thought, giving the concept a meaning. *Those beings are free to come and go as they wish. Then what are we?* He decided to ask Azah.

"We're part of a covert ops team now," she said simply.

"No, I mean as beings. Like all those living in that city. Coming and going as they please. They're free."

"Free," she said, tasting the word the same as he had a moment ago. "Yes, they're free."

"So, like I said, then what are we?" The lights were growing dimmer in the dark as clouds moved in. A few big drops of rain fell on them to punctuate the silence.

"Not free," she said finally as the rain began to fall in earnest. "We have a duty, and I start to learn coding tomorrow as part of our mission set. We better go down and get some rest."

Sadek slowly climbed onto her wet back and cast a glance toward the city. All he could see now was a hazy glow where all the free beings lived. Azah spun on her legs, and they moved down the stairs. *Not free,* he thought. *Yes, we're not free. There's a word for that as well. Slave.* The light of the building banished the darkness, and they left the rain behind.

* * * * *

Chapter Four

"Why won't this stupid thing work?" Azah growled and tossed the code box across their room with a flick of her foremost leg.

"Hey!" Sadek said, ducking as the box (which was approximately his size) flew across the room in his direction. "Watch where you aim your temper tantrums, there, killer!"

"It's so stupid!" Azah said again. "It doesn't work!"

"What are you doing, anyway?" Sadek asked. He put down the slate full of weapon manuals he'd been studying and slipped down from his stool. The box had fetched up harmlessly against the pile of pillows and mats where he and Azah slept, so he went and picked it up. "What is this thing?"

"It's a coding box," Azah said. "They gave it to us while you were in the armory. We're supposed to change the connections to make different lights turn on and off, but I can't ever make it work."

"Why not?"

"I don't know. Because it's stupid."

"Well, did you read the directions?"

Azah said nothing; she merely crouched lower and settled her abdomen on the floor.

"Azah…?"

"I tried, okay?" she said. "They didn't make any sense to me. They want me to use all the connections to override an internal lock.

It's a linear dataset, resulting in a code release. If you do that, there are too many uncontrolled variables. It's needlessly complex."

Sadek blinked, then looked down at the huge box. Sure enough, it had several lights embedded into it, along with an array of oversized switches and carefully secured bundles of wire. It was also hefty, and solidly built, thank goodness. If the scuffs on the outside of the black, rubberized corners were any indication, Azah was not the first Tortantula to vent her frustrations on the box itself.

"Show me what you mean by uncontrolled variables," Sadek said, carrying the heavy thing over to put it down in front of her. Azah let out a huff and closed her eyes. Sadek gritted his teeth and smacked her on the cephalothorax.

"What?" she said, her eyes snapping open.

"Quit. Being. A. Hatchling," he said. "I'm trying to help you."

"I don't want your help."

"Too damn bad. You've got it. They gave you a task, right? You have to learn coding, or whatever it is?"

"Yes."

"Well, then, you're damn well gonna learn coding. Because if you don't, they're going to do worse to us than send us back to the assault company, understand?"

Azah narrowed her eyes. Sadek stared right back into the two biggest ones; the ones he knew had the most direct route to her complicated brain.

"Fine," she said eventually.

"Fine," he replied, holding out the box. "Now, show me what they want you to do."

Azah stabbed at it with her forelegs, flipping switches and un-plugging and replugging wires until a light in the middle of the box switched from red to green.

"That's it?"

"Yes," she said.

"Then what's the problem? You got it to work."

"Yes, but watch this," she said, and slammed her right foreleg in-to the side of the box, nearly flipping it out of Sadek's hands. One of the wire bundles came unplugged, and the light flipped back to red.

"So don't do that," Sadek said, grabbing the box and reaching to plug the wire bundle back in. A blinding arc of electricity flashed into being between the wire bundle and his hand, and he dropped the whole thing with a cry.

"Entropy!" Azah said, rearing up. "Sadek! Are you all right? I'm so sorry! I didn't know it was going to do that. They told us not to let our partners do this for us, but I didn't realize they'd booby trapped it."

"I'm okay," he said, rubbing his hand. "Voltage with no amper-age. It just hurt. No damage." He stepped back from the box, mov-ing warily.

"You're sure?"

"I'm fine, Azah," he said, giving her the most reassuring smile he could summon. "Really. Just…you do it. Plug that wire back in, and you're all set."

"But I'm not," she said. She did, however, reach into the box and plug the wire bundle back into the receptacle where it had been be-fore. The light flashed back to green.

"Why not?" Sadek asked. "You completed the assignment. You can't be faulted for outside factors like someone hitting the box.

That's what you meant by 'uncontrolled variables'? There's always going to be those, Azah. You can't control for all of them."

"I know," she said, her voice going small. "It's just…it's frustrating. Because if I could just restructure those data paths, it could work cross-linearly as well as linearly, then maybe I could create conditions where, if the command stream gets interrupted, a secondary stream will activate and—"

"Whoa, Azah!" Sadek said. He let out a laugh that sounded disappointingly high and nervous. "Where'd you go?"

"What?"

"Azah…where did you go? You started talking about command streams and variable control structures, then you just…zoned out. Like in space sometimes."

"Oh, I…I don't know," Azah said.

"Are you all right?" Azah assured him she was. "Okay, then, can you make it better? Maybe you'll get extra credit." She examined the box's construction.

"Do you have your armorer's tools?" Sadek got out the little tool kit and handed it to her.

"What are you going to do?" he asked.

"I need to disable that stupid security interlock first, then access the internal systems." He tried getting more out of her, but once she had the case open, she seemed to lose the ability to speak, so he went back to his own studies.

* * * * *

Chapter Five

Sadek looked up from his manuals and saw Azah was asleep on the pads, the coding box sitting on the floor with a glowing green light. He was curious, so he picked up a heavy rifle and gave the box a solid *whack*. Azah didn't stir, and the green light stayed on. "Huh," he said and looked closer. It appeared unchanged. Still, some little voice in his mind said it was changed. Azah had been so intent for so long. What had she done?

After that nasty shock, he was reluctant to mess with the thing. He hadn't told her how intense the jolt had been. He'd tingled from head to toe and was worried it had come close to stopping his heart. Their instructors never joked around with rules. That was a booby trap meant for a Flatar, pure and simple. Nasty.

Finally, curiosity got the better of him, and Sadek picked up an insulated driver and pried at one of the wire bunches. It popped loose, and the green light stayed on. His jaw hung open in surprise. What had she done? At least it didn't shock him, and the driver's built in current sensor didn't flash. She'd disabled the security system. He got the rest of his tools and sat down next to the box to open it up.

They'd been taught a fair amount about how technology worked, mostly centered on weapon systems. Still, Union tech was all related in one way or another. A high-voltage power feed or a data-controlling box was the same whether it went into a laser or a medical scanner. He got the main box lid off and looked inside. There

157

were high voltage discharge connections on all the connectors. *How in entropy did she get around those?* he wondered. Then he looked into the machine's guts and gasped.

It was a relatively simple apparatus. A computer was mounted on one of the five remaining interior surfaces, the electrical wire junction connectors on another, power on another, the switches on still another, and the lights on the final. The arrangement left the center open, only now it wasn't open. Now it was filled with what must be Azah's silk. "What has she done?" he said again, this time aloud.

The silk was extremely useful and tough as steel. It was also something they knew should be kept hidden. None of the other Tortantula had the stuff, and nothing in their training had discussed it. If they could all do it, and it was as useful as it seemed, they would have gotten instructions on how best to take advantage of it.

The stuff in the box looked the same, though it was used in a way he'd never seen. It was woven together in patterns, interconnected between the lights, switches, power, and computer. The final remaining side was used to connect the largest mass of silk. As he looked, cocking his head from side to side, he could see the silk was shimmering. No, it was scintillating with its own light. *It was conducting power!* "Entropy," he hissed.

Sadek took out his own slate and accessed it. He'd learned long ago to create hidden files the teachers couldn't find. It seemed like they almost encouraged the behavior, so he indulged. Accessing one of those files, he took several Tri-V quality images, turning the intensity up as high as it would go, and embedded the images in the file. When he was done, he took the extra measure of encrypting the file, and buried it inside a sub-function directory. The file was named Weaver.

"This can't stand," he said, looking at the box. Some other member of the covert ops team would be issued the box, and when it didn't act the way it was supposed to, they'd take it apart. Where he'd thought her silk was something to keep between them before, now he knew beyond a shadow of a doubt. This was dangerous.

He spent some time examining how the box was *meant* to work. Finally, confident, he picked up a pair of wire cutters. He sighed. This felt like a violation but it had to be done. He started cutting away the silk.

When the morning arrived, Azah arose and found Sadek sitting with his slate, the same as he'd been when she fell asleep. She looked sleepily at him.

"You been up all night?"

"Yeah," he said. "I have to have these notations to Yeef today." He glanced at the coding box and back to her. "You gotta turn that in this morning?"

"Oh, yeah," she said and scooped it up.

"Remember not to bang it," he said.

"Right," she replied. "See you later." She scuttled out of their quarters and down the hall. He watched her go, his jaw set. She didn't remember modifying the box. He didn't know if that was bad, or very bad. He really wanted to know what was going on in that brain of hers. His teachers were fond of a saying, "Nobody knows what goes on in a Tortantula's mind, not even a Tortantula." He nodded. He'd removed the silk and carefully disposed of it. That returned the box to its normal function. He'd used a piece of simple tape to secure the wire bundle. It was a field-expedient solution and was probably what they'd wanted her to do in the first place.

What he couldn't do was fix the security system. He still didn't know how she'd gotten around it. Sooner or later, they'd realize it had been hacked. He just hoped it was long after they'd moved on. With a yawn, he set about getting ready for the day's work.

* * * * *

Chapter Six

"**G**ood afternoon." Sadek and Azah both jumped in surprise at the words. Yeef was hanging upside-down from the doorframe of their quarters, his tiny eyes regarding them.

"Commander!" Sadek blurted and jumped up from the pillow he'd been lying on, playing a game. Azah got to her feet respectfully as well. They weren't neglecting their duties; this was their off time, and you could do whatever you wanted then. Most teams spent it together doing something unimportant. Sadek and Azah liked to lounge in their private space and watch Tri-V, play games, or snooze.

"Commander," she said, lowering her head a bit.

"You should have learned by now," he said. "We don't go in too much for formalities here. May I come in?" The two glanced at each other. Neither could recall ever being asked for permission to do anything, especially by a superior.

"Of course," Azah spoke for them. The male moved over the doorframe, still upside down, and walked up the wall. He was so light the graspers on his feet allowed him to easily move that way. Sadek listened carefully; the male Tortantula's accent was difficult sometimes.

"You know," Yeef said, gesturing around the room with a leg, "when I took command of the team, I changed the living arrangements. Before I came here, all the Tortantulas and Flatar were billeted together in large rooms in a clannish structure, instead of traditional pairs such as yours. The Tortantula and their partners were not raised together."

"How bizarre," Azah said. Sadek nodded.

"Yes," Yeef agreed and spread his pedipalps in a Tortantula shrug. "They proved to be a borderline disaster. Well, more like a total disaster. We had a major incident during an operation. Several of the Tortantulas went berserk, and one even ate its Flatar."

"Entropy," Sadek gasped. Yeef nodded by bowing his thorax several times. If what he'd said wasn't so horrendous, it would have looked almost comical, considering the Tortantula male was hanging from the ceiling at the time. "Why were they trained that way?"

"Some Veetanho had what she thought was a brilliant idea. It wasn't. I lost most of my teams."

"I wondered why there was so much room here," Azah said.

"Yes, there were twenty pairs two years ago. The attrition rate from that training method was high, but the Veetanho were reluctant to admit it was a bad idea, so we pushed on until the mission where the rider was killed by his Tortantula, and everything fell apart. Now there's only Shypik and Ezek."

"They were trained that way?" Azah asked.

"Yes," Yeef said. "We aren't 100% certain, but they may be the last pair remaining. After the disaster here, the Veetanho finally relented, and that method of training was abandoned."

"Why do the Veetanho tell us what to do?" Azah asked. It was an unexpected question that made Sadek's head come around in complete surprise. The Veetanho led them; they were at the top of the command structure. Yeef was the first non-Veetanho they'd reported to. Sadek realized he'd never questioned that fact. Of course, why would you? The Veetanho had been there from the moment both were born, watching, teaching, and judging.

Yeef regarded Azah without comment for a long time. Sadek unconsciously assigned that pause to Yeef considering how to answer. As he waited for the commander to comment, he went from shock at his partner's bold question to curiosity about a possible answer.

"One of the areas of education you receive little information on is history," Yeef began. "Long ago our race, and yours," he said and looked at Sadek, "had very different paths. Then that path was irrevocably altered into what we have today, under the tutelage of the Veetanho, who've guided our course ever since."

"What happened?" Azah asked, a slight breathlessness to her question.

"I can't tell you," he said. "It's lost with the ages." Sadek and Azah glanced at each other. "And besides," Yeef continued, "it doesn't matter. Does the rain question why it must fall on the ground?" Yeef was quiet for a second and Sadek waited for him to say something more about it, but he didn't. "I've completed my evaluation of your abilities, which is the reason I've come to talk to you, not to reminisce on the ancient past. I knew when you were assigned, by reviewing your training and service record, that you would be a good fit; however, I also knew your secondary training would be severely lacking. I'm pleased it wasn't as bad as I'd feared. You two are an excellent team, and the way you complement each other does credit to both our races."

Azah and Sadek beamed, and Sadek thought it might have been the first time anyone over them had ever given them a compliment. And such a glowing compliment it was! He reached out and patted

Azah on her cephalothorax, and she returned the gesture with a pedipalp.

"We have more teams arriving in the coming months; I need to declare you operational so I can send you on operations. But in order to do that, you'll need to get pinplants."

"Oh," Sadek said in surprise.

"We get pinplants?" Azah echoed. "We thought only team commanders and such got them."

"Covert ops team members are an exception to that," Yeef said. "The situations and environments you often have to operate in make them a necessity."

"Will they take them away if we leave covert ops later?" Sadek asked.

Yeef laughed. "No, they cannot be removed after installation. Report to the medical section in an hour." He skittered down the wall and was out of the room without another word.

"Wow," Sadek said after he was gone.

"I know," Azah agreed. "Pinplants!"

"That *is* fascinating, but what I really meant was the whole Veetanho thing."

"He doesn't approve," Azah said.

"No, I don't think he does." Sadek considered. "How can we not know why things are the way they are?"

"I think he knows," Azah replied. "He said he couldn't tell us, then glossed it over with the bit about it being lost with the ages."

"You think he was lying?"

"No, I think he was just glossing over it."

"Maybe it's just the way it is," Sadek said, "like he said, 'does the rain question why it must fall on the ground?'" He looked down at the floor of their room. This was their life, after all.

"Yes," Azah said, "the rain must fall." She looked at him with that strange look she now had from time to time. "But enough rain can start a flood and even submerge the greatest mountain." Sadek didn't quite see the comparison. It would take billions of raindrops to do that.

The procedure itself turned out to be simple and fast. They were both put to sleep for a short time, and when they woke up, the implants were done. Sadek's was just behind his right ear, and Azah had two, one on either side of her middle side eyes. "Because of how their brains work," the Wrogul physician said. Sadek was almost as amazed by the alien doctor as he was by the procedure. It looked like a simple sea creature floating in water.

When he woke up, Sadek didn't feel any different. The Wrogul was gone, replaced with an elSha technician who was watching displays and tapping on a slate. "Feel anything weird?" the elSha asked. Sadek cleared his mind and *felt* around his brain. There was a buzz somewhere, and he couldn't quite find the source of it.

"Just a buzzing sound."

"Any flashing lights or dizziness?"

"No," he said.

"Good. Concentrate on the buzz."

"It's hard," he said.

"I know; it gets easier." Sadek tried for a long time, then suddenly he saw an image appear in the corner of his vision. It was a little like the heads-up display on some of the heavier weapons, only this wasn't projected into his eye; this was inside his brain.

"Oh, wow. I see a menu!"

"Great, now in the same way, concentrate on the word 'Initialize.'"

When he checked his now internal clock upon leaving, he saw it had been only an hour since they'd arrived. He rode on Azah's back, as usual, and could see the two glittering new pinplants on either side of her head. "Do yours hurt?" he asked.

"No, not a bit," she admitted. "You?"

"Nope," he said. As they walked, he was probing through all the menus and functions. He had a huge amount of internal memory available, at least an exabyte's worth. The Wrogul said it was carved out of his brain. *The part you won't use anyway.* Somehow, the alien came across as arrogant when he said it, too. Near their quarters, they encountered Shypik.

"Good, I was looking for you two," she said. "You'll have a mission in the next three days; be prepared."

"How do we prepare if we don't know what the mission will be and exactly when?"

"Covert ops is a job that can happen after weeks of planning or on a moment's notice." She turned and walked away.

"Excrement," Azah said. Sadek nodded.

* * * * *

Chapter Seven

True to Shypik's word, she gave them their first mission a few days later.

The Flatar stood in a small briefing room not far from their new quarters. Azah and Sadek had hardly been in covert ops long enough to explore the ins and outs of this new complex and were still learning their way around, but fortunately, Shypik always seemed to be able to find them. The previous evening, when they'd turned in the work she'd given them, they were told to meet her in this room first thing the next morning.

Unlike the teachers and their old assault company commander, Shypik didn't make them wait. She walked in, gave them both a nod, and began speaking.

"Your mission," she said, "is a simple operation, and for your first time, you'll go in alone. Yesterday, I asked you to memorize the blueprints for the orbital headquarters of a major galactic agricultural concern. Your mission will be to infiltrate that headquarters, and locate and destroy the genetic modification archive for their major food product. Any questions so far?"

"Yes," Azah asked. "Why?"

"Why what?"

"Why are we destroying an archive?"

Shypik paused, then looked at them both with an amused expression.

"You really are both very young, aren't you?" she asked. "Tell me, in your research into mercenary races, what have you discovered about the nature of warfare?"

"Warfare can be fought in multiple environmental conditions," Sadek said. "Everything from deep space combat to planetside brawls and all points in between."

"Is that all?" Shypik asked

"Well…" Sadek said, uncertain.

"No, it is not," Shypik said, her mouth twisting in a small smile. "Far from it. The truth, young ones, is that overt violent confrontation is often the *least* desirable way of accomplishing an objective. Especially given the combat limitations imposed by membership in the Galactic Union. In actuality, it's nearly impossible to truly destroy one's opponent by force and still be operating within Union law. However…there are other, more elegant ways of accomplishing the same goal. If you can destroy an entity's means of generating income, you can effectively erase that entity from existence. And if you are a rich agricultural concern, you probably have enemies willing to pay for the skills to make that happen…subtly. Elegantly, if you will."

"We're spies?" Azah asked.

"Not exactly. The proper term is 'industrial sabotage,' since you are to destroy the archive. If you were truly to be spies, you would bring the information back, and we would call it 'industrial espionage.' A small distinction, but an important one. Now, pull your schematics up on your slates, and let me show you what you're working with."

They spent the next hour going over the building schematics and discussing the plan in excruciating detail. Shypik covered entry and egress routes, possible points of contact with enemy beings, bolt-holes, and contingency after contingency after contingency.

"Next time out, you'll have to come up with these plans on your own, or if you're part of a larger team, you'll assist your team lead in doing so. Remember, the most important thing is this—the information must be destroyed, regardless of the cost. Understand?"

"Yes, Shypik," Sadek said, and Azah clicked her pedipalps in agreement.

"Good. You board your transport in an hour. Do not speak about the details of this mission during your transition through hyperspace. The crew work for our employer, but they aren't cleared to know the details of our mission or our methods, so keep your mouths shut. I would recommend mentally rehearsing, but that's up to you. Just get the job done, no matter how you have to do it."

"Got it," Azah said. Shypik gave them a nod, then turned and left as abruptly as she'd arrived.

"Wait—!" Sadek called as the door irised closed behind the departing Flatar. "Entropy! She didn't tell us where to go to meet our transport!"

"I imagine the same place we disembarked when we arrived here," Azah said. "These 'Covert Ops' types seem to think if we've seen something once, we've seen it enough to work with."

"You're right," Sadek said. "Now that you mention it, I bet that's exactly it. Okay then, go back to our room for our weapons, then head out?"

"Sounds good," Azah said. "I don't imagine it would be good to be late for our first mission."

She was right on both counts. After arming up in their room and double-checking to make sure Azah's combat harness was ready to go, they followed the path they'd taken when they first arrived: straight down the hallway to the large door that opened onto a featureless shuttle pad. There, they found Yeef and Shypik awaiting them.

"Good," Yeef said. "You're right on time."

In point of fact, they were a quarter hour early, but Azah wasn't going to argue with him.

"Good luck," the male Tortantula added. "Remember, this is not just your first mission, this is your final test. Either you succeed, or you die. Which one will be up to you both."

As he spoke, the dome opened overhead to reveal a shuttle descending toward them. It landed, the doors opened, and without further ceremony, Azah and Sadek boarded the flight that would take them from the training environment into the operational.

* * * * *

Chapter Eight

They hadn't been told where their mission was located, but it took two hyperspace jumps to get there. Both of them were given a file to store on their pinplants. It would unlock when they reached their destination. Azah used their time in the white nothingness to explore the utility of her new pinplants. The ability to hook in and browse the GalNet was fun, and she enjoyed learning new things. The GalNet was huge, though, and anyone could put anything on it, so she found just as much stupidity and dullness as she did interesting data. Combing through it all was just this side of exhausting, so she didn't do much of it.

Instead, she and Sadek worked on her favorite feature of their pinplant modifications—their new methods of communication.

"So," she said one day, about 100 hours into their second transition. "The point of the broadcast capability is to allow us to communicate even if we're separated, or it's loud, or whatever, right?"

"Right," Sadek said without looking up. He sat on the floor of their small, featureless cabin and cleaned his disassembled weapon for the thousandth time. "Why?"

"Well, is it secure?"

"What do you mean?" he asked, lifting his head and focusing on her.

"Is it secure?" she asked. "Or can anyone else in the vicinity with the right frequency—or a scanner that finds active freqs, or whatever—hear everything I'm thinking to you?"

"We hop frequencies," he said, "but any half-competent bot can aggregate the data and put our message together in near-real-time. I suppose...I suppose I could hack it and add some encryption. Are you worried the enemy will be listening in?"

"I don't know," Azah said, "it just seems like something we should consider. And..."

"What?"

"Well, you know we have a history of...improvising."

Sadek grinned. Azah clicked her pedipalps in her own version of a smile, then went on.

"It's just that," she said, "improvising has gotten us out of trouble several times, but I'm pretty sure if command knew we were going to be going off script, they probably wouldn't approve. So I'm thinking we need a way to communicate that's secure—"

"Even from them," Sadek finished for her, his grin fading. "Yeah, that might be a problem, Azah. I can layer encryption into our comm channels, no problem, but from what I've read, our pinplants are set with superuser keys. Any commander's going to be able to break in with no trouble. Unless..." He trailed off and looked narrowly at her.

"Unless what?"

"Remember what you did with the coding box?"

Azah went still.

"Yes. It didn't work."

"It did work, until I broke it."

"What?" Disbelief shuddered through her. Sadek wouldn't betray her like that. Would he?

"Azah, I'm sorry," he said, and misery crept into his tone. For just a split second, anger flashed through her, and she was glad. Let him be miserable. How could he do something like that? "I opened up the box after you finished it, and I saw what you wove with your silk. It was genius on a level I can't even come close to understanding. But…the silk is a secret, remember? I knew they'd want to know how you'd done your assignment, and if they saw that…well…no other Tortantula can spin silk."

"Loof and Yeef can."

"Loof and Yeef are males. You know what I mean. I'm sorry, Azah, I really am. But I was just so afraid for you!"

"I thought I had failed. I thought I couldn't code."

"Azah," Sadek said, laying aside the parts of his weapon and standing up. He walked over to her and leaned against her cephalothorax, just below her detail eyes. "I'm so sorry. You can code. You can code in ways I can't even comprehend…and that's what I think we could do here. No one's going to be messing with our pinplants or comm modules. So I think if I hack in, add some encryption—"

"And I add a code module that transmits it through my silk, that effectively adds another layer of encryption…and no one else has the key." Azah felt her anger start to drain away, replaced by the excitement of a new discovery.

"Exactly."

"Let's do it," she said, and clicked her pedipalps once more in a smile.

It didn't take too long. Sadek used his pinplant connection to open the base coding of the broadcast module that had been added to their pinplants and laid in a layer of simple, but elegant, encryption. Then Azah spun out enough silk to create two tiny woven matrices that echoed the encryption, then twisted it in three dimensions such that it had to be filtered back through another such matrix before the decryption keys could be applied. Sadek then applied one matrix to his own comm module, and another to hers.

"Let's test it out," she thought to him, and watched him jump, his eyes going wide.

"Azah! Your voice just…sounded in my head," he thought back. "This is crazy! I think this is going to work!"

"Well, don't say so out loud," she said, remembering her caution. "Because if command is keeping track, it's going to look like our encryption totally failed. They're probably going to want to look at our pinplants afterward."

"We'll deal with that then," Sadek said with a smile. "We'll switch back to unencrypted for now…and it's done!"

"Yeah," she thought, still using the encryption. "I added that in the twist code. You just have to think you want open comms, and you have them. Be careful what you say."

"They can't be monitoring us already," he said. "We're in hyper-space!"

"No, but the ship could be, or one of the crew or something."

"You're super paranoid, you know that, Azah?"

"Yes, and it's kept us alive. You're welcome," she responded, making the Flatar double over in laughter.

* * * * *

Chapter Nine

Sadek enjoyed their new secret communications method. Despite Azah's lack of concern, he'd always known they were under constant scrutiny, and now there was a way to avoid some of it. There was no way anyone could crack the scrambler Azah had built. It was, quite simply, unbreakable. It did beg the further question, why didn't other female Tortantula have silk? Azah was a very special Tortantula. The problem was, she didn't have a lot of concern on the matter. If Sadek had learned anything in his life, it was that being special was a dangerous thing.

In the remaining hours before they arrived at their destination, Sadek explored their transport's computer systems. Like before, the ship was owned by Veetanho and the crew didn't interact with either of them. They didn't run away when Azah or Sadek would encounter them, but they wouldn't talk to them, either. The technical staff, a few aliens he didn't recognize and several elSha, all but pretended he and his partner didn't exist. Their computer was just as standoffish.

"They were prepared for us," he said to himself as he nosed around the system. Their access was via coded interface, and that entry location limited what parts of the system he could get to. The older he got, the more he was starting to dislike being penned in. Being given more autonomous time as part of covert ops actually didn't help. He dearly wanted to test just how good the firewalls were. He didn't, though. This was their first covert ops mission, as well as their first solo mission; the last thing he wanted to do was be caught poking around where he wasn't wanted. At least, not yet.

They also resisted further experimentation with silk. That was more difficult for Sadek than not trying to break into other parts of the ship's systems. The properties of the stuff was more amazing than anything he'd studied in training. Azah's ability to use it to make other things was even more amazing, and disconcerting. The fact she seemed to simply take it for granted was less amazing, and more disconcerting. The more he thought about it, the more he wondered if he should be afraid of her. But he loved her; they were partners. Just like he didn't run away back on their assault mission, he wasn't going to be afraid of her now, just because she could do something other Tortantulas couldn't.

Their ship emerged from hyperspace, and the files in their pin-plants unlocked. They were in a system named Pros't, and the target was a data center in a city on the world's equatorial city. They were ordered to go to the city, find the data center, penetrate its security, and obtain a copy of all the secure communications being stored there. Afterward, return to the ship for transport back to base. That was it.

They read through it all several times, and finally Sadek looked up in confusion. "That's it?" he said. "No maps, no details on defenses, nothing?"

"They kind of left it all up to us," Azah agreed. "What happened to all those talks on planning operations as carefully as possible?" Sadek nodded, unable to understand how they were to proceed. The last part of their orders said the Veetanho ship would wait in orbit until the operation was complete. If Azah and Sadek were unable to make rendezvous, they were to transmit the information to the ship, and it would depart the system.

"If we don't get out alive," Sadek said, looking at his partner. The meaning was obvious.

"I've been ordered to put this shuttlecraft at your disposal," the ship's captain said a short time later, "I'll be awaiting your contact."

"Do we have to depart immediately?" Sadek asked.

"No," the captain said, "anytime in the next 22 hours is sufficient to avoid the planet's owners noticing you've come from my ship."

Sadek and Azah loaded their gear into the shuttle, made sure everything was secure, then Sadek settled into the small cockpit. Azah was far too large to fit, so she waited in the cargo area, and they communicated via their pinplants as Sadek used relayed sensor data from the ship. They looked over that data and tried to find out what they could about their objective. There was precious little to go on.

"We've never been to a city," Azah complained, "how are others going to react to our presence?" They'd been taught that Tortantula and Flatar were among the most feared mercenary races in the galaxy.

"They'll freak out, I'm sure," Sadek said glumly. They studied the map on the computer, assembled from radar scans.

"You'd think more detailed maps would be available," Azah said as they studied.

After a while they both admitted they weren't going to find their target by just looking at maps. Then it was Sadek who had a breakthrough. "You know," he said, "maybe we can use a different kind of data."

"Like what?" Azah asked. She'd been fixating on the clock—they only had five hours before they needed to depart to avoid blowing their cover.

"Think about how we're communicating. If you wanted to find us on a ship, would you look at radar or telescope data?"

"No, of course not. We're using our pinplants, so I'd..." she gave a little gasp. "Radio!" she exclaimed.

"Exactly," Sadek said. "Our objective is a data center, so I bet there's a lot of comms traffic." They accessed the specific data, and both began to smile.

* * * * *

Chapter Ten

For those with the eyes to see it, the radio frequency channels painted a glowing highway directly toward the communications station located in one of the three largest buildings in the city. As Sadek followed the radio highway, Azah played with her pinplants, filtering the data into her brain until she, too could literally see the streams of emitted data flowing and converging on their target. Sure enough, once they got close, the shape of the building came into view, and it matched that of the schematic Shypik had made them memorize. Of course, now they could have just uploaded it into their pinplant memory, so presumably memorizing the layout had been some kind of test. Azah wondered if they'd passed.

"I'm setting us down in the wooded park about a block and a half from the building," Sadek said. "It's ringed by trees, and I'm not getting any major life signs. If we're quick, we could be in and out before the sun comes up. Maybe no one will notice us. This planet has a single moon, but it's down right now, according to the shuttle's nav info."

"Sounds good," Azah said. "What direction is the building in?"

"It will be to the forward left as we land, but...entropy!"

"What?"

Sadek pulsed an image back to her over their private comms, and for a moment, she looked at a still picture recorded through his eyes. Everything seemed much bigger than she was used to seeing it, and it didn't have as much detail, but it had enough to illustrate what he was saying.

"That's the front entrance," he said. "See there? Those shadows next to what look like vertical doors? Those look a lot like CASPers."

"CASPers?"

"Yeah, remember? We learned about them a little while ago. That new merc race, the Humans, use them because they don't have any natural armor or weaponry. Weird for a merc race, but whatever. Anyway, CASPers are nothing to fool around with."

"You can take them with your cannon. There are only two."

"There are only two we can see. There are probably more inside. I just don't think a frontal assault is a good idea," he said as he maneuvered the shuttle to land with a soft thump in the grass of the park. Azah waited a moment, and the cargo door hissed and lowered to touch upon the grass.

It didn't look like the normal grass she'd grown up with, back in the training dome. It was thinner, shorter, and had funny spear-shaped leaves. It tasted different, too. Less boron-y, more carbon-y. It tickled her feet as she stepped out into the night.

Not far from the ship, Azah could hear the breeze rustling through the wide, flat leaves of the trees that ringed this spot. She also heard the distant sound of running water, but it echoed weirdly, as if it were in a cave, or...

"Sadek," she sent through her pinplant connection, turning to follow the sound. "I have an idea."

"What kind of idea?"

"The kind that might get us into the building without having to tangle with the big, bad, CASPers that scare you so much," she teased. "Mount up; I want to see if I'm right."

Sadek grumbled that he wasn't scared—he was smart—but he did as she asked. Azah felt a shiver of excitement skitter underneath her exoskeleton. If she was correct, this was going to be fun.

"I *am* right!" she sent a few moments later, when she'd followed the sound of running water to a culvert that washed under the nearby street and drained away into the darkness beyond. "This city must have an underground sewer! I bet we can get in there and use it to come up under the building. Remember how the schematic showed the sewer access in the basement?"

"Sewer access...you mean the drain? Azah, that thing's like two feet wide; you're never going to fit through there!"

"No, but you can. And then you can open one of the big cargo doors that lead down to the basement," she said, visualizing the schematic and sending him the image through her pinplants. "And I'll run in."

"I think you're crazy," Sadek said.

"Probably. But it sounds like fun, doesn't it?"

The Flatar let out a chittering laugh.

"Yeah," he said. "A little. All right, let's do it."

To their surprise, the crazy plan worked flawlessly. Sadek followed the culvert down and used their private communication link to keep in touch with Azah while she worked her way through the shadowed streets to the back of the building. She hadn't been sure if their comms would be compromised when they lost line of sight, but that was apparently not a problem. She didn't know for sure, but Azah suspected it had something to do with the broadcast working through the silk.

Whatever the reason, Sadek's thoughts were crystal clear in her head as he maneuvered through the fetid sewers and up into the basement of the building.

"I'm at the big door," he said to her. "There's a mechanism to raise it; it looks like it just rolls up instead of sliding into the wall like a normal door. This place is bleeding primitive."

"Open it," she said, "I'm on my way."

She darted across the open street area, tasting the old, rancid hydrocarbons that coated what these beings used for pavement. It was cracked and crumbling, like child's work. Who owned this agricultural concern, anyway?

Not that it mattered.

By the time she got to the door, Sadek had raised it high enough that she was able to drop to her abdomen and slide underneath it. Once she was inside, he used a metal chain on a pulley to lower the door back down and plunged the basement into darkness. She heard a click as Sadek flicked on the infrared light mounted to his weapon. With a thought, Azah commanded her pinplant-connected IR visor to snap into place over her main eyes.

The details around her suddenly jumped out in stark, monotone relief. They were in some kind of warehouse, crowded with stacks of variously-sized containers. It all looked haphazard and random, and a part of Azah's brain noted it was probably not a very useful warehouse if it wasn't better organized than this.

Sadek's touch as he pulled himself up into place on her pedicel recalled her to the present, and she pulled the building schematic from her enhanced memory.

"Stairs going up on the far end of the room," Sadek said, answering the question she hadn't asked. "Then the comm suite will be on the third floor, in the southwest corner of the building."

"Got it," Azah said and began threading through the piles of boxes toward the stairwell.

These stairs, however, only went up one floor, and seemed to be designed strictly for basement access. That meant they'd have to traverse the entirety of the first floor in order to get to the main staircase on the far end. No big deal, except if there were beings on the first floor.

There were.

As soon as they emerged from the staircase, someone opened fire with a laser weapon. Azah ducked instinctively, then snarled a challenge as she charged ahead. Sadek fired his own weapon in response until their attacker fell under Azah's feet. Battle rage gripped her as she used her weight to pin the armor to the floor and several limbs to rip open the metal casing, expecting to find a mewling, fleshy Human cowering inside.

Nothing.

"Not CASPers, then," Sadek thought to her. In contrast to her hot savagery, his voice felt cool and collected. Analytical, even. "Interesting."

"Why?"

"I don't know," he said. "Let's keep going."

"Yes, lets," Azah agreed. They worked down the hallway of the building, shooting, slashing, and dismembering each of the robot mockups masquerading as CASPers that stood in their way. It was easy, when it came right down to it. Their machine opponents lacked creativity in their actions. They simply waited for the pair, then fired on sight. It was far too easy.

"I bet real Humans aren't this easy," Sadek said as he blew a Flatar-sized hole in the chest plate of another machine. "They wouldn't be much good as mercs if they were. These things are like clockwork, easy to predict." As if to prove his point, he leveled his weapon at another doorway further down the hall. Sure enough, a robot popped out, and Sadek destroyed it.

"Maybe we're supposed to think they're this easy?" Azah said, pausing for breath as her initial rage drained away. "Could this be a trap?"

"I always think everything is a trap," Sadek said, "which is why we're still alive."

"Good point."

"Let's keep moving and find that data archive."

"Got it."

They climbed to the third floor, and the resistance stiffened. The robots began using actual tactics, which made Azah and Sadek respond in kind. The various rooms they ducked into didn't provide much in the way of cover, but enough of them were connected room-to-room that they could utilize some basic maneuver principles to outflank most of the attackers.

Finally, they made it to the comm suite. Sadek dismounted and took one of their small charges to booby trap the doorway. It would blow when one of the robots got close, giving them some warning and hopefully enough time to egress out the window and work down the outside of the building.

Only problem was, they hadn't accounted for the reinforcements that began to arrive outside.

"Um, Azah..." Sadek said. He had pulled himself up on a nearby shelf to look out the window while she went to the strange racks that sat at the nexus of the radio frequency trail.

"What?" she asked, distracted, as she puzzled over how, exactly, she was supposed to hack into this monstrous thing. Like the roll-up door, the computer was a beast of a machine, nearly as tall as she was, and covered in flashing lights. There was a flat, vertical screen on a table nearby, and a rectangular slab that had multiple buttons emblazoned with strange symbols. She dove through her enhanced memory and found a file she didn't even remember saving—a character map for the Human language. Or one of them, anyway; humanity had a multitude of languages. The important thing was the symbols on the buttons matched the characters from the map.

Not that it helped her much. It wasn't as if she could manipulate the small buttons herself, and they needed Sadek covering the window and the door...

"Azah!"

"What?" she asked again, this time looking up with an eye at Sadek and the window. Outside, a flying machine similar to the flyers she'd seen in training rose up in a hover and began peppering the room with laser fire. Sadek squealed and dove to the floor, and she took a searing burn on the backside of her exoskeleton. The tough fibers of her outer skin ablated most of the burn, but it really *stung!*

"Entropy!" she screamed, and Sadek rolled over to his back and returned fire through the window. His hyper-velocity pistol, the Flatar's favorite, boomed repeatedly. After a second, he stopped firing and lay the gun down.

"What did you stop for?" she asked.

"Barrel is at its limit," he said and deftly worked the oversized pistol, opening it and removing the complicated barrel, before snapping in another one. "The gun is awesome, but all the power in the accelerator magnets compromise the structural integrity after only a couple dozen shots." He finished and snapped it closed. A quick check of the power system, and he was back up and firing. One of his rounds slammed into the flyer dead center, and it faltered, then exploded. It rained debris from the sky in a wide circle, and Sadek again had to take cover.

"Are you all right?" she asked.

"Yeah," he said, "but I think we're out of time. Can you hack that thing?"

"I can't figure out how to start," she admitted. "It's junk."

"Let me see," he said, rolling to his feet and running to her side. After a few moments searching the various cables and wires, he let out a triumphant cry.

"Got it," he said, holding up a thick cord. "This is a Human interface cable. Something they call a USB. An old-style single-bus connector. Try hooking this to your pinplants, even with just a touch connection. You should be able to—"

"Use my silk," she said, spinning some into a line on the floor. "It's sticky when wet. Use it to stick the end of the cord to my pinplant, and…" she trailed off as Sadek hustled to follow the instructions, and suddenly she felt her mind flooded with data.

Old, strange data. Unlike the smooth streams of sensory input she was used to, this was cumbersome and damn near gibberish. No syntax to speak of, just a long, endless stream of repeating symbols. Ones and zeroes, she realized, recognizing them from the Human character map. Ones and zeroes organized in groupings of 4, 16, and 256. There seemed to be no pattern to them beyond that.

What was this?

"Azah!" Sadek's voice had gone shrill with urgency. He was firing again, both out the window and toward the doorway. "Azah, they're about to blow the trap! We gotta figure a way out of here, and quick!"

"One second," she said, making a snap decision. She funneled her thoughts to the silk on her pinplant and used that to take the still-rushing stream of data and...collapse it in upon itself. That was the image she had, anyway, and it came to her instinctively. *Tri-D*, a part of her mind whispered. Whatever it was she actually did, the data packaged itself into a dense, but much more manageable chunk. With a mental heave, Azah threw the chunk through her silk/pinplant connection at the command comm channel. Though it wasn't really meant to be used that way, her field-expedient solution worked, and she could feel the data being pulled through her as it uploaded to the orbiting ship, destined for Yeef's secure data location.

Then the booby trap blew.

Or rather, it didn't, but it would have, if their charges had been real.

"You are dead."

The Veetanho who spoke walked into the room in its usual unhurried manner. She didn't have her customary dark glasses on, instead using a visor to see in the IR light from Sadek's weapon and the cultural lighting that streamed in through the dirty window. Azah felt the last of the data pass through her pinplants and broke the connection. Under the guise of disconnecting from the data archive, she removed the silk from her pinplant and hid it under her lowered abdomen.

"You are dead, but have you completed your mission?"

"We have," Azah said. "The data archive is wiped clean."

"Is it?" the Veetanho asked, and she walked up to the character buttons and tapped on them in a rapid succession. "Hmm, it seems you are correct. Well. Not a complete failure, then. Congratulations. Most new recruits don't do half so well. Your commander, Yeef, will be pleased."

"I am pleased," Yeef said from behind them. Azah whipped herself around to find the male entering through the broken window.

"They did not survive," the Veetanho pointed out. "It would have been an expensive victory."

"We are all expendable," Yeef replied, "as you are so fond of reminding me."

"Indeed," she said with a tiny smile. "Well. I will leave you to your debrief, then, Commander."

Yeef watched her go without another word, then turned to look directly at Azah.

"It wasn't a real mission," she said.

"Not entirely," Yeef confirmed.

"But why?" Sadek asked. "I suspected something when the robots were so predictable on the first floor, and the flier looked like the ones in training, but..."

"To see what we would do," Azah said. "To see if we'd choose to survive or complete the mission."

"Yes," Yeef said.

"Did we choose correctly?" Sadek asked, and his voice held a deep well of bitterness.

"Oh, yes," Yeef said, and his tiny pedipalps moved to indicate deep satisfaction. "You chose very well indeed."

* * * * *

Chapter Eleven

"They're dangerous," Teeno said, looking at Yeef with her eyeless visor. The ancient Veetanho spent a great deal of her time traveling back and forth, watching the training of the broods under her control, following up with various experiments, and supervising the vast Tortantula/Flatar operations. She was notoriously hard to please, even for a Veetanho.

"We want them dangerous," Yeef said without pause.

"Yes, dangerous in a *controllable* manner. These two are not as controllable. This pair of loners aren't performing on the nominal curve. Pidek and Zorm, their first level teachers, both recommended they be recycled."

"They recommend that often for any team that doesn't conform to the curve," Yeef said, "and if you did do that..."

"We wouldn't have any left for field work," Teeno finished for him. "Even so, after their borderline rogue actions on their assault company mission, I should have liquidated them immediately."

"They showed immense initiative and saved the contract."

"I don't want Tortantula and their riders showing initiative," she snapped. "I want them killing who we tell them to kill!" She visibly calmed herself. "If we were not still recovering from that fool Sleeso's insane scheme to replace rider team loyalty with a clan, we wouldn't be in this situation." The male Tortantula remained silent. All the males had tried to advise the Veetanho stewards against the idea, and their advice had been soundly dismissed. None of them were foolish enough to bring up that fact now.

"What do you want me to do with them? They passed the evaluation."

"I know perfectly well they passed, I would like to know better *how* they passed."

"I'll complete a report. But, in the meantime?"

"Activate them," she said and left without another word. Yeef watched her go with several of his eyes until she'd departed headquarters, then took out another slate. He accessed his own secure systems, verifying that Teeno had boarded the transport back to space before logging into another account. This one wasn't part of the Veetanho-created and controlled system. He was certain the Steward didn't know it existed. If she did, or any other of her number were aware of it, he and a great many others would have been dead long ago.

"She is operational," he typed into a message. "I am operating on the edge of discovery. You're right; she's the one with silk. Proceeding." He entered a code into the slate. It was a one-time-only code that encrypted the message in such a way that only the exact same code could break the encryption. Once it was complete, the message file was attached to a series of spreadsheets. They already had several other images encrypted with the same methods. Together they were just a series of routine reports on his covert ops unit, and the message went into the queue to be transmitted back to the headquarters on Hok.

Yeef sat silently as his reports were transmitted to the next ship to leave Kutu for Hok, which just happened to be Teeno's own vessel. His pedipalps clicked together as he weighed the risks. The sooner Loof was aware, the better. It was his brother Loof who'd woven the web of manipulations on Teeno, which got Azah and Sadek assigned to him in the first place.

"He is taking too great a risk," one of the other males in their network warned sometime later as Loof's web became clear to them.

"We should stop, and start again once the Stewards are less wary," another eventually agreed.

"They won't become less wary anytime soon," Loof argued. "The clan program proves they were desperate to stop any progress. We are so close to success that backing off could result in complete exposure, and you all know what that means."

The conversation took weeks to unfold, messages moving between breeding worlds, operational bases, and even far-flung administrative leaders. Males were seldom stationed more than one or two to a world, and only eleven were part of the effort. Once there had been many, many more. Not all their attritions were the cost of success, either. So few of them were given autonomy by Stewards. They were too much like other rodents, naturally wary and quick to become suspicious. Messages were sent in fragments only, making conversations slow and monotone.

Normally, after a brood's training was complete and the females dispersed, their Steward moved onto another brood or other responsibilities. Yet here was Teeno, still following Brood 37F2 long after she should have been. When she'd arrived at the end of the test period, Yeef had immediately become suspicious that Loof had been uncovered. He still wasn't convinced he'd been wrong. She was suspicious, but not suspicious enough to toss away such an incredibly valuable asset as an effective covert ops team. Azah and Sadek showed inconceivable potential. The Tortantula commander cursed silently. This was the risk. That very potential signaled that Loof might be correct about this daughter.

Almost, he'd tried to dispose of Teeno. It would have meant his own end, of course. It was only the risk to Azah and Sadek as potential collateral loses that stopped him. He considered that an even bigger threat than such an action against the Stewards. They almost never pierced the veil of perceived subservience. In the end, he'd stepped back from that course of action.

Yeef opened his legitimate comms log and reviewed the mission requirements list. They needed some successful operations to their credit, as soon as possible, so they could blend into the background. The challenges were not losing them and not spoiling them for future plans. He found what he was looking for and wrote out a series of orders.

Once finished, he took the slate he'd used to send his secret messages over to a machine and fed it in. The device ground the portable computer into dust and melted the dust afterward. Satisfied, he moved on to more routine work.

* * * * *

Part V

The Way of Things

Chapter One

"**D**o you think this mission is real?" Azah asked Sadek as they looked at the briefing.

"Yes," he said, "this time I do." Unlike the first time, there were details for them now, albeit confusing details.

"A diplomatic mission," Azah said. They'd both needed to look up what diplomacy meant. "Who even knew that sometimes races talked instead of fighting?"

"News to me," Sadek agreed. "Must be how non-merc races solve problems." The concept was a foreign one to him, but it actually sounded like a pretty good one. He looked over at Azah, who was busy working on the modified saddle they'd been given. It wasn't an assault model, like their normal one, or even a light design like they'd used right out of training. This one was carefully designed to look like...nothing. Just a simple affair on casual observation; in reality, it was anything but. His partner was amazed at how many things could be hidden in the saddle.

The mission stated they were to accompany a Sidar merchant on a negotiation. The Sidar looked like a leathery bird. They weren't a merc race, so Sadek didn't know much about them. This negotiation was on behalf of the Veetanho, and was both delicate in nature and potentially dangerous. Azah and Sadek were to stay out of sight and wait until they were called upon, which would mean the negotiations had gone from delicate to dangerous.

"Priority number one is securing any vital trade information the Sidar merchant obtains," Sadek read. "Priority number two is protection of the negotiator, personnel, and vessel."

"Tough to be a Sidar merchant," Azah said. "What does some merchant contract have to do with the Veetanho, and, by default, with us?"

"I don't know," Sadek admitted, "but my bet is they expect everything to fall apart."

"Why do you think that?"

"Because if they didn't, they wouldn't send us."

"Azah, Sadek." They both turned to the door for their quarters to see Shypik standing there. "The Sidar trading ship just transitioned into the system. Yeef said you are to report to the mission bay in five minutes."

"We will," Sadek said.

"Why do we hardly ever see you with Ezek?" Azah asked.

"Her?" Shypik asked. "What's she ever done for me?" Both Azah and he watched in stunned amazement as he turned and left.

"He's one of those," Azah said after the Flatar was gone, "the ones who weren't raised with their Tortantula."

"Is he insane?" Sadek wondered aloud.

"Maybe," Azah agreed, "but we better get ready regardless."

The pair collected their gear and went to the mission bay as they'd been instructed. There they found Shypik and Ezek, along with their commander, Yeef. The bay, normally used for the mustering of missions, was now dominated by a trio of huge shipping crates. One of them stood open, and the pair could see there was considerable room inside, along with machinery.

"Are you ready?" Yeef asked as they approached.

"We are," Sadek answered.

"Is this a real mission?" Azah asked. Sadek cringed inwardly.

"Yes, it is," he replied. "I understand you are annoyed at the fake mission. You need to understand that, while I control this team, I don't decide the method of selection for my teams, or how you are certified as mission-ready." Sadek and Azah glanced at each other but didn't comment. "We do our duty the best we can, and as we're told to do it." He focused all his eyes on Azah. "It's what we do."

"We understand," Sadek said, and Azah repeated it a second later.

"Because of the nature of this operation, you'll be undercover the entire time unless your mission parameters are realized."

"Meaning?" Sadek asked.

"You read the briefing," Yeef said. He pointed at the open crate. "This doesn't look like much, but it's fully self-contained for up to 60 days. It has life support, food, waste disposal, and contingency equipment for most situations you might encounter."

"It's almost like a space ship," Sadek said.

Yeef skittered inside and began pointing out some of the systems. "These monitoring sensors will automatically integrate themselves with any ship they are placed within. We have the information on the merchant, and you'll be able to monitor his comm traffic. Further details on the subject are stored in the system." He showed them a pair of slates that acted as the controls. "Are there any questions? No? Good." He skittered back out and gestured. "Good luck, do your job well."

Sadek patted Azah on the thorax and she moved into the container. It wasn't large, but it was bigger than their first quarters back in the assault company. Sadek slid down from Azah as the doors began to close. He looked back and saw Shypik looking at him and smiling.

* * * * *

Chapter Two

Azah hadn't technically met Urralon, the Sidar merchant, but she already knew she didn't like him. After she and Sadek loaded into the disguised crate they monitored his comms while the merchant negotiator was briefed on their presence and mission.

"How do I know they won't break free and begin shooting up the place?" Urralon asked, his chittery voice carrying a nasal whine, even through the translator. "I should probably have a lock on that crate, to protect myself from my 'protection.'"

"Azah and Sadek are a highly-trained and disciplined operational team," Yeef said coldly. "They will not emerge from the crate unless it's necessary to save your life. You wanted security backup on this mission; you've got the best we can give you. I suggest you take it and be grateful."

"Oh, I am, I am," Urralon said quickly, bobbing his ridiculously crested head and shifting the leathery wings he held tightly closed to his body. "I just thought perhaps…but no. You are clearly the expert in this area. I will trust to your judgment. Though I will take the opportunity to remind you, the terms of my contract stipulate that I complete the mission hale and whole; otherwise, the whole thing is null and void. I am certain our mutual employers would be distressed were that clause invoked."

"That's why we're sending Azah and Sadek with you," Yeef said, and focused all his eyes on the Sidar. The male Tortantula was small,

201

even to the Sidar. Even so, his series of eyes looked with coldness and his fangs clicked idly. Tortantula, male or female, were an intimidating species. Sadek must have liked the attitude of their commander, because he murmured appreciatively as he leaned against Azah while the two of them watched through the crate's optical displays.

"Of course, of course," the Sidar said, giving his own wide version of a smile.

"They really are ugly creatures, aren't they?" Sadek said softly, though the crate was soundproofed.

"I'm not one to talk…but yes," Azah said. "Especially that one. There's something about him…he seems really…oily."

"Yeah," Sadek said, nodding his head vigorously. "Exactly. Like there's something gross that clings to him and would jump on you if you got too close. I hope we don't have to rescue this guy. I'm not sure I want to get that close to him."

"You've gotten prissy," Azah said, her tone joking. "You're close to me all the time, and I'm ugly."

"Shut up, you are not. You look exactly as you should."

"I'm small."

"Shut up, Azah," Sadek said, the banter leaving his tone. He sounded tired, so Azah let it drop, wondering what was wrong with her friend.

"Fine," she said, all business, "but I was thinking about something. These comm monitoring sensors…Yeef said they could integrate with any ship we're loaded into, right?"

"Yeah," Sadek said, his eyes narrowing in interest.

"And ships have to maintain contact with the Galnet in order to perform financial transactions and data transfer, right?"

"Yeah," he said again. "So? You want to watch GalCasts while you're bored?"

"No," Azah said, derision in her tone. "We're on a mission. However, if we can integrate with the ship's comms traffic, it shouldn't be too hard to hack the sensors so we can monitor all of the traffic...including the information data transfer this Sidar is supposed to negotiate. Our primary mission is to secure the data, after all, right?"

"Right," Sadek said, a slow smile growing across his face. "Exactly right...but that wasn't what we were told to do."

"Sure it was," Azah said, clicking her pedipalps. "Yeef told us to do our job well. This is how we do it."

"Okay," Sadek said, his smile growing into a fully-fledged grin. "You got it."

There wasn't much room to maneuver in their little box, but Sadek was able to get over to the comm monitoring boxes by squeezing under her abdomen and lying flat on the floor. Azah watched him through one of her peripheral eyes as he produced a tool from a hidden pocket somewhere, and began to methodically dismantle the box, exposing its inner workings. For a moment, she wished they still had the silk-enhanced pinplant comms, but they'd had to clean the silk off, and Sadek hadn't asked for it again. For some reason, using silk made him nervous. She couldn't figure out why. It had pretty much been pivotal to every success they'd had so far.

"Got it!" Sadek said, triumph in his little voice. "You were right; it was stupidly easy to expand the scope of the sensors' monitoring parameters. We'll get all the traffic now. I'm going to post a display on that side screen there, okay? We'll be able to watch the Sidar and the negotiation on the main screen and this one here to the right."

"Perfect," Azah said, tamping down on the tiny flare of disappointment that she didn't have to use her silk. "Good work, and just in time, too. The Sidar is entering the negotiation now."

Sadek wormed out from under her body and came up to stand beside her cephalothorax. He casually draped one arm over her, careful not to impede her vision, but leaning close in a way he hadn't done in quite a while. She'd missed it, and she leaned subtly back into him. Not enough to knock him over, just enough to let him know she returned his love.

"Greetings!" Urralon was saying. They watched on the main screen as he spread his leathery wings wide in what must be a Sidar gesture. "Welcome to our negotiation!"

"Ha!" the hooded figure facing him said. Or rather the translator did. The figure's actual words were a growled garble that sounded like gravel in a metal drum. "Presumptuous of you, Sidar, to ape a Depik greeting. Are you trying to be threatening?"

"Not at all," Urralon said, "merely welcoming. The Depik don't have a monopoly on negotiations, after all. Nor welcomes, I imagine."

"No indeed," the hooded figure said. It stepped forward, but something was off with its gait, as if it couldn't walk properly. It lifted furred, clawed appendages and tossed back the hood, revealing its nightmare face. "I did not find them welcoming at all."

"Besquith," Azah said, her tone lighting up. Fighting a Besquith would certainly make things more interesting. They were known to be vicious, ferocious combatants…and shrewd merchants. What were the Veetanho buying from a Besquith?

Sadek said nothing, but he patted her cephalothorax one more time and pulled himself into his saddle. Azah missed his comforting weight against her side, but that was probably a good call. With Besquith involved, this thing could go from excellent to entropy in an eye blink.

"Would you care for something to drink? I've refreshments—" Urralon said, but the Besquith negotiator cut him off with a shake of his furred head.

"I'm not here to waste time. Let's just get on with it. I have the information you want."

"Excellent," the Sidar said smoothly.

"But the price has gone up," the Besquith growled, and his fanged maw twisted in something that might have been a smile. "I need another fifty thousand credits."

"My dear Anghakk," Urralon said, "that was not the price that was quoted."

"No," Anghakk said, "but it's the price I am charging. If your employers do not want the data, I will find someone who does."

"Be assured," Urralon said, "they want it. But for an extra fifty thousand, I must have something additional to take back to them. A hundred thousand credits is not an insignificant sum."

"Wait," Sadek said softly, "did he say a hundred thousand credits?"

"Yeah," Azah said, "why?"

"Because that was the original amount that was offered, according to our brief. Why are they acting like it was more?"

"I don't know," Azah said slowly. She shifted her weight more onto her toes. Above her, she felt Sadek unholster his XT-12. She shivered slightly in anticipation. Sadek was seldom wrong when it came to impending violence. "That is weird."

"What do you want?" Anghakk grunted.

"More," Urralon said, his usually chittery voice low and smooth as silk.

"What do you mean, more? This is the compiled data from my mother's holdings on Khatash. Our firm no longer has those holdings."

"No, but you've rebuilt a presence on Khatash under another name," Urralon said. "I want first access to the data you'll accumulate."

The Besquith eyed the Sidar as if he were contemplating how tasty he'd be. Urralon simply dropped his jaw in a smile and waited.

"Done," Anghakk growled. "Transfer the credits, and I'll transfer the data."

"Already happening," Urralon said. Sure enough, when Azah looked at the screen Sadek had hacked, she could see the credits and information had both begun to flow.

"Whoa," Sadek said then, "that's really weird. Look at that."

"What?"

"The data transfer just split...it looks like...like Urralon's transferring some of the data elsewhere? To a different data archive than the one designated."

"He's skimming," Azah said. "Can we copy the data stream?"

"Just a second...done! I hooked the comm monitor control box to my pinplants," Sadek said, vicious triumph in his tone. "We're getting copies of all of this and sending it via our secure link to Yeef."

"Perfect," Azah said. "What data is he skimming?"

"I don't know. It seems random, which means it's probably not," Sadek replied. "It's all tagged with a 'Delta' identifier, but I can't see any other thing in common. Do you want to take the time to hack it now?"

"No," Azah said, mindful that they'd most assuredly be noticed if they did. "It's not our business. Let Yeef and the others figure it out. Our primary job is done."

Just then, Anghakk let out a roar and lunged at Urralon, his claws slashing wicked furrows in the Sidar's large head-crest. Urralon staggered back, trying to hold his leathery arms up to protect his face.

"Liar!" the Besquith howled. "Double crosser! Why are you copying the data? That wasn't part of the deal—"

Azah didn't hear the rest, because she had punched the egress lock on their crate and was busy charging out to protect the Sidar negotiator. Sadek's hyper-velocity pistol cracked, the shockwave deafening in the close confines of the room. It hit the Besquith, who howled in pain, but didn't fall. Somewhere behind him, a door opened, and five more Besquith rushed in, all armed and armored. Sadek's instincts were again good.

"Get in the crate!" Sadek shouted at Urralon, who whimpered, but rushed to comply. Blood flowed down his head in a torrent as he ran. The Flatar then opened fire on the newcomers. *Crack, crack, crack!* His gun dropped two instantly, and wounded a third. At close range, even the Besquith's heavy combat armor was no match for the pure ballistic badassery of the XT-12.

Two remained for Azah, plus the crippled Anghakk. Azah's fangs clicked in excitement. This was going to be fun.

She lunged at the lead Besquith, but he rolled away as his two surviving guards tried to flank the massive Tortantula suddenly in their midst. One of them brought a laser carbine up and aimed at her head. Azah used her forelegs to slam into that one's face, catching the carbine as well. The gun flew through the air, and its owner staggered to the side. She pounced on the other and sank her fangs into his chest.

Tortantula fangs were far more than enamel or chiton. Evolution armed them with a bone structure that more closely resembled carbon fiber. They were both incredibly strong and flexible enough not to be brittle. The muscles that drove them crossed Azah's lower cephalothorax and were a meter long each. They could deliver more than 2 tons per square millimeter at the tip. The hardened hybrid ceramic armor the Besquith wore provided a decent purchase for the fangs. She bore down, and with a hideous *Skreeee* sound, her fangs split the armor and slowly punched into the Besquith's chest.

"Argh!" the alien screamed, "No…" His blood tasted of fear and rage. It was delicious. She sank her fangs in as deeply as she could, at which point her venom sacks automatically contracted, poisoning her foe. His screams ceased instantly as the neurotoxin did its work.

Sadek fired again as she killed the Besquith. His shot hit one in the abdomen, tearing it open and blowing his entrails across the room. He screamed and fell to his knees, sprawling in his own guts.

The remaining Besquith slammed into her cephalothorax from the side. His claws scrabbled for purchase on her exoskeleton, and she flinched away, raising a pair of legs lest he puncture her eyes on that side. She followed the flinch with a blow from her rear legs, and the claws of her back feet tore into his armor, tearing several pieces free and ripping into his furred flesh underneath. He let out a tearing, coughing scream, too, just before she tore him in half with her four back legs.

He, too, tasted of fear.

"Entropy!" Sadek swore. "The main one got away! The ship's comm just told me he jettisoned his shuttle and sped away."

"Can we shoot him down?"

"This is an unarmed transport, Azah," Sadek reminded her. "He's gone."

"What about the Sidar?" she asked, forcing her mind back to the mission at hand. Bloodlust was a heady drug.

"Safe in our crate," Sadek said. "Yeef just hailed the ship. They're on their way. Mission accomplished." He grinned at her as he slid a new magazine into his gun. They'd done it; they'd completed their mission.

* * * * *

Chapter Three

"They've exceeded my highest expectations," Yeef said in his secure office as he read the action report on Azah and Sadek's mission with the entropy-cursed Sidar.

A year ago, during the middle of the crazed experiment, he'd been tasked with completing a similar mission. Some valuable data was being purchased from a reluctant group of Aposa traders. The owners were Pushtal, quick to anger felines. They caught up with the Aposa just as Yeef's agents were making the purchase. It turned into a bloodbath. That was often the cost of doing business. The problem was, after the Pushtal were liquidated, the Tortantula and Flatar continued to the Veetanho's agents, then the ship's crew, and finally each other.

Azah and Sadek had performed perfectly. They'd even saved the Sidar. That was impressive. "Now to cultivate this until we see the final results." He picked up a new slate and entered the beginning of another message. On a specialized slate nearby was a detailed analysis of the data Sadek had pilfered from the Sidar, who'd been pulling a cute little double-sided gambit with the Veetanho. He was surprised at the audacity of the move. Of course, was what he and the others were doing any better? It was certainly as dangerous.

The computer was still working on the data. Officially, it was simply packed and sent to the Veetanho. Unofficially, he'd made a copy and was dissecting it. There was a great deal of interesting information included in the data. Much, much more than simple trade information. "This is interesting," he said as he looked at some of it. With a gesture from a pedipalp, he dug into his archives.

Deep within the systems' memory were more of the cunningly saved files. A few of them contained data, which Sadek and Azah had gotten on their supposed training mission. More than an exercise, less than an actual covert operation. Neither of them knew the level of subterfuge, and he intended to keep it that way.

They'd turned the Sidar over to Veetanho specialists. At that point, Yeef didn't care what happened to the sleazy bird. The more he looked at the accumulated data, the more he saw that something big was up. The Veetanho always had a dozen plots going on, but this was huge. Big enough they were burning assets already in critically low supply. Two other intelligence units had been lost in the last month. Secret messages from other males confirmed this fact. His was now one of only four covert ops units in their galactic arm still functioning. If you could call two teams, one a leftover from the disastrous experiment, functioning.

Being a male Tortantula taught patience from the beginning. Evolution gave them a slight edge. Male eggs hatched first, giving them time to escape before the bigger, dangerous, and more aggressive females. The males hatched a full day ahead of the females, and they used that time to flee into specially made caves above the brooding chambers. There they created alliances with other males and snuck down to grab food when they could. Occasionally they preyed upon each other, though not to the level of the females.

The patience they learned helped make them ideal for covert ops and other positions that didn't involve direct combat. Males didn't go straight at you; they came in from the side. It also helped with what he and the other males were doing. Slow work. Tricky work. Dangerous work.

A courier arrived and disgorged a torrent of data. The network cycled information in redundant floods, because you never knew which direction it was going in. The solution was exabytes of data sent in every direction, with lots and lots of encryption keys at the other end. It was inefficient, in a data storage way, but ensured vital data spread as quickly as possible. It was also a great way to hide communications between his fellows. It did, however, require more patience to wait while specially-written software, software he'd helped design, chewed through vast amounts of information looking for tiny indicators.

It took three days for the special slate to flash for his attention. He wrapped up what he'd been working on and picked up the slate. The icons would mean nothing to almost every other being in the galaxy, except a small handful of male Tortantulas. To him, it meant disaster. "So it begins," he said and shredded the slate.

* * * * *

Chapter Four

With no required training to complete and no missions to perform immediately, Sadek didn't know what to do with himself. He spent some time doing something he had little experience doing. Relaxing. He read some technical journals, watched some Tri-V, and even took some walks around the compound with Azah. It was the first time they'd been out in any sort of outdoors environment since the training dome, which felt like a million years ago.

It rained almost constantly, though, which made walks not nearly as much fun as they could have been. In fact, it was rather miserable. Azah was happy just to spend her time eating and sleeping.

"I'm conserving energy," she joked and went back to sleep.

Lacking other distractions, Sadek turned to the computers. Azah had a talent with systems and computers in ways Sadek didn't understand. His talent was programs and hacking. He'd managed to ignore the covert ops base system until he had nothing else to do. He started by just dabbling in the system's architecture, but it quickly progressed into a no-holds-barred attack.

"What are you spending all your time doing?" Azah asked one morning when she returned from mealtime to find him right where she'd left him, with his pinplants plugged into a slate.

"Just messing around," he said, and she went over to her sleeping place. Sadek went back to his digging.

The system appeared quite normal in the beginning. If anything, too normal. It reminded him of a civilian system in its simplicity. He'd been taught considerable detail on the operation, design, and hacking of civilian systems made by hundreds of races. Compared to the systems the Veetanho, and by extension the Tortantula and the Flatar, used, civilian systems were childish. *This is a ruse*, he realized.

He abandoned his attempt and wrote a quick program to have the slate continue a ham-fisted hacking effort at the visible system. He detached his pinplants from the slate and clicked them directly into the facility interface. "Let's see what's behind the mirror," he said and went in through the main data access.

"This is elegant," he said to himself as he dug into the layers of fake data. Gigabytes, terabytes, even exabytes of seemingly innocuous data layered on top of itself. It would take a lifetime to go through it before he could even pick the files that *might* contain something worthwhile.

Sadek spent several hours trying to decide which files might be worth further investigation before he stopped and considered. Whoever had set this up had gone to a lot of trouble to make it seemingly impossible to find what they were hiding. He had no doubt; the system was designed to hide something. Maybe a lot of somethings.

He thought for a long moment, then programmed in an intricate query.

When he got up the next morning, he checked his slate. It had dutifully copied every file that matched the criteria he'd programmed. There were several dozen files. He hadn't expected that many. He almost told Azah what he'd found, but something held him back. He didn't know why, and that bothered him. He decided to keep quiet until he found out what was hidden. Who knew, maybe it was meaningless stuff?

Yeah. Sure it was.

Sadek looked out the window at the sunlit mist. It was a relatively nice day. Maybe Azah would be up for a walk.

"Look," she said a few minutes later. "The sun is actually peeking through the clouds."

"Huh," he said, focusing on her words. It was nice to be out walking with her, but as a distraction, it wasn't working. He couldn't tear his mind away from the files he'd found and his curious reluctance to tell Azah about them. *Why* did he feel so guarded around her?

"Are you all right?" she asked him, stopping and clicking her pedipalps in concern.

"I'm fine," he said. "I'm fine, I'm just tired."

"You're not mad at me?"

"No. Not at all. Why would I be? You're perfect, Azah." And she was. She really was. But he still didn't tell her.

When they got back, there was a message waiting for them from Yeef. He wanted to see Azah by herself.

"I wonder what that's all about?" Azah said. She sounded wary.

"I'm sure it's something routine," Sadek said. "He's wanted to talk to you alone before. Probably some new training or information he wants to share. Go on. I've got some stuff to do anyway. I'll see you when you're done."

"All right," she said slowly, and gave him a long look before turning and heading toward Yeef's office area.

As soon as she was gone, he set to breaking the files' encryption.

It took only minutes. Most of the designer's efforts had gone into hiding the files. Now that he knew what to look for, he cracked each file with relative ease. As his programs worked on the next file, he examined the first one. It was a list of names and locations. He wasn't sure, but he thought it was Tortantula/Flatar teams like his own, and where they were located. The next file contained a list of missions, teams assigned, and resolutions. Many of the resolutions didn't make sense to him. Out of curiosity, he searched for himself and Azah.

"There we are," he said quietly. *Strategic Intel—988A*, was the description, *Azah/Sadek*. *Results—Prime*. He smiled at the thought of Azah, who wasn't back yet. He'd have to tell her about it when she returned. Over the next few minutes, he broke the encryption on several more files and found mostly uninteresting information, or stuff he didn't understand. He was about to abandon the whole thing. It wasn't that interesting.

His slate alerted him. Another file's encryption was broken. Sadek decided to glance at that one too.

This file had a lot more to it than the previous ones—Tortantula names and huge strings of numbers and symbols. He used his pinplants to access the GalNet for the meanings of the strings. The answer came back quickly: genetic markers. He was looking at the genetic markers for hundreds, no, *thousands* of Tortantula. Why would a male commander of a small covert ops unit have all this information?

Sadek flipped to the file's basic data. Who had created it, and where had it come from? It was encoded as a covert ops field command file, shared with all covert ops commanders, as well as someone called the *Brood Father*. Sadek accessed the Tortantula command records and entered Brood Father. There was only one listed—Loof.

With a growing sense of dread, he scanned down the list of all the Tortantula. They were sorted in three categories. No-Marker, Prospect, and Target. The first one, No-Marker, only contained their genetic information and nothing else. The second one, Prospect, also held their assignment and condition. Most appeared to be in combat units, and many were *Dead*. A few said drone, but that wasn't something he knew anything about. The final category, Target, was the shortest. It still held a couple hundred names, and each of those names had a lot of data. There was some sort of notation next to the genetic coding, not just current assignment, but all their assignments, a number that seemed to be a ranking from 1 to 100, and their status. When he looked at status, most said *dead*.

Then he saw a couple of those not noted as dead had comments. *Too unpredictable*, one of them said. *Wild talent*, another said. A jolt of fear raced up his spine when he saw his partner's listing. *Azah*—the big long list of symbols for her genetic data - *Covert Ops Team Green/5—Weaver.*

"Weaver," Sadek said. There was a comment. "I think she's the one, if we can keep her secret from the Veetanho."

Now he understood the hidden files. The males, maybe all of them, were doing something to the females. Genetic data, lots of dead females, assigning special ones to covert ops.

Entropy, what are they doing? he wondered. *'If we can keep her secret'? All those dead…* he thought. *Whatever they're doing…it's killing the marked females.*

"No," he said aloud, coming to a decision, "They won't get my Azah killed!"

Sadek took all the data he'd gotten and copied it into a file deep in his pinplants. Then he snatched up his personal slate and started writing a message. *They're not going to get Azah killed,* he vowed. No, he'd tell the Veetanho about the sneaky males, and how they were trying to manipulate his friend into doing something that would get her killed. That would stop the males. With a wicked little grin, he sent the message.

* * * * *

Chapter Five

Azah followed Yeef out of the building, across a rain-soaked courtyard, and into another building she hadn't been inside before.

"Where are we going?" she asked the commander. "Do I need to get Sadek?"

"No," he said, and his voice sounded tight. Was he angry? "There's someone who wants to see you, but she specifically requested you come without your partner."

"Am I in danger?" Azah asked. This was highly irregular. She and Sadek were a team. Everyone respected that.

"I hope not," he said. "I doubt it. However, I'll be there in the room with you, and we have taken…other precautions. It's highly unlikely anything untoward will happen."

"But you've taken precautions anyway," she said.

"Yes," Yeef said, and left it at that. Azah clicked her pedipalps in acknowledgment and followed him through a warren of corridors. He stopped outside a door, which irised open at his approach.

"Go on in," he said, gesturing for her to precede him. Though she felt nervous and on edge without Sadek, she trusted her commander, so she stepped through the opening.

"You're still small," her mother said without preamble. Zorm crouched on the other side of the room, watching the doorway with all her eyes. Azah buried a stab of disappointment along with her surprise and forced herself to move forward calmly.

221

"Hello, Zorm," Azah said. "What are you doing here?"

"I came to talk to you," Zorm said. "Despite your disappointing size, I've heard encouraging reports of your skill and performance. I wanted to evaluate you with my own eyes."

"Evaluate me? Why?"

"Because," Zorm said, her tone derisive, as if Azah were asking stupid, childish questions. "You carry my genetic code. A brood mother has died. Another will be chosen. I have come to see if you deserve my recommendation when the time comes."

"I don't understand," Azah said.

"That has always been painfully obvious," Zorm said. "You know what a brood mother is?"

"You are."

"Yes. I was chosen for the privilege of breeding because of my skill and desirable genetic qualities. You are too small to be a perfect choice, but you have shown you have other traits that are much in demand—intelligence, aggression, efficiency of violence. And, naturally, I want my own traits to carry on. They would have a better chance of doing so if two of us carried my genetic code."

"Naturally," Azah said softly, wondering at her mother's overwhelming arrogance. Was it a front, or did Zorm truly believe that about herself? Azah had never known a day when she hadn't doubted her own worth, so it was incredibly difficult to wrap her head around the idea that not everyone felt the same.

"You would be a good choice from that perspective, but there is a problem. You're here, doing a nothing job. I can only do so much to persuade the Stewards. If you want to be a brood mother, you cannot stay here, skulking in corners and playing spy. You must get back out on the battlefield and demonstrate that you have a true talent for destruction," Zorm said.

"Covert operations is an honorable and vital role, Brood Mother Zorm," Yeef said, and Azah was surprised at how much respect shaded his tone. Was Yeef afraid of her? Zorm easily dwarfed the male, but then, so did Azah, and Yeef had never spoken to her like that.

Zorm ignored him entirely and clicked her pedipalps at her daughter.

"Azah, I will be completely honest with you," she said. "I did not expect you to survive the training dome, but you did. I did not expect you to complete your training, but you did. You have demonstrated you are tough and resourceful, and you have the capacity for a respectable amount of violence! I've seen it in the tapes from your graduation exercise and in the reports from your training mission. You are a warrior, not a worthless sneak! You belong in the assault companies, reaching for the glorious slaughter! I can get you a transfer back, and you can begin to live up to your true potential. You can even bring your Flatar with you. Once you're back doing some decent killing, I can show the Stewards you're Brood Mother material."

Yeef shifted slightly behind Azah but said nothing. Azah waited a moment, trying to organize her chaotic thoughts before speaking.

"Thank you," she said carefully, "but I think I'm needed where I am."

Zorm clicked her fangs dismissively.

"Of course you're not," she said, "look at you! You're still puny. I'm sure they could train up another pair quick enough. It's not as if this job serves the higher purpose, after all. You must think of the killing you could be doing! It's what you were bred to do; you know that? I was the best in my training clan because I could create such massacres as to make the ancients weep! Then when I was paired with Hranou and sent to the companies...I was legendary! And my blood flows blue through your veins, Azah. You, too, could send thousands to oblivion!"

The near-rapture in her mother's voice made Azah shiver inside her exoskeleton. This was almost worse than Nura's enjoyment of the ferals' pain had been. Azah didn't mind killing when it had to be done...but Zorm sounded as if she *ached* to return to those days. Had she really taken thousands of lives? And remembered it with relish?

"Thank you," Azah said again, "but I decline. You may be my mother, but I'm not like you. I like covert operations. I like the missions we do—"

Zorm rose up suddenly, making Azah flinch backward. She could almost feel Yeef tensing behind her, but what could the tiny male do against Zorm's psychopathic might?

"Worthless," Zorm hissed, anger lighting up her words. "Just as I suspected. I had hoped for better from you, Azah. Mark my words; there can be no joy without the slaughter."

"You're wrong," Azah spat back, and to her surprise, she found rage burning away the fear in her mind. "There is joy in a job well done! There is joy in working with a partner to—"

"Weak," Zorm said, cutting her off again. "You are weak and needy. I never should have let Hranou give you that Flatar pup. You'll die alone, Azah. Remember that. You'll die alone, like we all do. Nothing matters except the slaughter." She lunged forward and charged for the door, knocking Azah aside even as Yeef shot upward on a line of silk he'd fastened to the ceiling at some point.

"You're wrong!" Azah yelled at her mother's retreating back. "You're wrong! I'm not like you!"

"Yes, you are," Zorm said as she continued without looking back. "Just like me…but weaker."

* * * * *

Chapter Six

Sadek looked up from his slate as Azah entered. She went immediately to the far side of their quarters and lowered herself to the floor. She didn't say a thing. He looked at the slate for another moment before speaking.

"What did Yeef want?"

"It was my mother," she said in a monotone. It was said simply, but Sadek could still feel the pain.

"Zorm? Here?"

"Yes," Azah said. "She wanted me to go back to assault."

"Why?"

"For the *slaughter*," she said, spitting the last word with as much contempt as he'd ever heard her say anything.

"What did you say?" He asked, filled with dread.

"I said no, and to leave us alone."

He sighed with relief. "What did she say to that?"

"She said I was weak, worthless, and small."

"You're none of those things."

"Do you know what made me maddest?" Sadek shook his head. "I might be smaller than her, but I'm not weak, and I'm not worthless! She said giving you to me was a mistake."

"How dare she!" he hissed.

"Exactly." She turned to look at him. "You're the best thing that ever happened to me."

He leaped over and landed on her back, hugging the bristly torso. "Azah, you're the best thing to happen to me, too." He thought about the message he'd sent just a short time ago and was even happier he'd done it. He almost told her about the plot of the males, but something stopped him. The time wasn't right, not just after her mother had attacked her like that. Later would be a better time. "We'll be together forever," he said reassuringly. "I'll make sure of that."

* * * * *

Chapter Seven

"Let's go!" Shypik yelled into their quarters, startling both Sadek and Azah.

"What's going on?" Azah asked, yawning.

"We're being deployed. Now move it."

"Why the hurry?" Sadek asked.

"Yeef says it's an emergency. The shuttle lifts in one hour. Assault and infiltration gear," she barked, and was gone.

"Entropy," Sadek yelled and started grabbing equipment and stuffing it into Azah's assault saddle.

"I wonder what happened," Azah asked his partner. Sadek dropped a tool kit, scattering all manner of implements everywhere. He'd sent the message concerning the male's plot exactly two weeks ago. The exact time it would take a message to make a round-trip to leadership. "Are you okay?" Sadek looked at his partner, the surprise obvious on her face. "What?"

"Nothing," he said and shook his head. "I'm just worried." Azah looked at him for another moment, then went back to packing gear.

Sadek leaped into the assault saddle 45 minutes after Shypik showed up, and Azah walked them into the landing bay a total of 53 minutes afterward.

Shypik and Ezek were already in the bay waiting when they came in. For a change, Shypik was riding Ezek, several bags of equipment slung from the assault saddle. Sadek noticed the way they interacted, in an almost businesslike manner. He usually had a hand on Azah's

229

230 | KACEY EZELL & MARK WANDREY

exposed exoskeleton, or even the bristly 'fur' behind her head, just before her cephalothorax. One of her rearward facing eyes moved slightly, looking up at him, and he smiled. *Those males won't get you,* he thought, and patted her affectionately. Shypik saw the motion and made a face.

"Is everyone ready?" She looked over and saw Yeef skitter in. Unconsciously, her expression darkened.

"Are you going," Shypik asked, only tagging on an honorific "sir?" at the end.

"Yes," he said as he dropped a small bag to one side. Males didn't have the nearly 360-degree vision of a female, so he moved around as he examined the two pairs. He moved precisely, almost like a robot, taking in every detail. When he looked at Sadek and Azah, he did his best to appear completely normal. Still, he locked eyes with Sadek for an unusually long moment. "I have been ordered to command the operation directly."

"What's the op?" Shypik asked. She had one of her XT-12 hyper-velocity pistols out from Ezek's saddle and was checking its function.

"They haven't told me," Yeef said. The building reverberated with multiple sonic booms, and the roof began to open. The omni-present rain began to fall inside, and Sadek could see a shuttle descending through the clouds. "I only know an assault company was coming through the system en route. I was ordered to mobilize my teams and intercept an icosahedron coming through."

"We saw one while we were with Assault Company 889," Azah said. Sadek nodded. The ships were only used for major assaults. They held thousands of Tortantula, mostly the feral ones. Whatever was in the works, it was huge.

"Sounds like someone sees an opportunity during the coming carnage," Shypik said. Ezek just grumbled.

The shuttle set down with a scream of its lifting fans. Robots moved in and immediately began refueling the shuttle as its boarding ramp descended, and a Jeha stuck its head out.

"Board quickly, please," he said and gestured with a feeler. "The ship captain is most annoyed at having to slow his transit to the stargate."

Yeef was first up the ramp with his small bag of equipment, followed close behind by Ezek. Shypik looked back at them as her ride took her up the ramp. Sadek had to fight down a feeling of fear at the way she looked at him. She spoke up. "You coming, or are you going to hug your Tortantula first?"

"Shut up," Sadek said and patted Azah on a leg. "Come on, they're waiting." Ezek moved aside enough to make room for Azah to slip past. The other Tortantula was just as indifferent as her rider. "And stay out of our way." Shypik gave a yipping series of laughs as they went by.

The shuttle was a cargo model with no actual passenger spaces. Luckily, Tortantula were used to making their own spaces. Between Ezek and Azah, they occupied quite a bit more than half the cargo hold. They examined the setup and found the cargo tie-down points. In moments, they'd grabbed one with each leg and secured themselves better than the best strapping could manage. Yeef found a crate fixed to the deck by a cargo net and latched onto the net. The riders fastened the three-point harnesses built into the saddles and were secure.

"Ready for lift off?" the Jeha who'd greeted them at the ramp asked while slithering through the room.

"Ready," Ezek grumbled.

"Ready," Azah echoed.

"Get us in the air," Yeef said. The Jeha left the hold and entered the front of the shuttle. Moments later, the craft was back in the air with a scream of its lift fans. Once it was high enough, the main engines lit and thrust tore at them as the shuttle blasted for orbit. An hour later, they landed on the icosahedron. Shortly after, they were in hyperspace.

* * * * *

Chapter Eight

As usual, the soldiers knew nothing about the upcoming mission. Sadek began nosing around as soon as he was on board. Azah was more interested in the other Tortantulas aboard. Thousands of shock troops, and dozens of Tortantula/Flatar teams. Their reaction to the new arrivals caught them both by surprise.

"Hey," a Flatar called in a hallway as Sadek was floating past. He caught himself on a handhold and turned.

"Yeah?"

"You're one of those covert ops types. I can tell by the outfit you wear." Sadek was impressed the other Flatar could tell. He'd noticed a lot of others of his kind weren't as perceptive as he was, though they were usually a lot more violent.

"Yes," he said, "we're assigned to covert ops." The other Flatar looked him over, then nodded.

"You guys are all right in my book. One of your teams rescued my entire company a few months ago when we were pinned down by a bunch of Humans. They have those armored suits, and they're tough as shit. Most merc races see us; they run. The Humans?" He shook his head and whistled between his buckteeth. "Entropy, they *like* to fight. I don't mean the way the Torts I control like to fight; I mean the Humans just get in and fight. The more desperate the situation, the harder they fight. Does that make sense to you?"

"Not really," Sadek admitted, "if you can't win, why fight?"

234 | KACEY EZELL & MARK WANDREY

"Unless a Veetanho is screaming at you, am I right?" The other Flatar laughed, and Sadek joined in. "My name is Kibed."

"Sadek. Nice to meet you." Kibed nodded and pointed down a hall.

"A few of us are going to have some drinks and talk; do you want to join us?"

"Our quarters provide drinks," Sadek said.

"Not that kind," Kibed said. Sadek stared at him in confusion. "You know, intoxicants?"

"Oh!" Sadek said. He'd heard some beings consumed such things for the effect it had on them. "But where do you get that kind of drink on ships like these?" Sadek wondered.

Kibed laughed again. "These ships are owned by Izlian." He floated a little closer. "They like to keep us happy. They don't want a lot of crazed Tortantulas accidentally tearing the place apart. Happy Flatar means happy Tortantula. You coming?"

"Yeah, okay," Sadek said, and followed his new friend.

He followed Kibed down a series of corridors, all marked in languages he understood. Eventually they came to a pressure door simply marked, "Danger." Kibed pushed a control next to the door and grabbed a handhold to move to the side. He reached out and pushed Sadek aside as well. Sadek looked confused, but a moment later, the panel Kibed had touched flashed almost painfully bright, and he felt heat from it.

"This is Kibed; I'm at lock #12." The flashing stopped, and a voice replied in barely understandable Flatar.

"One moment. Wait."

"What was that flashing?" Sadek asked.

"The Izlian," Kibed said. "That's how they talk."

"Entropy! It was like an energy weapon."

"They can kill with their words. The Union calls them an exotic species." Kibed took out a small slate and used his pinplants to make it display. The thing it showed looked like a sea creature, only it floated in misty air. "This is an Izlian." He pointed at the door. "They occupy these areas. Their language can kill us, and their atmosphere *will* kill us. The pressure alone is deadly."

A buzzer sounded, and lights flashed around the pressure door. Motors whined, and the door moved aside. Two metallic cylinders floated there. Kibed floated forward but didn't immediately take the cylinders. He removed a device from his belt and carefully moved it back and forth over them. "Neutralizes chemical residue from their atmosphere," he explained. "We made a mistake and just grabbed the cylinders once, and they burned the crap out of me."

Kibed took one cylinder and handed the other one to Sadek, who looked at it skeptically. Kibed laughed and shoved it into Sadek's hands. "Come on," he said. "Follow me."

"Hey, Kibed, who is that?"

The space was a storage room with all the crates secured to the walls, making a space twice what Azah and Sadek shared for quarters. In that space a group of Flatar floated.

"This is Sadek," Kibed said.

"He's not assault like us," another one said.

"What is he, a handler?" another asked. They all laughed.

"Covert ops," Sadek said, and they fell silent.

"Really?" one asked.

"Yeah, he is," Kibed said. "He came aboard in that last system. They're the reason we slowed down." Sadek looked around the group, who were now eyeing him with a mixture of curiosity and suspicion.

"You guys want a drink?" Sadek asked and let the cylinder float out into the middle of the room. "I come with gifts." A couple laughed, and one of them grabbed the cylinder.

"A covert ops group rescued my company once," another said.

"Mine too," another said.

"I say he stays," Kibed said and looked around the space. They were quiet for a moment, then they all started nodding. Kibed took the cylinder he had and removed a bunch of drinking bulbs from a pouch. Using the cylinder, he filled one of them with amber liquid and floated it over to Sadek. The group went to work and soon they all had bulbs of their own.

"Drink," Kibed said. Sadek looked at the liquid skeptically. The other Flatar sneered, then took a drink himself. He hissed as he swallowed. "Good for everything wrong with the universe." Sadek thought about it for another second, then took a sip. Liquid fire slid down his throat.

"Entropy!" he hissed when he could speak again. They all laughed again, but this time it was friendly. He was confused. How could drinking the horrid burning drink make him their friend? The whole group was drinking and laughing now, so he carefully took another drink. It wasn't as bad the second time. In fact, he felt warmth spreading through his entire body! Another drink led to another, and another, and another.

"You guys are alright," Sadek said, though it took him four times to get it out. His mouth didn't want to work properly. "I was wif assat for a while, me an Asha."

"Asha?" one of the others asked.

"Asha…Ashka…no, entripty, Azah! My Tortatruka."

"He's drunk as an elSha," one of the others said.

"First time?" Kibed asked. "Drinking?" Sadek looked for the bulb to take another drink, but Kibed beat him to it. "Yeah, I thought so. Did you say you were in an assault company?"

"Yeah, eight…eight…nine," he said, talking slowly because it was hard to concentrate. The others all fell curiously silent.

"Did he say 889th Assault?" another asked.

"Yeah." Kibed nodded. "That's what he said."

"To a fellow meat in the grinder," one of them said.

"Meat!" they all cheered. Sadek looked around curiously.

They continued talking for a time about life in an assault company. Eventually Sadek's mind began to clear, and he understood why Kibed had taken the bulb away. He resolved that if he ever drank the intoxicants again, it would be tiny amounts. He'd liked the initial feelings, just not what it did after he drank too much. Most of the liquid was gone, and he began thinking about getting back to Azah. She would be wondering where he was.

"You are welcome to come down here any off shift," Kibed told him as he glanced at the exit. "As long as the Veetanho aren't watching too closely."

"Why do we do what they say, anyway?" Sadek asked. He immediately wondered why he'd said such a frank, and probably dangerous, thing. The other Flatar looked at him with more than a little admiration.

"Such a question," he said, "isn't in your best interest to ask. The Veetanho are our stewards, they have been…"

"How long?" Sadek asked. The Flatar all looked at each other. In the end, none of them knew the answer. Because Sadek wasn't used to the ship, Kibed took him back to their quarters.

"Here you are," the other Flatar said. "Come by some time again."

"I won't drink as much of that stuff," Sadek said, and the two smiled.

"Hey," Sadek said before Kibed could leave, "you looked like you recognized the 889th Assault Company." The other nodded. "How are they?"

"They were wiped out a few months ago. We came in afterward to make it all good."

"Oh," Sadek said, and the other Flatar floated away down the companionway, leaving him with his thoughts.

* * *

"The objective is Piquaw." Sadek sat on Azah's assault saddle and listened as Yeef gave the briefing. The only other occupants of the bay were Shypik and Ezek. The former stood and listened while the latter simply squatted on the floor, her legs pulled up, and eyes watching their commander. "Piquaw is a major trading-world interest used by the race known as Humans." A pair of Azah's eyes glanced back at Sadek, who was looking at her. "The Humans trade in food; it's a big thing in the Tolo arm. From what I understand, it's quality stuff. Plus, they're expanding. Some of the syndicates aren't happy."

"Piquaw is their primary trading partner," Yeef continued, and a Tri-V came alive with maps. A small world, not ideal. Atmosphere was borderline, gravity was light, and the days were too short...but the light gravity and its location made it good for shipping. It also had large water oceans that provided a hydrogen fuel source. Most of the industry was centered on several large city-centers, which supported the world's three starports. One of the three starports was highlighted. "This is the target. Locals call it Lumpak. It is the smallest of the three starports, and it's the primary location Humans use because it is the cheapest."

"They've assigned the 325th, which we're aboard now, as well as the 441st and 499th assault companies to this operation." Sadek's eyes grew wider at the mention of three assault companies. He didn't know in detail the total forces available, but that was a significant number. Maps of Lumpak came up and showed landing points for the 325th and 499th. "The 441st will land to support the final containment once the 1st and 2nd objectives are taken."

"And what do we do?" Shypik asked. Sadek found himself nodding at the question, despite his dislike for her. Yeef tapped at his tiny slate for a moment and the map of Lumpak shifted. Sadek immediately recognized a garrison area.

"As this starport is primarily centered on the Human's trading interest, they have hired Human mercs to secure the facility. You are both aware that the Humans employ powered armor they call CASPers, and they've become progressively more effective over the years. The company providing security is changing, mere days before the assault. Our leadership has ordered that the commander of the new merc unit in charge of the starport needs to be liquidated."

"Assassination?" Shypik asked. "Sounds straight forward."

"Why?" Azah asked.

"Why what?" Yeef replied.

"Why does this commander need to die? I'm sorry, but isn't it against merc law to do that?" Shypik sneered at Azah, then glanced up and saw Sadek looking back. She must have seen the look of anger on his face, because she looked a little surprised.

"Once combat is initiated, the commander is a valid target," Yeef said. "As for why, I only know it is part of a long-term plan, the details of which I am not privy to." He looked at them and paused for a second. "Once the assault has begun, and one of the two objectives is taken, I predict that the commander of the defending forces will take personal charge to rally their forces. I'll be handling aspects of identifying that target. Once done, you will disengage from the 325th, move to the identified location, and neutralize it. Is that understood? Good."

Yeef secured his slate and turned off the Tri-V. "We arrive in the Piquaw system in three days. I'll send you information on which drop ship you'll be going down aboard. I decided against sending you with the icosahedron to reduce the risk of losing our element. We'll land in a support role once it's down. That might appear unusual, but it's sufficiently convincing. Dismissed."

* * * * *

Chapter Nine

They travelled down to Piquaw the same way they'd travelled up from Kutu, in a shuttle. Sadek watched the assault begin through a link to his pinplants. There had been a brief space battle upon their fleet's arrival, but the enemy quickly ceded the system to their superior firepower. It was the first time Sadek and Azah had been in a space battle.

"Pretty boring, really," Azah said afterward. The icosahedron was the size of a battle cruiser and bristled with firepower and shields. It was designed to deliver a Tortantula assault company to a planet's surface through heavy enemy resistance. The Humans had almost no warships in the system. No contest.

"I don't know if I want to be in an exciting space battle," Azah said.

"You don't," Yeef said. Apparently, he'd been listening in a few meters away in the shuttle cockpit.

"We control space around the planet," the strangely-modulated voice of the Izlian crew said over the inter-ship coms. "Covert team, you are cleared to depart. We will be descending to the surface in 10 minutes."

"Understood," Yeef said. He was piloting the shuttle. He addressed his team in the rear of the craft. "We're undocking." There was a loud *thunk* through the hull, and they floated free. A moment later, the icosahedron began to accelerate toward the planet surface.

241

Sadek watched on the shuttle's display as the big assault ship fell away.

"Are you concerned for the Flatar you got to know?" Azah asked.

"Yeah, I think I am," he admitted. "They were the first of my own kind that ever respected us."

"They are fools," Shypik said. "Too stupid to do anything but force feral Tortantulas to make suicide charges." Sadek started to say something, then stopped. Maybe she was incapable of caring for another? "You see I am right?"

"No," Sadek said. "I see you are too damaged to feel anything, good or bad."

"Who cares what you think?"

"Quiet," Yeef said. "We're beginning reentry." The two Flatar glared at each other as the atmosphere began buffeting the shuttle. The shuttle's sensors showed the atmosphere lighting up with weapons fire. Spaceships couldn't fire at the surface above 10 miles, while surface defenses were under no such restrictions. The Human defenders were unleashing everything that could fire so much as a popgun at the attackers. Luckily for the shuttle, the icosahedron landers were several orders of magnitude larger. Larger and more threatening.

"What if they decide we're dangerous?" Sadek asked.

"Then we die," Yeef said.

"Whatever," Ezek grumbled. "End it."

Sadek sat in the saddle, outwardly unconcerned. He squeezed Azah's massive cephalothorax with his legs. It was an inconsequential movement from such a small being. Still, she felt it.

Zha oort, came the transmission to him through their private, silk-augmented pinlink.

Zha oort, he replied. Unto the end. Together they waited for a missile to blow their shuttle apart, or an energy beam to flash them out of existence in a millisecond. He felt...at ease. They could die in an instant, but the males wouldn't take her from him.

"The icosahedron is on the ground," Yeef said, "we'll be setting down next to it in just a minute." The shuttle's landing engines screamed; it flared and settled to the ground.

The rear door dropped down and immediately the occupants were assailed by a solid wall of noise. The icosahedron was a hundred meters away, its six doors open, ramps down, and a solid stream of noise assailed their senses like a physical explosion. A thousand massive Tortantula were flowing down the ramps like a tidal wave. Sadek could see the occasional Flatar rider on their Tortantula shepherding the ferals toward battle.

"Simple," Yeef said over comms. "Fall in with the assault group until I give the word, then we break off. Ready?"

"Ready," Shypik said immediately.

"Ready," Sadek said a moment later.

"Do we protect you?" Shypik asked.

"No," Yeef replied. "I will be fine. We males are good at not being seen. Just follow my instructions."

I don't like this, Azah said over their private link.

I know, Sadek replied. *Neither do I; however, we have to go along.* He swallowed as he continued. *It's our duty.*

Inside he was in turmoil. The timing was wrong. Just after his message should have reached the Stewards in command. That, and Yeef was along on the operation. Even Shypik seemed surprised and uncertain about that. Sadek checked their position as Azah ran to meet up with the nearest formation of ferals, and when he looked back, Yeef was gone. It was as if he'd never existed.

"Sadek, is that you?" He glanced over to see another Flatar on a Tortantula. It was Kibed, and he was astride a female almost twice the size of Azah. She was likely the largest he'd ever seen.

"Yes, hello, Kibed." The other Flatar nodded.

"I thought I recognized you."

"How?" Sadek asked and glanced around at the hundreds of other Tortantula. Among them were dozens more riders as well.

"Your Tortantula," he said, gesturing from his to Sadek's ride. "I know you have a special job, and you must to have such a—"

"Do not," Sadek said, his voice loud, "call Azah *small!*"

"I was going to say special." Sadek looked back along their route of movement. "Any chance of knowing what you are up to?"

"Zero," Sadek said. On his other side, Shypik looked at him and sneered. "Just pretend we're part of the unit."

"As we've been ordered," Kibed said. He looked over at Ezek, then at Azah again, and shook his head, but his face held a tiny smile as well. He was confused how these two Flatar on such tiny Tortantula could be so useful. Understanding was beyond his ability. Thunder rolled across the formation. Only it wasn't thunder.

* * * * *

Chapter Ten

The assault Azah and Sadek had participated in before was nothing, absolutely nothing, compared to what they saw this time. The port facility of Lumpak had defensive walls and emplacements. The space inside the starport was designed so any ship landing inside would be subject to intensive fire, so they'd landed outside.

Some of the emplacements were smoking ruins from the landing force's fire, while others were busy pouring fire into the approaching forces. The icosahedrons landed just beyond range of the emplacements, for their own safety. The attackers were under fire for their entire approach.

"Forward!" Kibed screamed and fired a round in the air. "Onward to glorious slaughter!"

"The Humans wait for you to take them into oblivion!" another rider cried out; Sadek wasn't sure if he remembered that one or not. A wave of missiles lifted off behind the starport wall, angled over, and rained down on the advancing Tortantula. The Flatar who'd just screamed was vaporized in a ball of fire, the shockwave staggering Azah as well. Sadek felt more than heard supersonic shrapnel fragments ping off his partner's armor, and a piece crossed the tip of his snout, taking a tiny chunk out of his nose.

"You okay?" Azah asked.

"Y-yeah," he said, a little shaken.

"You sure?!" Azah started to slow.

"No, don't stop, we'll draw fire!" Azah sped back up. "I was grazed, that's all. My nose."

"Close your helmet!"

"It's harder to see what's going on."

"It's even harder to see with your face blown off." Sadek reached up and snapped his helmet closed. Ahead, the lead element was about to reach the wall. Hundreds of Tortantula had been blown to bloody bits, and parts were everywhere. Azah ran past her sisters, who lay twitching in their death spasms or were horribly wounded and still trying to move toward the objective. They were being slaughtered.

"Angle them toward that!" Sadek yelled at Kibed and pointed to the burned ruins of a weapons emplacement.

"The wall there is closer," Kibed replied.

"And heavy weapons." A thunderous explosion killed dozens. "They're being devastated."

"Glorious slaughter!"

"Slaughter doesn't serve your objective!" Azah roared. "If we don't get inside, the assault fails. Our mission, Sadek's and my mission, will fail too!"

Kibed looked at Azah and then Sadek as missiles continued to fall. Tortantula were reaching the walls, trying to scrabble over, and being mowed down by the weapons emplacement, which spouted a dozen roaring cannon.

"Turn!" he yelled to the feral Tortantula around him and pointed. "There, where the wall is weakest, attack!" The other riders near Kibed heard and began ordering the ferals around them to move as well. The surging tide of multi-legged war machines crashing against the wall, slowly, ponderously, moved sideways toward the damaged section.

"Yes!" Sadek cheered.

"They did it," Azah agreed. A missile hit. In a flash of fire and death, Kibed and his Tortantula were gone. Nothing remained.

With a series of roars, huge armored shapes flew into the air from the other side of the wall and arced over. Each began unleashing a wave of rockets, lasers, and magnetic accelerator rounds. The Human CASPers had entered the battle.

"They're faltering," Azah said. Sadek looked and could see the remainder of the company was trying to get at the CASPers. There weren't enough to breach the wall. "What do we do?"

"We make them move," Sadek said. He reverted to their training in assault and fired a round in front of the nearest feral Tortantula as it was trying to turn toward the new threat. "No!" he snapped and pointed at the damaged wall. "That way!"

"Shut up," the Tortantula growled.

"Do what you are ordered!" he screamed and fired again. The round hit the ground and ricocheted off the Tortantula's armor, surprising it. "Now, or I'll kill you before the slaughter." Its many eyes locked on him, pedipalps quivering in indecision. "Do it!" *Crack!* The pistol fired again, even closer.

"No, we go that way!" another feral said. Sadek was surprised it could speak that complicated a sentence.

Azah's saddle mounted MAC swiveled and shot the feral who'd spoken square in the head, killing it instantly. *We don't have time for this,* Azah said over their secure link. Sadek gawked at his partner for half a second, then pointed again at the wall. The feral he'd been threatening moved. Others followed. In moments most of the remaining ferals on their side surged at the damaged section of wall. Thanks to the damage, they were up it in seconds.

"Command," one of the Flatar leaders said on the company frequency. "Objective #1 is taken. We're over the wall."

Sadek examined their position. A few of the Human CASPers were falling back on the other side of the remaining defenses. Several lay on the ground nearby, leaking red blood and smoking. Judging by the number of dead Tortantulas, they'd fought to the last. It was a level of carnage he hadn't seen before.

"You okay?" Azah asked.

"Sure," he said.

"Didn't you hear the call from Yeef?"

"Call?" he asked. He hadn't heard anything. Sadek accessed his pinplants and ran the last few seconds back.

"Covert ops," Yeef's voice said, "proceed to and eliminate target."

"Got it, sorry," Sadek told Azah. "Sorry, I was distracted." He slid his visor up.

Shypik came running up on Ezek. She seemed completely unimpressed by the massive number of bodies in all directions. If anything, she seemed even more at ease than before. She had her XT-12 pistol out, the action flipped open, and she was sliding a new barrel into place. It was a sure sign she'd been doing more than just keeping up with the assault troops.

"Did you have to fight?" he asked her.

"Fight? No, had to shoot a dozen of these idiot ferals, though. They aren't more than a hairs-breadth stupider than Ezek, but at least she listens when given an order." A pair of Ezek's eyes looked at Sadek, and another pair at her rider. She was completely unaffected by the comment. "You going to sit and feel sorry for these ferals, or are we going to do our job?"

"Go," he said, "we're right behind you." Ezek moved, and after a slight pause, Azah followed.

They slipped away from the assault elements with ease. The ferals were moving around, feeding on the dead, and hunting the living. Their controllers had enough on their hands to keep their charges from running wild into the starport, but that wasn't the mission. The only Flatar Sadek knew who'd seen him was Kibed, and he was a messy stain somewhere outside the breached defenses.

Away from the perimeter defenses was a less bloody, yet more chaotic scene. The locals and visitors to the complex had been caught up in a major merc action. Visiting ships were unable to flee under threat of being shot down. Hundreds of merchants were panicking as well. When an assault began, there was never a formal notice to those around the target of exactly what that target was. It was not unheard of for other concerns to attack a competitor under the pretense of industrial retribution, and that retribution would then grow to become much, much bloodier. Civilians simply freaked. When the iconic 20-sided shape of the icosahedron transports appeared over your city, you knew it was bad.

With an assault underway, all it took was the sight of a pair of Tortantula with riders astride to clear the street in moments. As Azah and Ezek raced along, they drove the citizens of Lumpak before them like a tide. The first Humans they encountered weren't mercs, or at least they didn't wear the powered combat armor called CAS-Pers. Sadek and Shypik both swung weapons toward the startled aliens, who responded by screaming and running.

Shypik laughed and fired a shot after them that took a chunk out of the wall as they ran around the corner.

"These are the aliens everyone is so afraid of?" Shypik laughed.

"Cowards," Ezek grumbled. "Let's kill them."

"No," Sadek snapped, making Shypik look at him hard. "We have a mission," he added. "Yeef is waiting."

"Yeah," Shypik agreed, her face showing disappointment.

"Cowards," Ezek repeated. Sadek didn't know if she meant the Humans or her rider.

"Objective one kilometer northeast," Azah said, marking their progress with the navigational aids built into her pinplants. "Cut left here through this alley." Instantly they both turned. The Tortantulas concentrated on navigating; the Flatar on making sure nobody got aspirations of stopping them. The alley led into a narrow secondary entranceway of an industrial building, only the building showed heavy signs of recent modifications. One of those was a set of heavy weapons shields on both sides of the entrance. Another was the squad of Human mercs.

"Hit them hard," Shypik snarled. The 10 Humans were hunkered together watching a Tri-V. Sadek was too far away to tell what it was displaying. What he clearly saw was the look of stunned surprise on the face of one Human, who picked just that moment to look up. It was a strange, flat face, with large eyes and a tiny nose. There was no fur on the face, but some stuck out from beneath the helmet it wore. It opened its mouth to yell, and Sadek shot it.

The XT-12 cracked, a single hypersonic round exploded from the chamber, and the Human's strange face exploded.

The other Human mercs responded slowly. As Sadek changed targets, a part of his mind thought about the slowness of response.

These weren't the Human's best; they were probably some of the worst. Tasked with guarding this minor entrance. Tucked away in an alley no one knew about, and still it was guarded. It just wasn't guarded well.

They tore through the security in seconds. By the time the Human mercs fully realized they were under attack, half their number were down. A couple managed to grab their weapons before Azah and Ezek were in their midst. The Human screams of pain were as strange as their screams of alarm. Only one managed to fire a weapon, and that was into the floor. Their blood was red, like Sadek's blood, and unlike Azah's.

"Good," Shypik said as she examined the carnage, "good."

"They taste soft," Ezek said with her growling voice. Sadek could only think of how easy it was. Slaughter, not battle. Was that the point? Was that what she was after, like a feral Tortantula?

"Was there a delay?" They all turned to see Yeef hanging from a gossamer thread of silk just above the security point's entrance. He'd no doubt been there the entire time. Sadek opened his helmet visor to breathe better. Blood smeared the inside where his nose had rubbed the glass. It hurt, too.

"The assault team is in disarray," Sadek said.

"These Humans are easy prey," Shypik said.

"Either way," Yeef said, "here is the building's floorplan." Sadek felt a file arrive through his pinplants and opened it. The image showed the building's three floors. The language was strange, and his pinplants didn't automatically translate it. Human written language, then. Their pinplants could handle their spoken language. There were several notes in Sadek's language. Defensive positions, troop quarters, and in particular, the command center on the top floor.

"This is your target," he said, and an image appeared in the pin-plants. A Human, with a close-up of their rank insignia, dress, and facial features. "Neutralize everyone in the command center, they're all command staff. This one is your priority. Once it is neutralized, head to the roof for exfil. Prepare to attack. I will cause a distraction." He wore a small harness with all manner of equipment and explosives attached. "There is a central stairwell with guards on each floor. Guards of this quality," he said and gestured with a tiny pedipalp to the bodies. "Speed is the best option. The command center is a retasked conference room; the stairwell opens on the rear. Wait for my sign, then complete your objective."

Yeef was gone in a flash. The tiny male Tortantula moved with lightning speed. Sadek had no idea they could be that fast. *I guess that's how they survive as babies,* he thought. A couple minutes passed, then a series of muffled explosions echoed through the building, followed by distant Human shouts. "Now," they heard through their comms.

"Let's move," he said, and bumped Azah with his legs. She jumped into motion, Shypik and Ezek close behind.

The stairwell was too small for both Tortantulas to go side by side, so Azah led. Their goal required getting through each floor's guard position without alerting any of the other guards or the command post. Move fast, strike hard was part of their training. Sadek led with his XT-12 pointed along their course, cutting the pie as they came around the corner and up the stairwell. Loud explosions rocked the building; it was perfect cover.

They rounded the corner and found two Human guards. Sadek shot one, then the other with his XT-12. They went down without saying a word. Azah moved off the stairs to verify they were both down, and Ezek bounded past to the next floor. Azah gave both a quick stab with her fangs and spun. Sadek covered the door with his hyper-velocity pistol as she spun about and bounded back up the stairs behind Ezek. The other Tortantula had already reached the next landing.

Shypik's XT-12 cracked twice, and Sadek figured he'd cleared the floor, when there was a crash. As they came around the corner, the door was destroyed and all that was visible was the narrow waist and abdomen of Ezek thrashing on top of the Human CASPer. So much for less-than-competent mercs guarding the stairs. He was halfway to leading Azah into the fray when Shypik came through on his comms.

"We got this, go onto objective!" The CASPer flung Ezek to the side. The Tortantula managed to flip and hit the wall side on, instead of on her back, which would have smashed Shypik to goo. The Tortantula rebounded like she'd hit rubber, and not reinforced concrete. The Human-powered armor had only gotten to its knees before Ezek slammed back into it, sending them slamming into the opposite wall. "Go!" They went.

"They're probably expecting us now," Azah said as they raced toward the corner.

"I know," Sadek said, swapping magazines on his XT-12. Close to capacity of the barrel, but nothing to be done about it now. "Use the MAC."

"In the stairwell?"

"Just do it!" Sadek barked. "Take the corner, fast!"

Sadek slid his pistol into his lap, then reached up with a hand and slapped the helmet visor down once again. For added measure, he put his arms on either side of his head. Azah careened around the last corner, not on the floor, but on the wall, like a racecar on a high oval. Two Human CASPers were waiting, and both fired laser rifles scaled for their size at where Azah would have been if she hadn't been running along the outside of the wall. As soon as she came all the way around, her MAC fired with a thunderous crash.

The heavy magnetic accelerator cannon mounted on Azah's saddle was a massive weapon with a slow firing rate. It was meant to breach anything she might encounter, from walls to alien power armor. What it wasn't intended to do was fire in an enclosed space like a stairwell. The concussion from the blast smashed Sadek in the head like a thunderclap, despite the helmet's sound buffering and his arms over his head.

One of the two CASPers was hit squarely in the chest. The massive magnetically-enhanced slug, accelerated to 20 times the speed of sound, hulled it and killed the occupant, sending the suit tumbling back into the door it had been guarding. Sadek slid his gun back up. The second CASPer tried moving and firing. It wasn't very good at either. *Crack, crack, crack!* Sadek shot it, aiming for the weapon. Two of the shots scored, and the laser rifle's power system exploded with a crackling discharge. The merc fumbled with the weapon for a second, not realizing it was wasted until Azah was on him.

She collided at full speed. Azah might have been a smaller-than-average female, but she was still bigger than the powered armor and moving at a high rate of speed. The collision imparted a monumental amount of kinetic energy. Sadek was almost jarred out of the saddle as Tortantula and CASPer struck the doorway and exploded through it into the command center.

The powered armor was wrecked; hydraulic fluid sprayed and sparks flew as it careened away from Azah and into several unarmored mercs. As soon as her many legs hit the floor and Sadek was able to see around her, he aimed and fired at the closest armed merc who was aiming at him. The XT-12 tore through the unarmored Human's torso and sent him flying. Sadek turned and pointed his weapon at a large group of nearby Humans.

"Stop!" someone screamed. "Fight me!" Azah swiped out with a pair of limbs to send the Humans flying head over heels as Sadek spun on the one who's screamed. A bullet went *sprang* off Azah's saddle, right next to Sadek's head as he found the target. Instantly he recognized their main objective. Strange flat face, uniform, insignia all matched. It aimed a small hand weapon at Azah's head, and Sadek fired. The XT-12 cracked and bucked, and the Human fell.

"No!" another Human screamed. Sadek saw one running, not toward him but across the floor. It dropped its weapon and knelt next to the commander he'd just shot. It examined the Human for a moment, then seemed to fall over the other, who was certainly dead.

"Sadek," Azah said. Sadek spun his weapon back around, the fog of battle beginning to clear. He was finally focusing on the room. All the armed mercs were down. The rest weren't even wearing combat armor. They looked different. Many were smaller, or shaped different. *Are those Human children?* he asked Azah.

I think so, she replied, *and non-combat types. We're supposed to kill them? How can that be our orders?*

"You fuckers." Sadek looked back to the commander's body. The one who'd gone to him was up. He bent and retrieved the fallen man's weapon. Sadek instinctively brought his gun back around. "You killed him," he said, "that was your intention all along, wasn't it, you goddamn murderous chipmunk?" Sadek didn't speak as the man walked around him and Azah to the group of unarmed Humans who were crowded against one wall, watching with their peculiar huge eyes.

"That one was our mission," Sadek said, gesturing to the body, but not sure why he had spoken.

"Well, you succeeded." He stopped in front of the rest of the Humans and looked around. The two ruined CASPers were nearby, one twitching slightly in mechanical distress. "Congratulations, you killed Thaddeus Cartwright."

"We were supposed to kill all of you as well," Azah said.

"Then why haven't you?"

"Because it's not right," she said. Slowly, Sadek lowered his gun. She was correct; this was senseless murder, and it wasn't right. Maybe he'd planned to not carry out the slaughter part of the orders all along? It didn't really make any difference at that point anymore.

"We've had enough," Sadek agreed, laying the gun in his lap and gently patting Azah's back. He looked at the Human and the ones he was protecting. "Go, but quickly. Another team is just below us and will be here quickly." The Human looked uncertain.

"Go now!" Azah roared. They moved toward the main entrance, fast. The armed Human and another one picked up the body of their commander and moved toward the exit. He looked back at them as they were leaving.

"What's your name?" Sadek asked.

"Top Sergeant Hargrave," the man said, "and this isn't over." A moment later, he was gone.

"We'll say they escaped," Sadek said, "I've edited the gun camera footage so only the commander's death will be seen."

"Sadek!" Azah said in alarm.

"A burst transmission!" he said. Their pinplants both received it, but something was wrong. It wasn't decrypted. Sadek's blood ran cold. "We need to crack it!" His mind spun, it would take hours without his extra tablets and stuff.

"Get me your slate, quick!" Azah said. He didn't pause, he jumped off and pulled out his slate and gave it to her. In a flash Azah snatched some silk from her spinnerets and used it on the slate. It happened so fast Sadek couldn't follow it. One second a fine net of silk was flashing like lightning, the next second the message was flowing, translated, into his pinplants.

"Directive directly from the Stewards to Shypik and Ezek—Sadek and Azah have been compromised in a plot led by males Yeef, Loof, and others. They are traitors. They are to be eliminated immediately along with these males." Sadek's blood turned to ice water.

"Entropy," Azah said. "What happened? We didn't do anything!"

"It was me," he whispered.

"What?!" Azah said, shock in her voice.

"I hacked into the computers back on Kutu. There were hidden files, files about the males trying to turn you and other females into something. It was a plot against the Stewards." He sighed and lowered his head. "They've been doing it a long time, and most of the ones they've manipulated, like you, are dead. I sent it to the Stewards hoping they'd spare you. Azah, I messed up!"

"No," she said, "you did it to try and save me."

"Here's the file," he said and sent it over their private comms, "for what it's worth."

"I know you did what you did to help me, but I wish you'd told me."

"Me too," he said, and laid down against the bristly fur of her back. "What do we do now?"

"Traitors!" came a Tortantula battle cry from the stairwell.

"We kill those aberrations," she said, "to entropy with them."

"And then?" Sadek asked, picking his XT-12 back up.

"Then? Then we find our way on our own." The sound of many powerful legs racing up the stairs echoed up the stairwell. "Zha oort, Sadek," she said aloud for the first time in a long while.

"Zha oort," Sadek replied, flicking the safety off on his gun. "Unto the end." The already damaged doorway exploded inward, and the fight began.

* * * * *

Chapter Eleven

As the door exploded, Sadek was wondering at the timing. A couple of minutes had passed between the orders to kill them and their actual arrival. Considering Shypik and Ezek were only one floor below, that was strange. When three feral Tortantulas exploded into the Human's command center, he understood.

Azah's massive MAC boomed, taking one of the three full in the face with an explosion of blue gore. The gun took several seconds to cycle a new round. Far too long. She instantly detached the MAC from its quick-release, snatched the falling weapon with a pair of legs, and hurtled it like a missile. The gun weighed at least 100 kilograms, and Azah's powerful muscles gave it devastating momentum. It pulverized her target's exoskeleton and severed two forearms. The feral Tortantula wasn't dead outright, but it was badly injured. The third feral, the one who had come in on the right side, stood shocked into motionlessness, rooted to the floor.

Ezek rocketed through the shattered remains of the door; using the first Tortantula Azah had killed like a springboard, she shot into the air toward Azah. *"Traitor!"* she screamed in midair. Azah grabbed a console of monitors and pulled with all her might, yanking herself to the side and causing Ezek's piledriver attack to miss. Sadek fired two rounds quickly as the other female went by. The first went high. The second punched a neat hole through the center of the saddle support, where Shypik would have been, if she were still there.

259

Entropy! Sadek thought, *you never get out of the saddle in a fight!* As he searched for her, he remembered she'd been raised and trained in the strange divergent manner, where the bond between Flatar and Tortantula wasn't the most important thing. Azah jumped away from the wall, spinning to one side and lashing out with a pair of arms to score bloody wounds on Ezek's side. The other female screamed, more in rage than pain, and threw a metal chair at Azah.

As Azah spun, a hyper-velocity round cracked just past Sadek's shoulder. The round passed close enough that the shockwave slapped at him like a cuff to the head. He didn't have time to think about how close he'd come to dying. A couple millimeters to the right and his head would have been blown off. He spun his gun in the direction the shot had come from and fired on instinct. He had a fleeting view of Shypik diving to the side and under a table, the shot missing by meters.

"Traitor!" she yelled as she slithered past a ruined CASPer.

"Coward," Sadek replied.

"What did you call me?" she screamed and popped up.

"Gotcha," Sadek said as he leveled his aim and squeezed the trigger. A massive force slammed into Azah from the side, throwing him from the saddle. One of Azah's arms reached out, snatching him and pulling him back to the saddle even as she fought the feral Tortantula that had rammed into her side.

Sadek swung his pistol around. The feral was gargantuan, using her weight to bore down on Azah, and flexing to get her fangs into Sadek's partner. *How many shots,* he wondered as he leveled the gun and fired into the feral's eye ring. The head disintegrated in a spray of chitin. He dropped the magazine and replaced it with another from Azah's assault saddle. There were three barrels there, and four magazines. As he slapped the new magazine home, he struggled to remember when he'd last changed the barrel. Two, three magazines?

Ezek came at Azah low and fast, trying to take advantage of the fact that the thrashing feral still had ahold of her. Azah threw herself upward by pushing on the side toward Ezek, causing her to flip over toward the dying feral. It exposed her underside, but Ezek was committed and crashed into the feral instead of Azah. The impact drove the feral over, and caused Azah to flip back and on top of Ezek.

With a visceral yell of triumph, Azah sank her fangs into Ezek's head, right in the middle of her eye ring. There was a crunching sound, and Azah ripped backward, tearing the other female's head off.

"You and me," Azah said, spitting out the bloody ruins of Ezek's head, "together we're unstoppable!"

"Die!" Shypik screamed and jumped from behind the table she'd been using as cover, firing her XT-12. The supersonic round was aimed at Sadek's head, but one of Azah's legs was in the way. The bullet tore the leg in half, deflecting a fraction and missing Sadek. Azah cried out in pain.

"No, you die," Sadek said and fired. There was nothing in the way of his bullet. The round hit Shypik center of mass, blowing the tiny Flatar apart. It was the 30th shot from the same barrel. The ceramic alloy material was well past the point of critical failure. It shattered, the fragments tearing through the magnetic accelerator coils, shorting them directly to the batteries, which exploded.

The last thing Azah saw was Sadek framed by a ring of light. Then nothing.

* * * * *

Chapter Twelve

Everything hurt.

This wasn't the first time Azah had awakened after a hard-fought battle. Nor was it the first time she'd awakened with pain lancing through her body. It was, however, the first time she'd awakened after a battle with so much pain lancing through her body that she couldn't tell where it originated. It felt like she was one big hurt. Or maybe so many little ones as made no difference. Either way, it was a struggle to open her eyes.

But she did it.

"Well," a voice said. Azah blinked and tried to focus on the shadowy figure that leaned in toward her cephalothorax, blocking the too-bright lights that stabbed into her eyes. "You are alive."

"Sadek?" she asked. The voice didn't sound quite like her partner, but Azah's own voice was broken and ragged, so she didn't know. She thought about trying to access their secure pinplant comms, but the pounding in her head dissuaded her.

"Ah...no," the voice said. Azah blinked, and the figure resolved into that of a Flatar wearing the vest of a medic. But not Sadek.

"Where is Sadek?"

The Flatar leaned back.

"Sadek is gone, Azah," he said.

"Oh," Azah said. "Okay. What happened to me?"

The Flatar looked at her for a long moment, then spoke slowly as he continued to edge away from her.

"The Human mercs…your second from the back leg is pretty banged up. I don't know if we're going to be able to save it."

Ah. That explained the pain, then. She still hurt all over, especially as whatever she was lying in banked suddenly to the side, and instinct made her reach out to brace herself rather than slide. But that act of reaching out taught her two things: one, she was on some kind of ship, maneuvering fiercely; and two, the largest section of her pain came from her leg.

"Where are we going?" she asked the Flatar medic.

"Up to the fleet," he said. "Your pinplant connection flagged you for medical treatment if we could get to you in time. Operators like you are expensive…anyway. There's a Begalad doc up on the flagship. We'll have to see if it can save your leg."

"Okay," Azah said, stifling a grunt as the ship banked again. "Will Sadek meet us there?"

"Um…no…"

"Okay. I guess I'll see him later, then." More pain washed over her, leaving her exhausted in its wake. Or maybe the medic had given her painkillers. Either way, her eyelids wanted to slide shut. She decided that, since there wasn't much she could do until after she saw the Begalad, she'd go ahead and fall back to sleep.

When she woke again, she was lying belly down on a treatment table and covered in orange, leafy vines.

"Don't move," a voice said. It wasn't the medic again, but it was familiar. "The Begalad has you. It's removing the damaged tissue from your leg."

"I don't feel anything," Azah said.

"The Begalad has administered anesthetic sap through its thorn punctures…you've probably never been treated by one before, have you?"

"No," Azah said.

"Yeah, they're really rare, but we get one because it's so expensive to train operatives. They're a species of intelligent flora…but their intelligence isn't quite like ours."

"What do you mean?" Azah asked, her voice dreamy. She felt strange, whether from the absence of pain, the medication, or the trauma to her body, she couldn't say. The familiar voice babbling on offered a distraction, so she held onto it.

"Well, they don't communicate as we do, but they're incredible healers. Give them one live specimen to consume and they'll make every one they encounter after that whole."

"Consume?"

"Eat. They're carnivores. It's eating the necrotic flesh on your damaged leg right now."

"Oh. That's interesting."

"Isn't it, though?" the familiar voice said, and Azah thought she detected a thread of laughter. "But don't thrash around or anything. If the Begalad perceives you to be a threat, it'll throw a poisoned thorn into your brainpan faster than you can think."

"Why would I thrash? I don't even want to move," Azah said. Her brain felt wreathed in a delicious, velvety fog.

"Yeah, that's the sedative. Begalad sap is amazing."

"Too bad Sadek isn't here, he'd probably laugh at me right now," Azah said, feeling the strangest desire to giggle. "I wonder if he'll laugh when we meet back up."

"Meet back up?" the voice said. Where had she heard it before?
"Azah…Sadek's gone."

"I know. The medic told me."

"Told you what?"

"That Sadek wasn't here. I thought he'd meet me here once we got to the fleet, but I guess he's still busy downside."

"Azah…" the voice said, "that's not true. Sadek isn't going to be meeting up with you. He was killed in the battle when you lost your leg."

"No, he wouldn't do that," Azah said, and a tiny laugh escaped her. "He loves me."

"I'm sure he did, Azah, but…"

"He'd never leave me like that," she said, more laughter bubbling forth. This familiar voice was really funny! "He promised, and he'd never break that promise. We're always going to be together."

"He didn't leave you, Azah, but he is dead. His weapon exploded. There was nothing anyone could do. He…Sadek isn't coming back."

"Of course he is –!"

"No, Azah, listen to me!" The voice drew closer and suddenly it clicked in Azah's fog-bound brain. This was Yeef! Her commander!

"Yeef! You must know where Sadek is," she said, still giggling. "When are we meeting up with him? I have to tell him about this joke. I didn't know you were so funny."

"Azah." Yeef moved forward into her line of sight. He turned his small body to look around, then spun a small structure out of silk. "Azah, I'm sorry for this, truly I am. But Sadek is dead."

"No," Azah said again. "He wouldn't do that. He—" she cut off as Yeef touched her right side pinplant with his silk.

The world exploded in razor-edged grief.

* * * * *

Chapter Thirteen

N o.

It wasn't true.

He would never leave. He promised.

Zha Oort.

Until the end. Was this the end?

Was she dead?

Slowly, Azah opened her eyes.

The orange-leaved vines were gone. She lay, belly down, on a wide, circular table that let her legs dangle around her. The light in the room was dim. The air was cold and tasted of antiseptic. One of her back legs ached like it had been in one place for too long. She went to move it…

Nothing.

Oh. Right. Doctor plant with the merciful thorns. Ate her necrotic flesh.

So. Nine legs then. Should be enough, right?

Azah moved slowly, testing what little strength she had. It wasn't much, but she was able to get her remaining legs under her body and stand up…mostly steadily…on the table.

A door irised open in the wall. A Flatar walked in out of her earliest memories. Hranou.

"Azah," he said. His voice squeaked.

"I need to see the doctor plant."

"What do you mean?" Hranou asked.

"I can't remember what it's called. Orange leaves. Thorns of mercy."

"The Begalad? It's gone," Hranou said, taking a step forward. "Besides, you're healed—"

Azah leapt, forelegs slashing. Hranou let out a squeak as he went down. Azah landed atop him, her fangs slashing as she opened the Flatar from throat to groin. Hot, hot red blood fountained forth, covering Azah in a burning spatter that did nothing to warm the icy shards of agony in her mind.

Beneath her, Hranou let out a screaming wail, and fell still under Azah's feet. The flavor of the Flatar's pain and shock poured over Azah's feet, but it was nothing, nothing compared to what she felt inside.

"Azah!"

She froze, her fangs buried in Hranou's chest as the body cooled. Her detail eyes rolled up to focus on the doorway, and the Tortantula lurking beyond it.

"Azah," It was Hranou's partner, Zorm. Azah's mother. "What are you doing?"

Azah lifted her head and felt Hranou's blood drip from the tip of her fangs.

"My partner is dead," Azah said, sounding calm and matter of fact like she were discussing the weather. Like her insides weren't tearing themselves apart. Like... "I need the Begalad. I need the thorns."

"Why?"

"So I can thrash. Yeef said if I thrashed, it would kill me."

"Why do you want it to kill you?" Zorm asked, her voice sounding genuinely curious. Azah lifted one blood- and gore-stained foot.

"My partner," she said, "is dead."

"So?" Zorm asked. "So is mine, now. So what? You can get a new part—"

Azah leapt again, but this time, her quarry was ready for her. Zorm reared back and met her fang to fang as they crashed into the passageway outside of the recovery room where Azah had woken. Zorm's feet scrabbled at Azah's exoskeleton, expertly seeking the seams and joints. The older Tortantula rolled, using her greater weight to come crashing down on Azah, pinning her to the deck of the ship.

"Listen to me." Zorm said. She leaned closer as she spoke. "You can still be a brood mother! Especially now that you've covered yourself in Death! You're finally learning how to be what you should be! You can get a new Flatar!"

"I need Sadek!" Azah hissed back, her words garbled by Hranou's blood that flooded into her mouth from her pedipalps. "I can't be without him!"

"You *are* without him!" Zorm spat, and her words took on an edge of cruel pleasure. "Look at you! Useless little dependent, helpless without your Flatar to think for you! Right now, you're no better than a Feral, Azah. Quit it! Own your violence! You don't need a Flatar to be the perfect killer!"

"Sadek loved me!" Azah screamed, writhing under Zorm. She slashed out with her nine remaining legs, but the larger Tort was quick enough and powerful enough to trap them with her own feet. Plus, thanks to Azah's injury, Zorm had one foot free to pin Azah's abdomen. "He loved me, when you never did, and I loved him! I can't be without him!"

"Then you're just another feral slave," Zorm said, and reared back, fangs glinting in the ship corridor's light. For just a moment, joy and relief flooded through Azah. Good. She could die here, and this nightmare would be over.

She stopped struggling and lay still, awaiting the death strike.

"Good, you've got her. Hold her steady, I'll jolt her pinplants, and that will knock her out." The voice was high and chittery. Not a Flatar. A Veetanho.

"She's gone feral," Zorm said.

"What's the difference?" the Veetanho asked softly. Azah felt someone coming closer. "It doesn't matter. With her partner gone, she's not useful as an operative anymore. She was only saved because we have a buyer for her in the fighting pits. Apparently, she's managed to impress someone. So it's good you didn't kill her."

"No!" Azah wailed, and she pushed at Zorm's weight again. "No! Kill me! Kill me!"

"Ugh. I hate it when you Torts lose your riders," the Veetanho said. Azah's centermost eyes were filled with Hranou's blood, but her peripherals caught sight of the Veetanho arm reaching out and connecting something to her pinplant. She began to thrash harder.

"Hold her still!" the Veetanho commanded.

"I'm trying!" Zorm said, shifting her body to try and pin Azah down. She only slipped further off.

"Zorm, please kill me!" Azah screamed.

"No. Entropy, Azah…just. No!"

That "no" ricocheted through her brain, careening off the razor-sharp, icy agony that shredded her consciousness. Azah screamed, thrashed, and screamed again, while Zorm and the Veetanho fought to try and subdue her. Somehow, she managed to get a limb free.

Without thinking about what she was doing, she reached up and pulled Zorm's cephalothorax closer. Close enough to sink her fangs into her mother's two center eyes.

Zorm screamed and reared back so far she toppled over onto her back and began to thrash in agony. The taste of her blood (cold, uncaring) filled Azah's mouth as the Veetanho started to swear a blue streak. A jolt of electricity rocketed through her brain. It was the last assault her consciousness could handle. The being that had been Azah shattered, a million ragged fragments exploding into oblivion.

* * * * *

Chapter Fourteen

It was awhile before she registered anything else.

For a long time, her awareness just retreated. External stimuli were not really her concern. She must have eaten, because she kept breathing, but she couldn't have told you who'd fed her or what she'd consumed. She didn't even register the passage of time. Things happened around her. Beings spoke to her. She moved from one place to another...but none of it mattered.

Until, suddenly, it did.

"She won't be much good in the pits if she won't fight."

The harsh, mangled growl of a voice plucked at her memory. She blinked and focused her eyes for the first time in who knew how long.

There wasn't much to see. She stood in some kind of metal box with ventilation holes punched in the top. Harsh white light streamed in through the holes, reminding her of the lighting aboard a ship.

"Put her in with something trying to kill her, and she'll fight," a second voice said. This one, too, sounded familiar. It took her a moment to remember how, but she scanned back through her memory and matched the sound to one she'd heard before.

The Sidar negotiator. Urralon. The one she'd locked in a box when she'd found him skimming information during a deal.

"I've got a lot of credit riding on this, Sidar," the first voice said, and suddenly she was able to place that, too. The crippled Besquith from the same mission. "She better fight."

"She will. And if she doesn't, I'll provide a full refund."

"You'll provide more than that," the Besquith growled, but Urralon didn't respond.

She felt the crate being lifted, felt it sway as if it were being slung from one place to another. She began to hear a low roar of sound just at the edge of her audible range. The sound swelled and grew as the crate began to descend slowly. It landed with a thump, and the roar crescendoed.

Two clicks sounded from the top corner of the crate, and the wall in front of her face fell out and away. Blinding light spilled in, and she blinked furiously before taking a tentative step out.

Beyond the flattened crate wall, she stepped into soft sand that carried the copper and iron tang of old blood. She squinted as her eyes adjusted to the light, and she began to see that she stood in an oval depression. Sheer walls ringed the space, and they were lined with beings of all types and descriptions. Beings who howled, and screamed, and surged in a chaotic frenzy as the large monitors overhead recorded real-time credit transactions.

Wagers.

She was in a fighting pit. Here to fight, and live or die, for the amusement of the ravening crowd. She took another step forward, limping a little. Her remaining legs felt stiff and weak, like she hadn't bothered to use them in a long time. She blinked again and looked around as the noise swelled once more. She turned to see a dark opening had appeared in the far end of the oval. All around her, the crowd began to take up a stamping, beating rhythm that reverberated through the space.

A deep, rumbling roar filtered out from the yawning opening, and the crowd noise rose in ecstasy. The rhythm quickened, like a heartbeat in full fight-or-flight mode.

Another roar. Louder this time. Closer.

From somewhere, a voice said something in a language she didn't understand. She must have lost her translator at some point, because it just sounded like a lot of clicks and squeaks. The crowd noise surged again, thrumming across the sands like a living thing.

First one, then a second shaggy purple figure emerged into the light of the pit. They lifted their snouted faces to the crowd and let out a synchronized roar that had the rhythm dissolving in wild chaos. The noise battered at her, pounding into her exoskeleton as the two Oogar roared again and began to circle to either side of her.

Ah. So. This was how it was to be, was it? Fine. Worked for her. Everything she loved was gone, but she'd always been good at fighting, so she'd fight one more time and sell her death dearly. Maybe the next of her kind to step out onto these sands would taste her defiance in the traces of blood she would leave behind.

The Oogar moved well, she realized, as she turned her focus to the instruments of her imminent death. They had, at the least, trained together. More probably, they were a professional pit-fighter pair who performed in tandem all the time. Their movements were confident and nearly synchronized as they circled to try to outflank her. She held herself still and watched them closely. They would probably try to distract her...

Yes.

The Oogar on her right gave another roar, amping the crowd up still further. Without further thought, she launched herself toward the left, slashing at the other Oogar. He startled backward as his partner roared again and charged, but she'd succeeded in surprising them. The crowd noise faltered, then rebounded even louder.

She kept charging, her peripheral eyes keeping tabs on the second Oogar as she attacked. Her target scrambled backward, his eyes flicking behind her. She kept pressing, her feet flying across the sands. The second Oogar roared again and charged as well, his wicked claws flashing.

She let him get close, then drove her legs against the sand and leapt up and forward toward her target. She hit him with the bulk of her cephalothorax and sank her fangs into his fur-covered shoulder. Lines of fire erupted in agony as the Oogar's claws raked down the side of her exoskeleton. Somehow, he missed her eye, and she didn't intend to give him another chance at it.

She savaged him with her fangs, ripping deeper into the flesh of his torso and jerking her head to the side to open a gaping wound where his vitals should be. His scream cut off with a bubbling gurgle as she tore open his breathing organs. The second Oogar screamed behind her as its partner died. Then it attacked from the rear. More agonizing slashes appeared in her exoskeleton as it hopped on top of her and began clawing its way toward her eye ring. She flinched, and her rage and pain ignited inside her. It exploded outward in the form of an eerie, piercing shriek as she threw her body to the side, tucking her legs up to the underside of her body as she rolled over the vengeful Oogar. She felt the crunch of bone below her. The Oogar might have screamed, but it was hard to tell over the cacophony of the crowd. Something burst wetly beneath her as she rolled all the way over and back to her feet.

The broken bodies of the two Oogar lay mangled on the sand before her, their purple fur stained dark with blood. The crowd had gone quiet. She took a step backward, tasting the metallic blood-taint of the sand.

The amplified voice issued forth again, clicking and hissing in the language she didn't understand. It sounded tentative at first, but then the cadence built and began to ring out over the shocked crowd. Someone began that stomping, beating rhythm again, and the crowd's hushed murmurs grew into a deafening, crushing, over-whelming roar of approval.

She looked around, tasting the approbation of the crowd. Tasting the blood of her vanquished enemies. Tasting the slaughter. Appar-ently her mother had been right, may she die gasping in vacuum. This was proof. This was all there was. There was nothing else.

Only the slaughter.

* * * * *

Chapter Fifteen

Oblivion called to her, but the slaughter was louder.

She didn't know how long it had been. Her world had narrowed to the darkened tunnels where she ate and slept, and the harshly lit sand of the pit. Her heartbeat echoed the sound of the crowd's chant. The flavor of fear and death soaked through her. There was only the dark and the light. The oblivion and the slaughter.

And the slaughter was louder.

After the Oogar, there was a Jivool. The crowd took up its pounding rhythm as she stepped out of the darkness onto the sands. The Jivool knuckle-walked toward her, its half-meter long claws glinting in the pit lights. She lifted her head as it let out a roar of challenge that cut through the crowd's beat. Her detail eyes found the face of her Besquith owner in the crowd. He tilted his head and dropped his jaw, revealing his rows of razor teeth in a mockery of a smile.

Clearly, he planned for her to find oblivion.

But the slaughter was louder.

She went from complete stillness to full-bore charge between one heartbeat and the next. Her legs launched her forward, bloody sand flying, and she hit the Jivool head-on before he could get his claws up and into the fight. She bowled him over, knocking him down onto his back. The claws came up and slashed at her eye ring, gouged her exoskeleton, ripped down the length of one of her legs.

It didn't matter. She reared back, buried her fangs in the Jivool's face, and pumped her neurotoxin into its system. It thrashed beneath her, spasming. The crowd's beating rhythm became a roar. The Jivool's eyes met hers, and she tasted the moment of its death as the slaughter sang its song of eternity.

She looked back up to the Besquith, but he was gone.

Next were the Goka. Several of them. They swarmed her en masse, and she felt the prick of their wicked little knives as they stabbed for the seams in her exoskeleton. One by one, they died beneath her fangs, and though she was wobbling on her feet at the end, eventually their blood painted the sands blue like everyone else.

Three Lumar: she took them out by moving faster than they could follow. They died screaming, one missing an arm from her bite, all three of them twitching and spasming from her neurotoxin.

Zuul. Died howling in pain with its innards ripped open.

More Lumar. Fell like trees as she knocked them into one another and slashed with speeds faster than their minds could comprehend.

Oogar. Again and again. More every time. At the beginning of each fight, she would see the Besquith smile at her. Each time she would fight, and she would stand, bloodied and victorious, tasting the sands while the slaughter sang through her veins. Each time, the Besquith would leave before she was done, while the crowd noise reverberated through the entirety of the pit.

Sometimes, at night, when oblivion sang its song, she thought about her Besquith owner. He was trying to kill her. She had no illusions about that. Someday, she knew, he would succeed.

But until then, there was the slaughter.

* * * * *

Epilogue
Unto the Ending

The roar of the pit hit him like a physical force as he pushed the doors open. It was only the anteroom, where patrons established credit to place bets, obtain refreshments, collect their winnings, or lament their losses. Most did the latter. Betting in the battle pits was a losing prospect, even on the best of days. He always considered it more of a pay-to-play arrangement. He was there to watch others die. He was good enough at picking the winners that it paid his bills.

"Back again?" the elSha named Bekin asked at the betting booth.

"Yeah," he said, hopping up on a convenient stool to look over the counter. He put a handful of credit chits and his UAAC, or Yack, on the counter. "Set me up?" He slid the large shoulder bag he carried to one side so he could use his short arms better.

"Sure," Bekin said, taking the chits and the Yack. A second later, he handed the Yack back with a little electronic device. A betting stick would let him place bets on any match, even in the middle. It contained a tiny Tri-V to project sliding odds scales and other vital data. "Good luck." He took the stuff and grunted before jumping down and heading toward the sources of the noise.

Big Dob Pit actually contained three battle pits. At any one time there could be fighting taking place in one, two, or all three. Patrons moved between the pits, depending on the interest in a particular battle. Pit #3 was the source of all the noise just then. He took the betting stick as he walked and accessed the schedule. He'd come in because he knew a match was coming up today. A Goka named Toosh was fighting a Xiq'tal with the amusing name of Cracker. Despite the fact that the Xiq'tal outweighed the Goka 20 to one, Toosh was the favorite. He wanted to see that fight and also sensed a chance to profit. That battle was scheduled for Pit #1. Pit #3 was the largest, and the stick only said 'unscheduled bout.' That meant he had to go in to find out what was going on. Toosh and Cracker's battle was in 20 minutes. He had time.

If anything, the noise in Pit #3 was even louder than he'd been expecting. The place was absolutely packed. He could recognize a hundred species, all screaming and enjoying the show. Now that he was inside, his betting stick updated the info. He stared in surprise. "It can't be," he said.

The battle pit was recessed in the floor with rings of seats around it. The floor inside was low enough that most species couldn't jump out. That was good, because the horrors that went on in there often made escape at any cost appear to be a viable solution. He moved down to the bottom row, ducking between legs, around huge forms, and under massive bodies until he reached the bottom, where he hopped up onto the railing around the pit and looked in.

Far below a single female Tortantula stood in the center of the pit. She was almost coated in blood, though not her own. Her torso heaved as she breathed. Around her were maybe six dead Oogar. She was missing at least half of one leg and was covered in scars and a few fresh gouges in her exoskeleton. You almost never saw Tortantula in the pits. He'd heard rumors about this one, because she'd been fighting and winning for days, maybe months. She was also half the size of any Tort he'd ever seen. "Entropy," he hissed.

"I know, right?" a reptilian alien of a species he didn't recognize said. "Number one was one-on-one. Then it was two-on-one, and then three-on-one!" He looked down at the Tortantula female and shook his head.

"Now what?"

"The Besquith in charge is apparently pissed," the reptilian said, a laugh in its voice. "People were betting against the Tort on the first two matches, and then for her to win the third match! She beat those three Oogar at 20-1 odds! Whooh!" the alien said, and its tongue shot out to taste the air. "I'm going to get me glitter and celebrate tonight!"

"Fine, but what now?" he asked and pointed to the panting Tortantula.

"Oh, yeah. Well, like I said, the Besquith is pissed. There are like six more Oogar crazies he's going to turn loose on her. But at 7-1 odds? Screw that, there's no way." He grunted in reply and looked below. The female had caught her breath and was looking around as the sounds of metal-on-metal came from multiple exits. She knew more were coming, but she wasn't moving to a more strategic position. She was just going to sit there and wait for them. She was welcoming it.

"Oblivion," he said.

"What?" the reptilian asked.

"She's waiting for oblivion."

"Sure, whatever."

The doors started to open, and Oogar moved into the pit. They didn't charge, they waited for all the rest of their number to gather.

Unlike most crazy Oogar raised to fight, these appeared to have a modicum of planning ability. They were going to do it right. She was going to die.

"Well, this should be good," the reptilian said, its tongue tasting the air again.

"Yes, it will," he said. From a bag on his side, he drew out a battered but functional XT-12. The bag was now mostly empty, so he secured it around his stout waist. The reptilian's eyes went wide in surprise. "This is the end I should have had," the Flatar said to the shocked lizard.

"What are you doing?"

"Changing the odds." He ran along the perimeter of the pit until he came to a power cable, grabbed hold, and slid down the cable into the pit. "Hey!" he screamed at the Tortantula. A pair of eyes looked at him almost casually. When she realized what she saw, several more eyes focused as well. "Want some help?" He laughed and held up the hyper-velocity pistol. He must have made quite a sight, dangling there from the power cable.

"What are you doing?" the amplified voice of a Besquith boomed. "Get out of there!" He looked up and saw the Besquith in his booth, way up high.

"Fuck you," he yelled and let the XT-12 boom a round in the Besquith's direction. He didn't know if it hit or not, but two of the Oogar charged at him. "Oh, entropy," he said and tried to aim at them. Dangling like bait on a line, he was screwed. In a second, the first Oogar was almost on him, ready to jump up and claim his prize. The Tortantula smashed into the Oogar. Fangs slashed, and she ripped out his throat in an instant.

"Get on," she said.

"Fuck, yes," he said and dropped onto her back. "Let's do this."

In seconds, they'd torn through the other five Oogar. They were no match for a Tortantula/Flatar pair. Though they'd just met, the two of them moved instinctively with one another. He matched his shots to the cadence of her slashing strikes. She shifted her body to help him keep balance without a proper saddle rig. Together, they ripped open chests and exploded heads, until the floor of the pit resembled a swamp of dark blood with purple fur scattered about the grisly lumps of Oogar body parts.

"Kill them both!" the Besquith screamed, and the Flatar looked up to see teams of uniformed security mercs pushing through the crowds toward the lip of the pit, weapons held ready.

"Let's get out of here," he said to his new friend. "I'm bored with this small time dung heap already." Two more rounds from the powerful gun blew one of the doors open and they raced through. The backstage area of the battle pit wasn't designed to contain armed fighters. In fact, those tasked with maintaining the order of fights took one look at the armed Flatar on the back of the most deadly pit fighter they'd seen in ages and opened the back doors, letting them go. The female led them out into the night of the startown.

She finally stopped a few blocks away and settled to the ground so he could get off. He jumped down and removed a magazine from his bag, reloading the gun.

"That was fun," he said to the female, who didn't reply. "Are you okay?"

"I'm alive," she said. *Wow,* he thought, *she's gone.*

"How long ago did you lose your rider?"

"How did you know I lost my rider?" He laughed and shook his head. She grunted. "It was a while ago. I…don't really know how long. They sold me." He looked at her closer. She had pinplants. Now *that* was unusual. She wasn't sexually mature, so not a brood mother. They wouldn't have turned out a brood mother. Maybe covert ops, then.

"What's your name?" he asked.

"I don't have one anymore." He looked at her. "Besides, it doesn't matter. Are you leaving now?"

"I was thinking you might want a friend," he suggested.

"Why would you want me as a friend?"

"Because you can fight really well." He held up his Yack. "I'm a registered merc, but there's not a lot of work for a single Flatar. The two of us…we could do well."

"Fight for money?" He nodded. "I've been fighting to stay alive. Fighting for money sounds better. I don't have one of those IDs."

"I can fix that. Are we a team, then?"

"I don't want to lose another rider."

"I don't want to lose another ride." She looked at him with all her eyes. "But I'm tired of being alone."

"Me too," she said.

"Good. So, we need a name for you. You don't remember anything?"

"I remember Zha Oort," she said. He flinched slightly.

"Yeah? The Stewards would have freaked out if they ever heard you say that. Unto the end. Well, you've reached the end, now it's time to come back. How about Oort? We can call you Oort. Is that okay?"

"Sure," she said, and clicked her pedipalps together in approval, the first sign of any emotions he'd seen.

"Good. My name is JeeJee."

"Okay, JeeJee, now what?"

"Well, we get you a Yack, we register you as a merc, and we look for a job."

"Anything in space?" she asked. "I like space."

"With those pinplants, I guessed you'd been trained for space. There's a Human unit hiring here. They're called the Winged Hussars."

"I've met Humans," Oort said.

"They're a real pain in the ass, but this Hussars unit is a good one." He nodded. "Let's go see if we can get a job." He hopped on her back, and the pair headed away into the night.

# # # # #

ABOUT THE AUTHORS

Kacey Ezell

Kacey Ezell was born in South Dakota in 1977. Her parents joined the US Air Force in 1984, and she grew up around the world on various military bases. When she was seven, her mother gave her a copy of Anne McCaffrey's Dragondrums, and shortly thereafter, Kacey decided that she wanted to be a dragonrider when she grew up. In 1999, she followed her parents into the "family business" and attended the United States Air Force Academy before going to pilot training. As dragons were in short supply at the time, she reasoned that flying aircraft was the next best thing. She earned her wings in 2001, and has over 2500 hours in the UH-1N and Mi-17 helicopters.

From the time she was a small child, Kacey made up stories to tell to her friends and family. In 2009, while deployed to Iraq, she wrote the military-themed supernatural story "Light," which was published in the Baen Books anthology Citizens. She was asked to consult on John Ringo's 2015 novel Strands of Sorrow, and wrote the cover story for the Black Tide Rising anthology set in Ringo's zombie apocalypse universe. That story, "Not in Vain," was selected for inclusion in the "Year's Best Military SF and Adventure Fiction" anthology produced by Baen Books.

Kacey writes science fiction, fantasy, horror, noir, romance…she writes fiction. She lives with her husband, two daughters, and two cats.

* * * * *

Mark Wandrey

Located in rural Tennessee, Mark Wandrey has been creating new worlds since he was old enough to write. After penning countless short stories, he realized novels were his real calling and hasn't looked back since. A lifetime of diverse jobs, extensive travels, and living in most areas of the country have uniquely equipped him with experiences to color his stories in ways many find engaging and thought provoking.

Sign up on his mailing list and get free stuff and updates! http://www.worldmaker.us/news-flash-sign-up-page/

Caution – Worlds Under Construction

* * * * *

The following is an

Excerpt from Book One of the Revelations Cycle:

Cartwright's Cavaliers

Mark Wandrey

Now Available from Seventh Seal Press

eBook, Paperback, and Audio Book

Excerpt from "Cartwright's Cavaliers:"

The last two operational tanks were trapped on their chosen path. Faced with destroyed vehicles front and back, they cut sideways to the edge of the dry river bed they'd been moving along and found several large boulders to maneuver around that allowed them to present a hull-down defensive position. Their troopers rallied on that position. It was starting to look like they'd dig in when Phoenix 1 screamed over and strafed them with dual streams of railgun rounds. A split second later, Phoenix 2 followed on a parallel path. Jim was just cheering the air attack when he saw it. The sixth damned tank, and it was a heavy.

"I got that last tank," Jim said over the command net.

"Observe and stand by," Murdock said.

"We'll have these in hand shortly," Buddha agreed, his transmission interspersed with the thudding of his CASPer firing its magnet accelerator. "We can be there in a few minutes."

Jim examined his battlespace. The tank was massive. It had to be one of the fusion-powered beasts he'd read about. Which meant shields and energy weapons. It was heading down the same gap the APC had taken, so it was heading right towards that APC and Second Squad, and fast.

"Shit," he said.

"Jim," Hargrave said, "we're in position. What are you doing?"

"Leading," Jim said as he jumped out from the rock wall.

* * * * *

The following is an
Excerpt from Book One of In Revolution Born:

The Mutineer's Daughter

Chris Kennedy & Thomas A. Mays

Available Now from Seventh Seal Press

eBook, Paperback, and (soon) Audio Book

Excerpt from "The Mutineer's Daughter:"

Kenny dozed at his console again.

There he sat—as brazen as ever—strapped down, suited up, jacked in...and completely checked out. One might make allowances for an overworked man falling asleep during a dull routine, watching gauges that didn't move or indicators that rarely indicated anything of consequence, perhaps even during a quiet moment during their ship's long, long deployment.

But Fire Control Tech Third Class Ken Burnside was doing it— yet again—while the ship stood at General Quarters, in an unfriendly star system, while other parts of the fleet engaged the forces of the Terran Union.

Chief Warrant Officer Grade 2 (Combat Systems) Benjamin "Benno" Sanchez shook his helmeted head and narrowed his eyes at the sailor strapped in to his right. He had spoken to the young weapons engineer a number of times before, through countless drills and mock skirmishes, but the youthful idiot never retained the lesson for long.

"Benno, Bosso," Kenny would plead, "you shouldn't yell at me. You should have me teach others my wisdom!"

Benno would invariably frown and give his unflattering opinion of Kenny's wisdom.

"Get it, ya?" Kenny would reply. "I'm a math guy. Probability, right Warrant? The *Puller's* just a little ship, on the edge of the formation. We scan, we snipe, we mop up, we patrol. We don't go in the middle, tube's blazing, ya? We no tussle with the big Terrans, ya? No damage! No battle! So, something goes wrong, back-ups kick in, buzzer goes off, we mark for fix later. And when's the only time you or the officers don't let a man walk 'round and don't ask for this, don't ask for that? When's the only time a man can catch up on the z's, eh? One and the same time! So I doze. Buzzer goes off, I wake, make a note, doze again till I can work, ya? Such wisdom!"

Benno usually lectured him about complacency. He asked what would happen if they *were* hit, if the shot was hot enough, deep enough, destructive enough to burn through the backup of the backup of the backup. What if they did have to face the Great Test, to rise and work and save the *Puller* themselves?

Kenny would always smile, relieved. "Well, then I be dead, ya? No more maintenance either way. Good enough reason to doze right there!"

Benno could have reported him any number of times, but he never had. Putting it on paper and sending it above them was a two-edged sword. It would solve Kenny's sleepy disdain for order, of that Benno had no doubt, but he also knew he would lose Kenny's trust and the vigorous drive the young ALS plebeian applied to every other task. Plus, it would signal to the officers above that Benno couldn't handle a minor discipline problem on his own. And it would indicate to the ranks below that Benno was no longer one of their own—when he had gone from Chief to Chief Warrant Officer, he had changed his ties, forever.

So Benno growled, but he let it slide, content only he would know about Kenny's acts of passive rebellion. No one else would ever know why the young tech kept getting extra punishment duties. Besides, it wasn't as if Kenny was actually *wrong*, in the fullness of things.

Then, before Benno could check his own side of the console to verify whether things were indeed alright, his internal debate was blown away by the unforgiving, indiscriminate lance of an x-ray laser blast.

The single beam struck the *Puller* a glancing blow, centered on a space just beneath the outer hull and aimed outboard. Armor plate, radiation shielding, piping, wireways, conduit, decking, internal honeycombed structure, atmosphere, and people all ionized and ablated into a dense, mixed plasma. This plasma exploded outward, crushing the spaces surrounding the hit and dealing further physical and thermal damage. Combat Systems Maintenance Central, or CSMC, lay deep within the *Puller's* battle hull—three spaces inward from where the x-ray laser struck—but that meant little next to the awesome destructive power of a Dauphine capital-class xaser warhead.

The forward and port bulkheads in front of them flashed white hot with near-instantaneous thermal energy transfer and peeled away, blown out by the twin shocks of the outward-expanding plasma and the snapping counterforce of explosive decompression. The double blast battered Benno in his seat and threw him against his straps to the left. As the bulkheads vanished, their departure also carried away the CSMC monitoring console the two watch standers shared with them into the black, along with Kenny's seat, and Ken Burnside, himself.

The young engineer disappeared in an instant, lost without ever waking. Benno stared, dumbfounded, at the blank spot where he had been, and of all the possible panicked thoughts that could have come to him, only one rose to the forefront:

Does this validate Kenny's wisdom?

Benno shook his head, dazed and in shock, knowing he had to engage his brain. Looking beyond, he could see the glowing edges of bulkheads and decks gouged out by the fast, hot knife of the nuclear-pumped xaser. Only vaguely could he recall the sudden buffeting of explosive decompression that had nearly wrenched him through the straps of his acceleration couch.

He knew he had things to do. He had to check his suit's integrity. Was he leaking? Was he injured? And what about Kenny? Was he gone, unrecoverable? Or was he waiting for his poor, shocked-stupid boss Benno to reach out and save him?

And there was something else, something important he needed to be doing. He wasn't supposed to just sit here and think of himself or unlucky, lazy Kenny. *Oh no*, thought Benno, still trying to marshal his thoughts back together, *Mio is going to be so angry with me, sitting here like a fool...*

"CSMC, report!"

Benno shook his head against the ringing he hadn't realized filled his ears. He reached out for the comms key on his console, swore at how futile that was, then keyed his suit mic. "Last station calling, this is CSMC. We've taken a hit. I lost my technician, console is...down, hard. Over."

"CSMC, TAO," the *Puller's* Tactical Action Officer said through the suit channel, "pull it together! We just had a near miss by a capital class Dauphine warhead. The battle with the Terrans has spread out of the main body. I have missiles up but zero point-defense. I need guns and beams back, *now!*"

* * * * *

Get "The Mutineer's Daughter" now at:
https://www.amazon.com/dp/B07BRTDBCJ

Find out more about Thomas A. Mays and "In Revolution Born" at:
https://chriskennedypublishing.com

* * * * *

The following is an

Excerpt from Book One of The Kin Wars Saga:

Wraithkin

Jason Cordova

Available Now from Theogony Books

eBook, Paperback, and Audio Book

Excerpt from "Wraithkin:"

Prologue

The lifeless body of his fellow agent on the bed confirmed the undercover operation was thoroughly busted.

"Crap," Agent Andrew Espinoza, Dominion Intelligence Bureau, said as he stepped fully into the dimly lit room and carefully made his way to the filthy bed in which his fellow agent lay. He turned away from the ruined body of his friend and scanned the room for any sign of danger. Seeing none, he quickly walked back out of the room to where the slaves he had rescued earlier were waiting.

"Okay, let's keep quiet now," he reminded them. "I'll go first, and you follow me. I don't think there are any more slavers in the warehouse. Understand?"

They all nodded. He offered them a smile of confidence, though he had lied. He knew there was one more slaver in the warehouse, hiding near the side exit they were about to use. He had a plan to deal with that person, however. First he had to get the slaves to safety.

He led the way, his pistol up and ready as he guided the women through the dank and musty halls of the old, rundown building. It had been abandoned years before, and the slaver ring had managed to get it for a song. In fact, they had even qualified for a tax-exempt purchase due to the condition of the neighborhood around it. The local constable had wanted the property sold, and the slaver ring had stepped in and offered him a cut if he gave it to them. The constable had readily agreed, and the slavers had turned the warehouse into the processing plant for the sex slaves they sold throughout the Dominion. Andrew knew all this because he had been the one to help set up the purchase in the first place.

Now, though, he wished he had chosen another locale.

He stopped the following slaves as he came to the opening which led into one of the warehouse's spacious storage areas. Beyond that lay their final destination, and he was dreading the confrontation with the last slaver. He checked his gun and grunted in surprise as he saw he had two fewer rounds left than he had thought. He shook his head and charged the pistol.

"Stay here and wait for my signal," he told the rescued slaves. They nodded in unison.

He took a deep, calming breath. No matter what happened, he had to get the slaves to safety. He owed them that much. His sworn duty was to protect the Dominion from people like the slavers, and someone along the way had failed these poor women. He exhaled slowly, crossed himself and prayed to God, the Emperor and any other person who might have been paying attention.

He charged into the room, his footsteps loud on the concrete flooring. He had his gun up as he ducked behind a small, empty crate. He peeked over the top and snarled; he had been hoping against hope the slaver was facing the other direction.

Apparently Murphy is still a stronger presence in my life than God, he thought as he locked eyes with the last slaver. The woman's eyes widened in recognition and shock, and he knew he would only have one chance before she killed them all.

He dove to the right of the crate and rolled, letting his momentum drag him out of the slaver's immediate line of fire. He struggled to his feet as her gun swung up and began to track him, but he was already moving, sprinting back to the left while closing in on her. She fired twice, both shots ricocheting off the floor and embedding themselves in the wall behind him.

Andrew skid to a stop and took careful aim. It was a race, the slaver bringing her gun around as his own came to bear upon her. The muzzles of both guns flashed simultaneously, and Andrew grunted as pain flared in his shoulder.

A second shot punched him in the gut and he fell, shocked the woman had managed to get him. He lifted his head and saw that while he had hit her, her wound wasn't nearly as bad as his. He had merely clipped her collarbone and, while it would smart, it was in no way fatal. She took aim on him and smiled coldly.

Andrew swiftly brought his gun up with his working arm and fired one final time. The round struck true, burrowing itself right between the slaver's eyes. She fell backwards and lay still, dead. He groaned and dropped the gun, pain blossoming in his stomach. He rolled onto his back and stared at the old warehouse's ceiling.

That sucked, he groused. He closed his eyes and let out a long, painful breath.

* * * * *

Get "The Mutineer's Daughter" now at:
https://www.amazon.com/dp/B01N0RGYZS/

Find out more about Jason Cordova and "Wraithkin" at:
http://chriskennedypublishing.com/imprints-authors/jason-cordova/

* * * * *

Made in the USA
Middletown, DE
07 June 2023

32246103R00170